"Quirky characters abound in this gentle romantic comedy with a hint of suspense. But it's the comic scenes featuring Shep that steal the show. . . . Readers who delight in tales about the bond between people and their dogs will enjoy spending time in Fossett."
—*Booklist* on *Please Don't Feed the Mayor*

"Filled with romance, drama, and family love, *The Dog Who Came for Christmas* is a fun, lighthearted read that is sure to give you warm fuzzy feelings."
—*Modern Dog* on *The Dog Who Came for Christmas*

***Boomer's Bucket List* is a**
***CLOSER WEEKLY* STAFF PICK!**

"Grab a treasured pet and a box of tissues before sitting down to read this endearing tale. Pethick has a knack for writing dogs with personality, and Boomer is no exception. Both witty and emotional, this touching novel is a journey through America's heartland. The romance takes a back seat while supporting the plot in all the best ways. . . . This is a great road trip read!"
—*RT Book Reviews* on *Boomer's Bucket List*

"A beautiful book filled with warmth, *Boomer's Bucket List* will tug at your heart strings for more reasons than one as you join Jennifer, Nathan, and Boomer in this journey filled with love, loss, and friendship."
—*Modern Dog* on *Boomer's Bucket List*

ALASKAN
CATCH

Also by Sue Pethick

Please Don't Feed the Mayor
The Dog Who Came for Christmas
Boomer's Bucket List
Pet Friendly

Published by Kensington Publishing Corporation

ALASKAN CATCH

Sue Pethick

KENSINGTON BOOKS
www.kensingtonbooks.com

KENSINGTON BOOKS are published by

Kensington Publishing Corp.
119 West 40th Street
New York, NY 10018

All Kensington titles, imprints, and distributed lines are available at special quantity discounts for bulk purchases for sales promotion, premiums, fundraising, educational, or institutional use.

Special book excerpts or customized printings can also be created to fit specific needs. For details, write or phone the office of the Kensington Sales Manager: Kensington Publishing Corp., 119 West 40th Street, New York, NY 10018. Attn. Sales Department. Phone: 1-800-221-2647.

Kensington and the K logo Reg. U.S. Pat. & TM Off.

ISBN-13: 978-1-4967-1983-6 (ebook)
ISBN-10: 1-4967-1983-2 (ebook)
Kensington Electronic Edition: October 2019

ISBN-13: 978-1-4967-1982-9
ISBN-10: 1-4967-1982-4
First Kensington Trade Paperback Printing: October 2019

10 9 8 7 6 5 4 3 2 1

Printed in the United States of America

For Doug and Amanda, with gratitude

Acknowledgments

In writing this book, I've been fortunate to have the support of a great team. A writer toils in solitude, but a book is the product of many dedicated individuals, every one of whom is crucial to its success. Among them this time are my agent, Doug Grad, and his former assistant, Amanda Blott, who suggested I write a story about a marine biologist and an Alaskan tender operator; my editor, Gary Goldstein, who trusted me to run with it, and his assistant, Liz May, who somehow manages to be equal parts diplomat and cheerleader—bless you.

My publicist, Vida Engstrand, keeps my name in front of the book-buying public, for which I'm inexpressibly grateful, and Paula Reedy is not only a wonderful production editor, but she writes me thoughtful notes about proofing my manuscripts that I always need, always read, and probably never adhere to perfectly, alas. Larissa Ackerman, Alexandra Nicolajsen, and Lauren Jernigan communicate, social mediate, and work their magic on my behalf, leaving me both humbled and grateful. No doubt, there are others on the Kensington team whose names I haven't included here. To you, also, I give my thanks.

Finally, love and thanks to my husband, Chris, whose wise counsel and gentle encouragement have often kept me going when I was ready to throw in the towel. How did I ever get so lucky?

ARRIVAL

Emily Prentice pressed her forehead against the airplane's window, hoping for a glimpse of the place she'd be calling home for the next three months. When she heard that the National Oceanic and Atmospheric Administration had an internship in Ketchikan, she'd jumped at the chance to go, but the truth was, she hadn't really thought much about what it would be like to live there. Now, seeing the snow-capped islands that hugged the coast like ships in a storm, she hoped she hadn't made a mistake. After twenty-three years in Southern California, what on earth was she doing in Alaska?

There'd been a fight about it, of course. There was always a fight when Emily made a decision her mother didn't approve of. Veronica Prentice had tried everything short of holding her breath and turning blue to keep her daughter from leaving home.

"What will I do without you?"

"Your friends will miss you."

"You're going to hate the cold!"

And the biggest one, of course:

"Won't Carter be lonely?"

The two of them would probably still be arguing about it if Uncle Danny hadn't stepped in.

Veronica would be fine, he assured her, and Emily and her friends could call or text each other every day. As for the cold, he was sure the new Canada Goose parka would keep his favorite niece toasty warm. And Carter? Well, with his final year of residency ahead of him, he'd probably be too busy at the hospital to notice she was gone.

Emily nestled back in her seat, smiling at the thought of the young man her mother called her "steady beau." Their parents had known each other since before she was born—the Trescotts had been the first to arrive the day her father died—but Carter had never been anything more than Chelsea's big brother until last year, when he'd kissed Emily at a New Year's Eve party and everything changed. Since then, their families had been acting as if the two of them would always be together.

And who knew? Maybe they would.

Nevertheless, whether or not Carter Trescott turned out to be "the one," Emily was determined to have a career of her own, and the job market for marine biology majors was limited to only a handful of research facilities. To find employment in San Diego, she'd have to have more than just good grades; she'd need experience and the endorsement of professionals in her field. Her adviser at Scripps had already written her a letter of recommendation and one of her professors had promised to do the same, but she figured the word of someone with practical expertise would carry more weight than a person in academia. Being an inspector at a fish cannery might not be the most glamorous job in the world, but it would add some much-needed work experience to her resume and prove that she wasn't afraid to get her hands dirty.

The thought of everything that awaited her when they

landed was making her feel antsy again. Emily picked up her book and started rereading the first chapter, hoping to distract herself, but it wasn't long before her attention began to drift.

If only her mother could find a boyfriend, she thought, both their lives would be so much easier. She knew how hard it must have been, being widowed at thirty-nine with a twelve-year-old to raise, and Emily appreciated everything her mother had done for her, but as time went on, her mother's care and concern had turned into manipulation and control. There were days when Emily felt as if she were being smothered by her mother's attention, to the point where she wanted to scream. Why couldn't she just let go?

As the airplane started its descent, the butterflies in her stomach took flight. Emily reached for her bottle of ginger ale and took a sip. She had to stop worrying about her mother, she told herself. It did nothing but keep her from concentrating on moving forward with her own plans, and she had no intention of letting this opportunity go to waste. Chances were, her mother was already consoling herself with some intensive retail therapy.

Shadows swept across the cabin as the plane banked toward Revillagigedo Island, a mitten-shaped swath of green with two small towns—Ketchikan and Saxman—clinging to its leeward edge. As the pressure in her ears increased, Emily took another sip of soda and put it away, then brought her seat back to its full, upright position. Minutes later, she closed her eyes and felt her body strain against the seatbelt as they touched down and the engines reversed, slowing the plane and allowing the pilot to taxi toward the terminal. Emily took out her phone and texted her mother with the news that she'd arrived safely, then turned it off and shoved it deep into her bag, determined not to take it out again until she'd arrived at her new quarters.

When the plane stopped and the flight attendants had secured the doors, Emily grabbed her bag and the parka her mother had insisted she carry onboard—*You're going to Alaska; people live in ice houses up there!*—then stepped out into the aisle. She thought she was heading out on a new adventure, a chance to live and work on her own in a part of the country where she'd never been before. Instead, her whole life was about to be turned upside down. And all because of a dog.

CHAPTER 1

Tim Garrett was waiting for her at the security gate, holding a hand-lettered sign that said: PRENTICE / NOAA. A tall, angular forty-something with springy brown hair and hazel eyes, Tim had interviewed Emily when she applied for the internship and he would be her supervisor while she was working at the cannery. She was surprised to see that he was wearing shorts.

"Welcome to Ketchikan," he said as she approached. "How was the flight?"

"Great!" Emily moved the parka to her left arm so she could shake hands. "Got a late start out of Sea-Tac, but we made good time once we were in the air."

"Come on." He pointed. "Baggage claim's this way."

Tim turned and strode through the terminal, his long legs making it hard for her to keep up. As she hurried after him, Emily juggled her bag and the bulky black parka, feeling like a dork. The sky outside was intensely blue; not an igloo in sight. Why hadn't she just packed the darned thing?

When they reached the baggage carousel, Tim checked his watch.

"With luck, this won't take long," he said. "The next ferry leaves in eighteen minutes."

Emily glanced out the window at the stretch of water that separated them from town.

"So, we're not actually in Ketchikan?"

He shook his head.

"Not enough flat land over there for a runway," he told her. "Planes land here and people and cars have to ferry over."

"Why don't they just build a bridge?"

"We tried. Remember 'The Bridge to Nowhere?' That was us." Tim chuckled ruefully. "Maybe I should have said, 'Welcome to Nowhere.'"

The first of Emily's bags slid onto the conveyor belt.

"I'll get it," Tim said when she pointed it out. "Let's go."

"Um, I've got another one," she said, feeling her face flush. "Sorry."

"Oh." He set the bag down and checked his watch again. "Sure. No problem."

Luckily, the second bag showed up seconds later. They caught the ferry in the nick of time.

"I'm afraid there's not much storage room in your quarters," Tim said, glancing in his mirror at the bags in back. "Things might be a little cramped."

"I'm sure it'll be fine."

Emily already felt foolish for bringing a parka that looked like it belonged to Nanook of the North. She wasn't going to let anyone accuse her of hogging up all the storage space, too.

"And don't worry about your stuff while we're at the cannery," he said. "Folks there know better than to mess with my car."

He reached around and grabbed a package off the back seat.

"Here you go," Tim said, dropping it into her lap. "Hope it's the right size. We'll pick you up a hard hat and some rubber boots when we get there."

Emily looked at the plastic bag in her lap: *ARAMARK lab coat WHITE Size S.*

"Go ahead," he told her. "Try it on."

Was this guy serious? She'd been on a plane all day; she'd just gotten there, for heaven's sake. She hadn't even had time to go to the *bathroom*. Besides, it was already after five o'clock. Wouldn't the cannery be closed?

"You mean we're going there *now?*"

"Sure," he said, grinning. "Gotta make hay while the sun shines, right?"

Emily looked out the window, where a blazing sun still sat high above the patchy white clouds. If memory served, twilight at that latitude wouldn't start until sometime after nine o'clock. There were still four hours of daylight left.

"Oh, yeah," she said, wilting slightly. "I guess I forgot."

A horn sounded the all clear and the ferry started its trip across the water.

"Would you like to get out?" Tim asked. "Stretch your legs? You've been cooped up for a while."

"That'd be nice, yes."

As she stepped out of the car, a stiff breeze tousled her hair, carrying with it the familiar smells of the ocean: seaweed and sand and driftwood. Emily took a deep breath and sighed contentedly. She'd been expecting Alaska to feel like a foreign country. Instead, she thought, it felt a lot like home.

It was almost six by the time they reached the cannery, an enormous white building perched along the quay. Tim pulled into the gravel parking lot and got out.

"My office is in here," he said, motioning toward a door in the back of the building. "Once you're suited up, I'll give you the grand tour."

Tim's "office" was a cluttered room about the size of a

closet, tucked away beside a door marked MECHANICAL. He grabbed a hard hat off the wall and handed it to Emily.

"See if this fits," he shouted over the racket coming from next door.

She put it on and jiggled her head.

"It feels a little loose."

He took it back and fiddled with the liner.

"Here," he said. "See if that helps."

Emily put it back on.

"Yes. That's better."

"Okay," Tim said with a wink. "Let's go see what you've gotten yourself into."

Even at that hour, the waterfront was a hive of activity. Boats with fish to sell were being secured to the dock, buyers and sellers were haggling over price, and greedy-eyed gulls were waiting for a chance to pilfer a meal. Farther along the dock, men in thigh-high boots grabbed containers of fish as they were passed up out of the holds, stacking them on hand carts that were taken through a pair of open doors on their right.

"We'll start at the beginning and move through each step of the process so you can see how things work," Tim said as they stepped inside.

The cannery floor was enormous—the length of a football field, at least—crisscrossed with conveyor belts and metal ducting and lit by rows of cold fluorescent lights. Workers in yellow slickers and rubber boots stood shoulder-to-shoulder at long metal tables while blood poured over their feet. The hiss and clang and hum of machinery were deafening.

Tim bent down so he wouldn't have to yell.

"This is the slime line. When the fish come in, they go to the belly slitters, head decapitators, and gut pullers before being washed, weighed, and graded."

Emily nodded, trying not to gag. The sight and smell of so much blood was nauseating. Tim gave her a kindly smile.

"Don't worry," he said. "You'll get used to it. Everyone does."

After a mercifully brief perusal of the slime line, they headed for the filleting stations, Emily picking her way carefully through the fish guts and blood on the floor. It occurred to her that if her mother could see what she was doing, she'd demand that her daughter stop this foolishness and come home at once. The thought made her all the more determined to stay.

From the filleting tables, they moved on to the feeder machine, then the patching tables, where the fish were readied for cooking. Tim's attitude was friendly and relaxed as he explained everything, but Emily noticed that he never stopped scanning the tables. When she caught a few of the workers eyeing him warily, she remembered something he'd told her at the interview. Because NOAA's inspectors had the power to shut down a cannery when problems were found, they were sometimes seen as the enemy. Fish spoiled quickly, and every hour a cannery was off-line was an hour it was losing product and the workers weren't getting paid. No wonder her friendly smiles weren't reciprocated, she thought. As far as these people were concerned, the two of them were trespassers.

Tim had just finished explaining how the cooked fish were sorted and loaded onto pallets when someone at the loading dock caught his eye.

"There's one of your roommates." He waved. "Uki! Come say hello."

A short woman with honey-colored skin and a fringe of blue-black hair nodded in response. As she walked over, paying no attention to the offal on the floor, Emily wondered how long it would take before she'd be as blasé about traipsing through fish guts.

Uki stopped in front of them and folded her arms.

"This is Emily Prentice," Tim said. "She just got here from San Diego."

"Hi," Emily said. "Nice to meet you."

Uki unfolded her arms just long enough to shake hands, then crossed them back over her chest.

Emily felt a twinge of anxiety. She'd never had a roommate before, and in spite of the horror stories her friends had told her, she'd been looking forward to it. Now, she wasn't so sure. The prospect of living for three months with someone who didn't like her was daunting.

"Hang on a second," Tim said, reaching for his phone.

He turned away, spoke a few words, and put it back in his pocket.

"Sorry. Looks like I'm needed elsewhere. Uki, why don't you and Emily go back to the intake area and get acquainted while I see what's going on?"

"Yeah, sure," Uki said. Then, to Emily: "Come on."

Somehow, the sight of fish blood sluicing over the slime line didn't seem quite as awful by the time she returned, and Emily realized that Tim was right when he told her she'd get used to it. Even the smell didn't seem so bad, but then, maybe she'd just reached some sort of saturation point. Once you were completely sick of something, how much worse could it get?

She saw two guys in the same type of lab coats and rubber boots that she and Uki were wearing standing just inside the open doors, watching a load of fish being brought in. Uki raised a hand in greeting and gave the guy on the left a playful shove.

"This is Emily," she said. "This is Dak and that's Noah."

"Hi," Emily said. "How's it going?"

"Where's Tim?" Dak said.

Uki shrugged. "Got a call. Said he'd meet us here later."

The other two exchanged glances.

"More problems on the line?"

Uki blew the bangs away from her face. "Must be. He looked kind of angry."

Emily frowned. "What kind of problems?"

The three of them stared at her.

"Just problems, okay?" Noah said. "Stuff that makes the inspectors look bad."

"The guys on the line don't want us here," Dak said. "They figure if they make us look bad enough, we'll leave."

"That doesn't make sense," Emily said. "By law, the cannery has to be inspected."

He shrugged. "Let's just say it's complicated."

Emily felt her lips tighten. She might be the newest member of the group, but these guys hadn't been there much longer than she had. If something serious was going on, she wanted to know.

Before she could say anything, though, Emily heard someone yell and saw movement off to her left—a huge black dog was careening toward them. Scrabbling on the slippery floor, unable to stop, the poor thing was headed straight for the slime line. If something wasn't done, she realized, it would be a disaster.

Uki screamed and Dak and Noah jumped back as Emily stepped into the dog's path. The impact knocked her back, but she held on, rotating her body and using the animal's weight and momentum to direct it away from the fish tables. As her shoulder hit the ground, she released the dog and continued the roll, coming to rest facedown on the concrete floor. Her lab coat was covered in fish slime, but she was unhurt—and so, apparently, was the dog.

As she lay there on the ground, Emily saw four furry legs walk over and felt a puff of warm breath snuffling her hair. She lifted her chin, and a giant pink tongue licked her face. Everyone in the building was staring at her.

Then someone started to laugh.

CHAPTER 2

Sam Reed was not having a good day.

When he and his Newfoundland, Bear, had gone down to the ship that morning, he'd found one of the tender's owners waiting for them. Travis Reznikoff was a good guy. Though ten years older than Sam, he had no problem deferring to his judgment when it came to the tender and—unlike the ship's co-owner—he rarely, if ever, criticized the decisions Sam made as captain. Nevertheless, when Sam spotted him up ahead on the dock, he knew it was bad news.

Bear galloped ahead and he and Travis play-wrestled until Sam caught up. Travis had known Bear since he was a pup and the two of them had formed a solid bond—something Sam had recently capitalized on when he sought permission to bring the dog with him onboard.

"Hey, Trav," Sam said as the two men shook hands. "What brings you down here?"

Travis gave Bear another pat and stood up. "Is Kallik around?"

Sam shook his head. "Don't think so. He doesn't usually get here this early."

"How's he doing?"

"In what way?"

Sam knew what Travis was getting at, but he wasn't in the mood to make this any easier. As captain of a tender, he was the middleman between the fishermen at sea and the processors on shore. Every day during fishing season, he and his crew headed out to buy the day's catch and bring it back to the docks to be sold to buyers from the canneries and fish processors. In theory, it was simple: you bought fish cheaper than you could sell it for, gave half the profit to the ship's owners, and split the rest with the engineer and crew. But just because it was simple, that didn't mean it was easy.

For one thing, sailing in Alaskan waters was dangerous. Weather systems that were barely a blip on the radar when they left Japan could spin into boat-battering monsters by the time they reached the northeastern Pacific, and transferring a fishing boat's catch into a tender's hold—a difficult job even in good weather—could quickly become life-threatening in a storm. With its hold full of fish, a tender rode low in the water, too, making it susceptible to being swamped. Add to that the physical strength and dexterity needed to move tons of slippery, cumbersome cargo, and it took an experienced crew to pull it all off. Sam had been hauling fish for most of his adult life—at twenty-seven, he was known as one of the safest captains in Ketchikan—and he resented having his judgment questioned.

Travis was scanning the ships in the harbor. "Jack thinks he should go."

Sam felt his fists clench. Jack Crompton, the ship's co-owner, was an impatient little man, quick to find fault and eager to place blame without knowing all the facts. If Sam had known what Jack was like when he was offered the captain's job, he never would have taken it. He squinted at Travis, trying to read his mood.

"What about you?"

"I've already told you: it's your call. If you think this is just a temporary situation, I'm willing to give him the benefit of the doubt. If not . . ."

He shrugged, leaving the rest unsaid.

Sam kicked the wooden dock and sent a splinter flying. Travis knew as well as he did that no one could guarantee Kallik's work would improve, but he figured the odds were better than even that it would. After three miscarriages, Marilyn was finally out of the woods with this latest pregnancy and Kallik was getting his head back in the game. Unfortunately, she'd also had to quit work, which meant the guy needed his job more than ever. The way Sam saw it, there was no way Kallik was going to blow it.

"How's it going with Bear onboard?" Travis said. "Any problems I should know about?"

Since breaking up with his girlfriend the month before, Sam had had no one to watch Bear while he was at work, and Travis had agreed to let the dog sail with him until he could find a dog sitter. This change of subject was a not-so-subtle reminder about who made the final decisions on the ship.

"Fine," Sam said. "No complaints from the crew."

"No luck finding a sitter, then?"

Sam shook his head. The truth was, the ship was probably safer with Bear onboard than without him. Newfies were natural rescue dogs, known to pull drowning victims from the water; if Sam had his way, the dog would be a permanent member of the crew.

"What's out there is mostly for smaller dogs," he said. "Bear doesn't do well when he's cooped up all day."

"Guess we'll just have to take it day to day, then." Travis glanced back at the ship. "You'll let me know if Kallik can't cut it, right? I've got the rest of the crew to think about."

"Don't worry," Sam said. "If there's ever any question, he'll be out of here in a heartbeat."

"Glad to hear it." Travis gave Bear a final pat. "I'll let you two get back to work."

His crew had shown up just as the boss was driving away. As Oscar and Ben walked down to the dock, Sam checked his watch. Travis's visit had used up the time he'd normally have spent checking the weather report and getting coffee and donuts for everyone. Now, they'd be taking off late—never a good idea in a business where time was money.

But things had only gotten worse from there. The weather report from NOAA included a warning about a cyclone forming near the International Date Line. At that distance, they'd be in no danger of a direct hit, but the rain and chop would slow the tender down and make transferring the catch more difficult. When Kallik arrived, he and Sam went into the wheelhouse to discuss their options.

"I don't think it'll be a problem," the engineer said as Sam showed him the map. "The water isn't warm enough yet to get it going. By next month, sure, but not this early in the season. I say we take our chances."

Sam frowned and reread the warning from NOAA. The same system had dumped two feet of water on Seoul before heading back out to sea, and it hadn't broken up as predicted. What's to say it wouldn't keep going? He shook his head.

"I don't like it," he said. "I'm going to prepare for heavy weather."

Kallik shrugged one shoulder. "We're already running late, man. You do that, we'll be the last ones out of here."

"Better safe than sorry," Sam said. "I'd rather be wrong than dead."

Kallik went out to secure the engine room. Sam took care

of the wheelhouse and went out to inform the crew. As he slid the door open, he looked back at Bear.

"Come on, boy. Better stretch your legs while you can."

Sam and the crew spent the next half an hour rigging the safety lines and hand ropes, securing any movable objects, and closing the deck openings, ports, and deadlights. As predicted, they were the last ship underway, but Sam thought the peace of mind was worth it. Unfortunately, though, the cyclone broke up almost as quickly as it formed, and the ships that had beaten them out of port took all the best fish. Even worse, by the time they made it back to shore, the day's by-catch quota had been met and half their haul had to be dumped. When the final figures were added up, Oscar and Ben were sullen.

"Don't worry about it, man," Kallik said as the crewmen stalked off. "We'll make it up tomorrow. Get an early start. You'll see."

Looking back, it must have been the tension caused by the unending string of disasters that caused Sam to react the way he did. Distracted by his crew's ill humor, he didn't notice the murderous seagulls that dive-bombed his dog, sending Bear running for cover through the open doors of the cannery. By the time Sam got there, all he saw was some skinny guy in a white coat as he landed facedown in a pile of fish guts. It was like something you'd see on a YouTube video. Sam couldn't keep from laughing.

Then Bear started licking fish slime off the guy's face, and as he sat up, a bunch of wavy brown hair tumbled down the back of his soiled lab coat. That's when Sam realized that the skinny guy on the floor wasn't a guy at all.

"Uh-oh."

Bear bounded toward him, fish slime sluicing off his thick coat as Sam hurried over, mumbling apologies to the line workers who stood and stared. As he reached down to give the girl a hand, she turned and smiled at him, her startling green eyes dancing.

"What the hell is going on?"

A tall, red-faced man in a hard hat was rushing toward him. The man crouched down next to the girl and flashed Sam a menacing look.

"Is that your dog? Get him out of here!"

Bear shied, baffled by the man's reaction. Sam took his collar and looked at the girl again.

"Are you okay?"

She glanced at the man beside her and nodded.

"Go on," the man snapped. "Get out of here, both of you. This is a food processing area. Animals aren't allowed in here."

"Okay, okay," Sam said. "Come on, Bear."

For a few seconds, the Newfoundland stood staring at the girl, refusing to leave. Then Sam gave his collar another, firmer tug. Bear turned reluctantly away and the two of them headed back out to the dock.

Yes, it had been a bad day, Sam thought, but even with everything that had gone wrong—a late start, questions about Kallik, the poor catch, plus Bear knocking the girl down and the trail of fish slime they were leaving in their wake—the day might not have been a complete disaster if at just that moment they hadn't run into Jack Crompton.

The tender's co-owner stood just outside the cannery doors, his face flushed, his thin black mustache bristling. When Sam and Bear walked out, he pointed a finger at them and his eyes narrowed.

"I want to talk to you."

CHAPTER 3

Back inside the cannery, things quickly returned to normal. Loads of fish were once again coming through the open doors, landing wetly on the metal tables, and the people on the slime line had returned to their work. If it hadn't been for the ache in her shoulder, Emily might have thought she'd dreamed the whole thing.

"Are you okay?" Tim said, helping her up.

"Yeah. Just shaken a little." She looked down at the ruined lab coat. "Can't say the same for this thing, though."

The others crowded around her, shaking their heads admiringly.

"That was awesome!" Uki told her.

"Yeah," Dak said. "How did you do that?"

Tim looked at them. "What are you guys talking about?"

"Her!"

"You didn't see it?"

"When that dog ran in here, she just, like, grabbed it and rolled it out of the way."

"It was like kung fu or something."

His eyebrows shot up as he gave Emily an incredulous look. "You did?"

She shrugged modestly. "It was aikido, actually. I've been a black belt for a couple of years. When I saw the dog coming toward me, I knew I had to do something."

The look on their faces—a combination of awe and disbelief—made her shy. If Emily's sensei had seen what she'd done, he'd have told her it was a pretty sloppy performance. The first principle of *tori* was to avoid an attack, not invite it as she had, and she'd misjudged the weight of the dog, too, making it harder for her to control what happened once the attack commenced. Nevertheless, as the two of them collided, she'd employed *aiki,* the joining of forces, to redirect the dog's momentum into a roll that had left it unhurt—the basic tenet of aikido. If only she hadn't lost her footing and tumbled onto the floor herself, she'd have considered it a perfect outcome.

"It was no big deal. More of a reflex than anything."

"Well, whatever it was," Uki said, "I want to get me some. That was a seriously big dog."

"Yeah," Noah added. "I thought it was going to kill you."

Tim darted a furious look at the open doors. "If that's the case, then I'm just glad you're okay. And I'm *very* glad that dog didn't make it to the slime tables. If it had, this whole place might have had to shut down."

Emily looked around. She remembered seeing a man rush over to help her before Tim showed up, but he and the dog had disappeared before she got to her feet. She wondered where they'd gone.

"Where is he, the guy with the dog?"

"Out on the dock," Tim said. "There was a man waiting for them when they stepped outside. My guess is he's getting his butt kicked."

"Maybe he thinks I got hurt." She took a step in that direction. "I should let them know I'm okay."

Tim laid a hand on her arm.

"Don't bother," he said. "What happens out there is none of our business."

Emily pursed her lips. She didn't like the idea of anyone being punished for something they didn't do, but it was only her first day there and Tim was her boss. Surely, he knew more about these things than she did.

"Of course," she told him. "I understand."

He gave her a long look and shook his head.

"Let's get you out of that lab coat and take you home. I think you've had enough for one day."

"Are you sure?"

She didn't want the others to think she was a slacker.

"Don't worry about it," Noah said.

"We're going out later for burgers and brew," Dak told her. "You should join us."

"Yeah," Uki said. "I want to hear more about this aikido thing."

Emily gave them a weak smile. She'd been tired when she got to the cannery and the aftereffects from the fall were starting to set in.

"Maybe," she said. "I'll let you know."

Her new home was about a mile from the cannery, a modest ranch house with three bedrooms, two bathrooms, and a one-car garage. Tim carried her suitcases in and set them down in the front room.

"Thanks for getting those," Emily said as she looked around. "So, three bedrooms and four girls. Do you know who I'm sharing with?"

He scratched the back of his head, looking abashed.

"I think the others already called dibs on the bedrooms, but the couch is a pullout. I hear it's pretty comfortable."

Emily waited, hoping he would tell her it was a joke, then

realized that he was serious. She wasn't really angry, she supposed, just disappointed. It wasn't the sort of thing she'd have done in their place, but perhaps they thought she wasn't going to show up. She could have been there the week before if her mother hadn't insisted she meet with the colorist who was helping her redecorate Emily's bedroom. The room was fine as far as Emily was concerned, but at least the project would give her mother something to do other than call and pester her while she was away.

"In that case," she said, "I think I'll take the coat closet. That should give me plenty of room for my stuff."

"Seems fair to me," he said.

After Tim drove off, Emily took a few minutes to check out the rest of the house. The bedrooms were tiny—barely big enough for their twin beds; she could see why no one wanted to share. The bathrooms, too, were small, but clean and functional. No hair on the floor or soap scum in the bath, nothing clogging up the drains.

Not yet, anyway.

The kitchen was also small—about the size of her bedroom closet at home. Emily thought they might have to cook in shifts to keep from stepping on one another. In the refrigerator, she found milk, eggs, cheese, and an assortment of lunch meat, all of it carefully labeled with one of the other girls' names. She made a mental note to buy a Sharpie when she was at the store.

There was a noticeable smell of fish in the room that didn't go away when she closed the refrigerator, and it took a second for Emily to realize that it was coming from her. Having shed the hard hat, boots, and soiled lab coat back at the cannery, she'd thought herself free of fish odor, but it must have seeped into the rest of her clothing, too. She'd been planning to wear the same clothes until bedtime, but now she found she couldn't wait to get them off. She grabbed a towel from one of her bags and went off to take a shower.

Her roommates had come home by the time Emily was clean and dressed. Rachel was a junior at the University of Washington and Kimberley and Uki were local girls taking classes at UAS. Rachel and Kim had already laid claim to the bathroom with a tub, they informed her; Emily and Uki would have to settle for showers.

"Fine with me," Emily said, giving Uki a quick grin. "I've always thought taking baths was a waste of time."

"We told the guys we'd meet them for dinner in half an hour," Rachel said. "You coming?"

"I don't know," she said. "Maybe."

"Come on. Uki told us about your kung fu moves at the cannery. We want to hear how it really went down."

It was tempting. Emily had eaten nothing since lunch and all she had there was a couple of granola bars she'd tucked into her bags. Nevertheless, she wasn't crazy about being prodded for more details about her encounter with the dog. She was sure that anything she said would pale in comparison to whatever overblown version of events they'd already heard.

"I'm pretty tired," she said. "Plus, I promised my mom I'd call. Maybe another time."

"Suit yourself."

Kimberley turned and started down the hall.

"Come on, Rach, let's get out of these clothes before I barf."

"I'd better jump in the shower, too," Uki said.

She glanced at Emily's bags.

"Sorry about the couch."

"It's fine," Emily said. "Don't worry about it."

When the other three were finally behind closed doors, Emily took out her phone and called home. She'd had a long, exhausting day, and the thought of being stuck there with nothing to eat but a couple of granola bars was making her homesick. As the phone started to ring, she took a seat on the couch and tucked her feet underneath her. Tim was right; it was pretty comfortable.

"Hey, Mom, it's me."

"Emmy! Sweetheart, how are you?"

"I'm fine," she said, swallowing the lump in her throat. She hadn't expected to feel so emotional.

"How was the flight? No turbulence? I heard there was a storm over the valley."

"No, it was really smooth," Emily said. "We got out of Sea-Tac a bit late, but we landed right on time."

"Yes, I got your text. I'm just surprised it took so long to hear from you. Is everything all right?"

"Sorry about that," she said. "I was at work."

"Work? But you just got there. Can't they give you a chance to catch your breath?"

"It's okay, Mom. I didn't mind. Besides, I could hardly say no. The other interns have been here for a week already."

"Oh. Well, I suppose that's my fault, isn't it?"

Emily sighed. Why did her mother always turn things around so that she was the victim?

"I didn't say that."

"No, but you didn't have to. You were upset that I asked you to stay and now you're blaming me because Ava couldn't meet with us sooner."

"I wasn't *blaming* you, just telling you why I didn't think it was a good idea to try and beg off work."

"If you say so."

"I do say so."

She felt her heart racing and tried to calm down. Why did she always let her mother get to her?

"Have you talked to Carter since you got in?" her mother asked.

Emily felt a stab of guilt. She hadn't even thought to call him.

"Not yet," she said.

"I saw him this afternoon. He said to say hi."

"I thought he was on call at the hospital this week."

"He is," her mother said. "I had to take Uncle Danny over there for some tests."

Since her father's death, Emily's uncle had been the closest thing she had to a father. The thought that there might be something wrong with him was like having a rug pulled out from under her.

"What kind of tests?"

"Oh, you know: routine stuff. When you get to be our ages, they give you tests for everything. Have you met the other girls yet? Are they nice?"

Emily glanced down the hallway. All of the other doors were closed.

"Yeah, they're okay."

"Not a very enthusiastic endorsement."

"I just met them so it's hard to tell, but yes. They're okay. They seem nice."

Aside from hogging up all the bedrooms.

"You know," her mother said, "you're lucky to have a beau like Carter. He's been very open-minded about this little junket of yours."

"What junket? I'm not on *vacation*. I've got a job."

"An internship isn't a *job*, sweetheart."

Emily felt her temper flash.

"It's *work,* okay? And if I do it well, it'll help me get a job near Carter. I thought that would make you happy."

"Emmy, have you eaten dinner?"

The sudden change of subject pulled her up short.

"What? No, not yet. Why?"

"I thought not. You always get cranky when you're hungry."

Emily gritted her teeth.

"I'm not *cranky.* I just had a tough day: up early, stuck in a plane for hours, then falling on my face at the—"

"*What?* You *fell?* Are you *hurt?*"

She shook her head. Why had she thought that calling her mother was a good idea?

"No. I'm fine, Mom. Honestly."

"I'll catch a plane. I can be there in the morning—"

"Calm down. I'm okay, all right? A dog ran into the cannery and knocked me down. It was no big deal."

"What was a *dog* doing in the cannery? Isn't that where they do the . . . things with the fish? Oh God, I'll never buy another can of tuna."

Uki stepped out of the bathroom and gave her a curious look. Emily pointed at the phone and mouthed the word *mother.* Uki nodded and walked into her bedroom.

"Mom, stop it," she hissed. "The dog didn't get into the fish; no one got hurt; everything is *fine.*"

"Well . . . if you're sure."

"Yes. I'm *sure.*"

Emily saw the doors at the end of the hallway open and Kimberley and Rachel stepped out. They'd changed their clothes and pulled their hair up in matching ponytails. She could smell their perfume from across the room.

"Look, I have to go," she said. "Don't worry, okay? I'll call you tomorrow."

The two girls were checking their phones as she hung up. Uki came out of her room, tucking her shirttail into her Levi's.

"You sure you won't join us?" Rachel said. "There's plenty of room in the car."

Emily's stomach growled—an unhappy marriage of hunger and frustration—and suddenly the thought of eating granola bars while stewing over the conversation with her mother was unbearable. Maybe being interrogated about her tangle with the dog wouldn't be so bad.

"Sounds good," she said. "Let me get my sweater."

CHAPTER 4

The sun was low in the sky by the time Sam and Bear showed up at Kallik's house. When he'd left the cannery that afternoon, Sam had taken his dog for a long walk, trying to cool down and decide what to do about work. First, Travis had given him grief about Kallik, then Crompton had come down on him about Bear; it was like being in a dysfunctional family with those two. He was tired of being second-guessed by guys who'd never hauled fish for a living and sick of working hard while somebody else took most of the profit. It was time to take charge of his future, and the only way to do that was with a ship of his own.

He'd been working on his plan for a while now, but so far, the dream had remained out of reach. The perfect ship would be gone before he could bid on it, or the price would be too high, or the seller too flaky. Interest rates that had held steady for years were suddenly going up, too, making any money he borrowed that much harder to pay back. Some days, it felt as if the whole universe were against him.

Marilyn answered the door when Sam knocked, her baby bump proudly displayed under a fitted T-shirt. Pregnancy suited her, he thought, filling out her thin face and making her cheeks glow. Kallik was thrilled, but Sam wasn't sure he'd have had the guts to try again after so many disappointments. Then again, maybe he'd feel braver if he were in their position. Kallik and Marilyn were both pure Tlingit—the First Nation of Ketchikan. For them, a baby represented more than just family, it meant the survival of their people. Sam just hoped that this time, the two of them would get the happy ending they deserved.

She leaned against the doorjamb and lifted an eyebrow.

"Well, if it isn't Sandy Sam and his shaggy companion. What brings you two here on this fine evening?"

He grinned.

"Any chance we could steal your husband away for a little while?"

"Didn't you already steal him away this morning?" she said, her eyes twinkling with mischief. "You and that boat are as bad as a mistress."

"No way," Kallik said, stepping up behind her. "I'd be home a lot more often if I only had a mistress to take care of."

He gave her a squeeze and looked at Sam.

"What's up, Skipper?"

"Got time to talk? Over a drink, maybe?"

"Ah, that sounds like a *serious* talk," Kallik said. "Let me get a jacket."

As her husband walked off, Marilyn reached out and gave Bear a snuggle. Sam had noticed that his dog was less boisterous around her since the pregnancy. Newfoundlands were especially attuned to human vulnerability; he wondered if Marilyn's condition was drawing out the dog's protective nature.

"Try not to bring my husband home too late," she said, patting her belly. "Me and Junior don't sleep well without him."

"Don't worry," Sam told her. "I'll keep an eye on the time."

Kallik returned and gave Marilyn a kiss on the cheek.

"Don't wait up for me, baby. This might take a while."

The two men headed down to the Sourdough, a place where locals could hang out, have a drink, and play pool without being hassled. They ordered their beers at the bar and took them to a table in back while Bear wandered off to visit some of the regulars. Sam pointed to the pictures of famous shipwrecks on the wall.

"Kind of makes you humble, doesn't it?"

Kallik nodded. "Being humble is the only way to stay alive on the water. You start thinking you're the one in charge, it's over, man."

Sam stared at the bottle in his hand. It had taken hours to work up the courage to share his plan with Kallik, and now that they were face-to-face, he was having a hard time getting started. Getting the engineer's buy-in was crucial for his plan to work; if the answer was no, he'd be done before he even got started. He took a second to scan the room before laying out his proposition. The last thing he wanted was for word to get back to the ship's co-owners and crew. Finding the right ship might still take time, no matter how eager he was, and neither one of them could afford to lose his job.

"I've decided to buy my own ship," he said. "Not some-day—now. As soon as I can get my hands on one."

Kallik took another sip of beer.

"You have the money?"

Sam shrugged. It was a fair, if uncomfortable, question.

"Not all of it," he said. "Not in cash, anyway, but rates are still low and my credit's good. I can borrow the rest and pay it back with the extra I'll be making as owner."

The engineer was making condensation patterns on the table with his bottle.

"I don't know, man. Debt's like a weight around your neck,

always pulling you down. You have a bad season, miss a few payments, you lose everything."

Sam clenched his teeth in frustration. He hadn't gone there to hear what he already knew; he was looking for support.

"Then again," Kallik continued, "most people who borrow do okay, and you've got other resources. I suppose you'd be fine."

"That's right," Sam said, relieved.

"You're still gonna need a crew, though, and the season's already started. Most guys out there have a ship by now."

"I'm not worried about finding a crew; there are always guys on the dock looking for work. The hard part will be finding an engineer."

Their eyes met.

"Will you do it?" Sam said. "If I find a ship, will you join me?"

Kallik took a deep breath and shook his head.

"I can't, man. I'd love to, you know that, but with the baby—"

"Come on. Travis and Jack have been giving you crap for months. You don't like working for them any more than I do."

The engineer nodded, then fixed Sam with a hard stare.

"Let me ask you something. You been talking about getting your own ship for as long as I've known you. What's the hurry all of a sudden?"

Sam looked down the row of tables and saw his dog padding toward them. Everyone Bear passed smiled or said hello or gave him a pat on the back. It had been that way on the ship, too. The crew liked having him around—Oscar even said that having a Newfoundland onboard was good luck. Why were Jack and Travis so anxious to get rid of him?

"You know they've been after me about having Bear onboard."

"I thought you guys worked that out."

"I thought so, too—at least temporarily—but then Bear got spooked and ran into the cannery this afternoon. He knocked some girl down."

"Aw, crap."

"I thought it would be okay. I mean, it didn't look like she was hurt, but that NOAA inspector showed up and started yelling at us to get out. Just my luck, Jack Crompton was standing right there on the dock."

Kallik shook his head.

"The guy went off on me like a bomb. Said Bear was a liability he couldn't afford. Told me not to bring him on the ship anymore."

"What are you going to do?"

Sam finished his beer and set the bottle aside. For the next few days, at least, it would be a moot point. After that day's poor harvest, the regional administrator had declared all fish in the area uncatchable in hopes of staying within the allowable ocean harvest goals for the season. Once that restriction was lifted, though, he'd be back on the water—without Bear.

"I don't know," he said. "I admit I haven't been looking that hard for a sitter, but it isn't easy to find someone with enough room for Bear. He can't just sit in a little cage all day. He needs to stretch his legs or he'll go crazy."

"What about Tiffany? She's got a place of her own now, doesn't she?"

"It wouldn't work," he said. "Too many issues."

Sam had actually considered asking his ex-girlfriend if she could take the dog, just for a while, but had decided against it. Tiffany and Bear still got along and the place where she was living had a decent-sized yard, but her drug habit had only gotten worse since the two of them broke up, and the guy she was living with was bad news. If Sam left Bear with them, he'd never be able to concentrate on running the ship. He couldn't afford to risk everyone's lives just so his dog could have a place to stay.

"Can't you just leave him at home?"

"I'll have to," Sam said. "At least until I can find someone to watch him. But Bear's a big guy, and he gets bored if no one's around. I don't want him getting out and wandering the streets while I'm gone."

Kallik was thoughtful a moment.

"Why don't I ask Marilyn if she knows somebody? There's a lot of girls in her women's circle who could use a few bucks working from home."

"That'd be great. Thanks."

"So, problem solved?"

Sam shrugged. "One of them, anyway."

Kallik lifted his empty bottle and gave it a waggle.

"Well, if you need me to solve another one, you'll have to buy me another one of these."

"You got it."

Sam got up to fetch them each another, stepping carefully over Bear, who had fallen asleep at their feet. When he returned, the dog lifted his head, blinked sleepily for a moment, then lay back down and continued his nap. Sam set the bottles down and took his seat. Kallik was looking at his phone.

"Everything okay?"

He nodded. "It's Marilyn. She's got another name she wants to run by me."

Marilyn had been looking for a traditional Tlingit name for the baby, something they could both agree on—so far, without luck.

"What's this one?"

"KaGák."

Sam repeated the word as best he could, trying to get the emphasis right.

"I like it," he said. "What's it mean?"

Kallik looked up. "Mouse."

"Uh-huh. So, what do you think?"

"Not sure yet. Giving kids the names of animals isn't my thing, but it's traditional, and Marilyn's always felt bad that she wasn't given a native name. Mostly, I just want something that doesn't sound like something nasty in English."

"Well, it's not too bad. Doesn't sound like anything a kid could make fun of, but then, kids can be pretty creative when it comes to making fun."

"I'll tell her it's a maybe."

He sent the text and put his phone away.

"So, problem number two?"

Sam hesitated. He hadn't been planning to mention Travis's visit when he asked Kallik to join him, but he figured it was better to get it out in the open rather than take the chance that someone would mention it later. As far as he was concerned, his engineer's performance issues were a thing of the past, but that didn't mean they'd gone unnoticed. The guy needed to know he was skating on thin ice.

"I got a visit from Travis this morning."

"So I heard." Kallik tilted the bottle neck toward him. "Oscar and Ben saw him leaving. They talk."

"He's concerned about some of the stuff that went on the last few months."

"With me?"

"Yeah. You know: tardiness, lack of focus. The equipment we lost in that storm."

Kallik's face collapsed in on itself.

"I already paid them back."

"I know that," Sam said. "I'm not blaming you."

"So, what did you say when Travis brought it all up again?"

"I told him the truth: you had a rough patch, but it's behind you now."

"Damn right. Why can't he let it go?"

"Because that's the way he is," Sam said. "That's the way they both are. They treat us like a bunch of little kids instead of professionals." He leaned forward to press his point. "That's why we need to get out of there—both of us. I need to know you're with me."

Kallik stared at the table and slowly shook his head.

"I can't, man. Marilyn would never forgive me. She'd say a bird in the hand is worth a dozen flying free."

"Yeah, well, what if the bird in your hand's about to fly away, too?"

The engineer's face flushed. When he looked up, his eyes were almost bugging out of his head. *What?*

Sam chewed his lip. He hadn't meant to say anything about Jack's threat, it had just popped out. Now that it was out there, though, he could hardly take it back.

"Travis told me that Jack wants to fire you. I don't know how serious he is. Maybe he will and maybe he won't, but I thought you should know."

Kallik opened his mouth.

"*And . . .*" Sam continued, "before you accuse me of playing dirty, I didn't tell you that so you'd agree to join me. I did it so you could be prepared in case the worst happens."

His assurance seemed to do the trick. The engineer's look of outrage subsided.

"I know that, man. You've always played straight with me. Sorry. I just—"

"Don't worry about it. I'd have thought the same thing."

The door to the bar flew open and a gaggle of young voices kicked the noise level up, disturbing the comfortable, low-key atmosphere. Sam turned and looked back over his shoulder.

"Who the hell is that?"

"College kids," Kallik said. "They were in here last week, too. Think they're locals now 'cause they're here for the summer."

Sam watched the four girls and two guys at the bar fishing out their IDs so they could buy drinks. One of the girls looked familiar.

"Oh, crap."

"What?"

"That girl, the one in back. She's the one Bear knocked down at the cannery." He turned away and hunched his shoulders. "I can't let her see me. She'll come over and rip me a new one."

The engineer craned his neck.

"Hey, she's cute. You sure you don't want to go over and say hi?"

"Positive."

Sam pulled up his shirt collar and turned his face to the wall.

Kallik chuckled. "Then I hate to tell you this, man, but even if she hasn't seen you, she's definitely seen your dog."

Sam reached down, but Bear was already on his feet. Before he could grab the dog's collar, he'd taken off. As the Newfoundland trotted over, the group at the bar greeted him like an old friend. Seconds later, the girl walked up and tapped him on the shoulder.

"Hey there. Remember me?"

Sam glanced up into the same emerald eyes he'd seen that afternoon.

"Yeah, I remember," he said. "You okay?"

She nodded. "Got a bruise on my shoulder, but that's my fault. I saw that guy giving you crap out on the dock. Sorry if you got in trouble."

How old was she? She seemed pretty poised for a college kid.

"It's fine," he said. "I was just worried about you."

"I'm Emily, by the way."

Emily stuck out her hand—it was really soft—and he shook it, feeling self-conscious about the calluses on his own.

"Sam," he said.

She hesitated a moment, glancing back at the others.

"Well, as long as there are no hard feelings . . ."

"No," he said. "No hard feelings."

"Okay. Well, I'll see you around, I guess."

"Yeah. Sure. See you."

She turned away and took a few steps, then looked back.

"By the way, what's your dog's name?"

"Bear."

"Bear." Emily nodded. "Yeah, that's a good name for him."

Sam's heart was pounding. As he turned back, Kallik grinned.

"Oh, my my, those green eyes. You look like a kid with his first crush."

Sam scowled. He'd never been able to hide his emotions; people always told him they could read his mind on his face.

"Come on," he said. "I promised your wife I'd get you home by bedtime."

CHAPTER 5

Emily found the rest of the interns crowded around a table for four that they'd augmented with a couple of borrowed chairs. Uki and the guys had started drinking back at the restaurant and their faces had the feverish glow of inebriation, Rachel was nursing her first beer of the evening, and designated driver Kimberley was having another Diet Coke. Emily set her beer on the table and took a seat.

"Sorry. I just needed to talk to that guy a second."

Rachel and Kimberley exchanged a look.

"You know Sam Reed?" Kimberley said.

"Is that his name? He just said it was Sam. Why?"

"He's a captain on one of the tenders. That was his dog we saw when we walked in."

"Yeah," Emily said. "That's the one that knocked me down at the cannery. I thought I should let him know I was all right."

The two of them were still staring at her.

"Did I miss something?"

"Kimberley knows him." Rachel smirked. "She thinks he's hot."

The rest of the group erupted with cries of, "*Ooh, Kimmie!*"

Kimberley ducked her head. "Cut it out, you guys."

Noah, who Emily suspected had designs on Kimberley himself, cast a dismissive glance at the door.

"Looked like any other tender jockey to me."

"Don't listen to him," Rachel said. "Men have no idea what women find attractive."

Emily shrugged. She had, in fact, found Sam rather good-looking, but she wasn't going to say that—especially now. Besides, she already had a boyfriend.

"So," Uki said. "Tell us more about aikido."

At the restaurant, they'd all been too busy eating to pump Emily for information. Now, it looked as if the subject was unavoidable. Word of her martial arts showdown with Bear had obviously been the topic of discussion after she left the cannery.

"You guys don't want to hear about that stuff."

"Why not? The way you turned that dog away from the slime line was cool. I mean, he must weigh almost as much as you do."

"Yeah," Rachel said. "Tell us what happened."

Emily stared at the bottle in her hand. What was there to say? What she'd done had been pure reflex—the result of hours of practice and repetition. When she thought about it now, the only clear memory she had—besides Bear—was of Sam running toward her, his sun-bleached hair flying, his strong arms reaching for her. To Emily, who was used to Carter's lithe build and finely wrought features, it was like having Thor show up to rescue her. She felt her face redden.

"In aikido, the first principle is to use as little force as necessary to stop an attack without hurting either yourself or your opponent. Unfortunately," she added, rolling her shoulder, "I wasn't entirely successful."

"*Without* hurting them?" Uki squeaked. "What's the point if you can't kick their butts?"

"Why do you have to be such a badass?" Noah said. "Try acting like a girl once in a while, will you?"

She narrowed her eyes at him.

"Native girls *are* badasses."

"Okay, okay," Rachel said. "Neutral corners, everyone. We haven't got much time here. Tim wants us on the docks by six."

A chorus of groans went up around the table, but it was far short of a mutiny. Emily figured it was still too early in the season for anyone to have developed a really bad attitude.

"Speaking of Tim," she said. "What was that call about this afternoon? You guys said something about problems at the cannery."

Dak nodded. "Tim hasn't said much about it, but Noah's brother interned there last year. He says it's been going on for a while."

"What's been going on?"

"We already told you," Noah said. "Stuff that makes the inspectors look bad."

Emily pursed her lips. She was getting tired of Noah's attitude.

"Okay, but what kind of stuff?"

"Reports from NOAA that have gone missing," Dak said. "Fish Tim okayed that gets pulled by the quality testers."

"So?" she said. "Stuff happens."

"Yeah, but it's been happening a lot more than it used to and always when Tim's there."

"You think someone's got it in for him?"

Glances darted around the table.

Dak shrugged. "Could be. Some of us think so, but like you said, it could just be a coincidence."

"The problem," Uki said, "is that there are people saying it's our fault."

"*Ours?*" Emily said. "How can it be our fault?"

"We're a distraction. Tim has to spend so much time holding our hands that he can't do his job." She shrugged. "At least, that's the rumor."

"But without internships . . . I mean, this might be the only way I can get a job in my field," Emily said.

Dak nodded. "This might be the only way anybody can get a job that isn't beholden to the canneries. Without independent inspectors, they'd be the ones in charge of how much fish gets processed and what kind of quality it is. I'm not saying they don't care, but if it hurts their bottom line . . ."

"So, what can we do about it?"

Noah laughed. "What are you talking about? *We* can't do anything. The only thing we can do is keep our heads down and hope the job lasts long enough to get a good reference out of it."

The rest of them nodded their resigned assent.

"Well, I'm not going to just sit back while the program gets canceled," Emily said. "I'm going to do something."

"Oh, really," Noah said. "Like what?"

She shrugged. "I don't know yet, but I'll think of something."

The other girls had long since gone to bed as Emily sat on the open couch, mulling over the problems at the cannery. It upset her to think that someone might be deliberately trying to wreck the internship program—not because it threatened her own position, but because shutting it down would prevent other young people from gaining valuable experience they couldn't get elsewhere. She knew the others thought she was joking when she said she'd find a solution, but she was dead serious. She'd never been one to do nothing when someone was being picked on. If she could find out who was making Tim look bad, then at least he'd have a chance to fight back.

Unfortunately, there was no way she could get close to anyone inside the cannery. Emily had seen the suspicious looks she'd gotten from the people there. Even if they knew something that would help, they'd probably figure it wasn't worth risking their jobs to share it—especially with an intern. And what if the problem included people on the dock, as well? She didn't know enough about how fish were caught, bought, and processed to even recognize a problem if she saw one. No, what she needed was someone who knew how the entire system worked and could recognize a discrepancy when they saw it.

What about Sam Reed?

He certainly knew how fish were bought and sold, and Emily knew that most people who worked in the fishing industry had worked in the canneries at one time or another. His dog had knocked her down that day, too, so he sort of owed her a favor, didn't he? Even if he couldn't help her, she thought, he might know someone else who could.

The thought of talking to Sam Reed again gave Emily a frisson, a feeling she immediately suppressed. She wasn't looking for an excuse to flirt with the guy. She wasn't Kimberley; she didn't care if Sam was "hot." She had a real problem on her hands and asking him for help was a legitimate path to a solution. Her interest in contacting him was completely professional.

Even if he did look a bit like Chris Hemsworth.

Thinking about talking to Sam Reed reminded Emily that she hadn't spoken to her own boyfriend that day. She rummaged around in her bag and took out her phone, frowning when she saw how low the battery was. Her mother had been after her for months to buy a new one, but there hadn't been time. She'd look for the charger, she told herself, just as soon as she'd checked her messages.

There were two from her mother and one from Tim reminding her to wear old clothes tomorrow, but nothing from Carter.

Probably too busy at the hospital, Emily told herself. She'd just send him a text.

Hope UR fine. TTYL?

In seconds, she got his reply. Emily squealed in delight as she read it.

Taking a break in the Drs lounge. Call me.

Emily felt giddy as she dialed his number. Carter picked up on the first ring.

"I wasn't sure if you'd be busy," she said. "Glad I caught you."

"Actually, things have been pretty slow tonight. I've just been hanging out in the lounge."

"You should have called," she said, trying not to sound critical. "I always love talking to you."

"Yeah, I guess I could have. Sorry."

"Well, the important thing is, we're talking now."

"Mmm-hmm."

She stretched out on the couch.

"It's been a long day. The flight took forever and then as soon as I landed, we went straight to the cannery. I didn't even have time to change."

"Uh-huh."

"The place is huge—and loud! And, oh God, all the blood and fish guts. I almost threw up."

"Hmm."

"Then this enormous dog ran in and knocked me down. I was able to keep it from getting into the fish, but at the last minute, I lost my balance and fell. My lab coat got covered in fish slime."

"Mmm."

Emily frowned. Somehow, she'd expected a bit more of a reaction.

"Carter, did you hear what I said?"

"Your flight was fine, you went to work, a dog knocked you down. Did I miss anything?"

"Well . . . no."

Emily sighed. This was a far cry from the fantasy of having Thor almost sweep her off her feet.

"I just thought you'd be more concerned," she said.

"Of course I'm *concerned,* but if you'd been seriously injured you would have said so. You're a big girl. I know you can take care of yourself."

Carter was right, Emily thought. She didn't need to be coddled and fussed over; she had her mother for that. Speaking of whom . . .

"I talked to my mom earlier. She told me she ran into you today."

"Hmm? When was that?"

"At the hospital. She had to take Uncle Danny in for some tests."

"Oh, right. That was during oncology rounds."

Emily sat up.

"*Oncology?* She told me they were just routine tests."

"Calm down, Em. I'm sure everything's fine."

"But oncology? Carter, that's cancer. What was my uncle doing there?"

"You know I can't tell you that. Patient confidentiality—"

"Carter, *please,*" she said. "This is my uncle we're talking about."

"I'm sorry, *Emily,* but I've already told you more than I should have. If you need more information about your uncle's treatment, you'll have to ask him."

Emily felt tears of frustration welling. She knew confidentiality was important, but this was a family member they were talking about. Couldn't Carter at least give her a hint? Why was he treating her like a stranger?

You're being ridiculous, she told herself. Of course he couldn't tell her anything. Confidentiality meant nothing if doctors could throw it out the window any time a family member asked them to. If anything, she should be admiring him for standing by his principles.

"You're right," she said. "I'm sorry. I'll give him a call and see what's what."

"Good girl."

She winced. Being called a "good girl" always made her feel like an obedient animal.

"Listen," he said. "It sounds like you need to get some rest. I'll try and call you in a couple of days, okay?"

"Sure," she said. "Talk to you then."

Emily hung up, feeling sick at heart. The idea that her uncle Danny might be seriously ill seemed impossible. He'd always been a bigger-than-life figure. Pink-cheeked and barrel-chested, with his dark hair slicked back and a cigar always smoldering somewhere nearby, he was a man to whom no one remained a stranger for long. Only those who knew him well understood that his hail-fellow-well-met exterior covered a painful episode: the death of his brother, Emily's father, for which he blamed himself.

She had to talk to him, find out for herself how sick he really was. Emily knew she'd never be able to sleep if she didn't. She looked at the time and bit her lip. Was eleven too late to call? Surely, he'd understand, she told herself. If he knew how upset she was, he'd want her to call and set her mind at ease. Or at least stop herself from imagining the worst.

The call went straight to his voice mail.

"Oh. Hi, Uncle Danny. It's me, Emily. I'm, uh, sorry to be calling so late, but—"

"Punkin'! I didn't see it was you. How are you, darling girl?"

As her uncle's voice boomed in her ear, Emily closed her eyes and felt a tear of relief run down her cheek. He sounded as strong and healthy as he always had. Why had she imagined there could be anything wrong? Nevertheless, she was glad she'd called.

"I hope I didn't wake you."

"*Psh*. You know I don't sleep. But you. There's nothing wrong, is there? You're not in trouble?"

"No, no. I'm fine. Just wanted to call and say hi."

"How's Alaska?" he said. "Met any Eskimos yet?"

She rolled her eyes. Uncle Danny could be a bit un-PC.

"No, but one of my roommates is part Tlingit."

"Oh, dear. I'd better put in my hearing aids. I thought you said she was a Klingon."

"No, *Tlingit*. It's hard to hear on the phone."

"I'm sorry. Didn't mean to offend."

"That's okay." She paused. "Listen, the reason I called is that Mom told me you were at the hospital for some tests today. Are you all right?"

"Of course I'm all right. Fit as a fiddle."

Emily frowned. Did his voice sound a little raspy, or was she just imagining things?

"You're sure?"

"Yes, yes. You know how doctors are when you have good insurance. Well, not your Carter, of course, but—"

"It's okay. I knew what you meant. So," she said, "you're really fine?"

"Yes."

"And you'd tell me if you weren't?"

"Well, I can't promise that, but I'd tell you if the end was near, and I'm still a long way from the finish line."

Emily took a deep breath and smiled. Carter must have been mistaken, she thought. It couldn't be easy to remember what part of the hospital you were in when you were sleep-deprived.

"Well, I'm glad to hear you're okay."

"And I'm glad you're doing well."

"I love you, Uncle Danny."

"I love you, too, dear heart. Sleep well."

CHAPTER 6

Pink cotton candy clouds dotted the pale blue sky the next morning as Sam and Bear walked into town. It had been full daylight for two hours and would remain so for another fifteen, so without fish to bring in, Sam had decided to spend some time checking out the "Ships for Sale" postings around town. A good ship wouldn't stay on the market for long; he'd need to keep his ear to the ground to find what he was looking for.

Kallik had promised to ask around and see if anyone he knew was looking to sell, and Sam had told him what he thought he could afford, but he'd probably go higher if the right one came along. It was a delicate balance. He didn't want to tip his hand to a seller who might have taken less, but neither did he want to miss out on the perfect ship if a few dollars more would make a difference. Sam wasn't too worried about carrying debt. Fishing wasn't his only source of income, and the way he saw it, the sooner he had his own ship, the more he'd be making and the faster he could pay it off. He looked down at the idle fishing tenders in the harbor, their crews busy doing maintenance until fishing resumed. Somewhere out there was the ship that would set him free, he thought. All he had to do was find it.

As they headed toward town, the smell of coffee mingling with the tang of the ocean made his stomach growl. Their first stop that morning would be Mollie's Café. Mollie Boone had been a fixture in Ketchikan for as long as Sam could remember, and it was generally agreed that she made the best salmon hash on the island. Most everyone who worked the fisheries came into Mollie's at least once a week; if one of them had mentioned a ship for sale, she would know it.

A series of long, low hoots told him a great gray owl was roosting close by. The enormous birds rarely flushed, preferring to stay hidden even when people came near. Occasionally, Sam would notice a dark shape in a tree and find a pair of yellow eyes staring down at him from one of its branches. This one was probably a female guarding her nest.

Bear lifted his head and growled as a thickset man stepped into the road ahead of them. His hair was grayer now than the last time they'd seen each other and the heavy beard had partially hidden the large red birthmark on the man's left cheek, but Sam had no trouble recognizing him.

"Morning, Captain Reed."

Sam took a firm hold of Bear's collar.

"What do you want, Logan?"

"Nothin'. Just out for a stroll, same as you."

Logan Marsh had been part of Sam's crew until halfway through the last season, when he'd nearly gotten them all killed. Like a lot of those who worked the ships, Logan was a drinker—something Sam had no problem with as long as a man did his job—but during an especially memorable bender, Logan had taken a fall, injuring his back and leaving him hooked on pain pills. Sam hadn't known the guy had a problem until the day the ship was caught in a storm and he discovered that Logan had sold the crew's safety equipment for drug money. When they finally made it back to shore—battered and near-drowned—Sam had fired him on the spot. Since then, Logan Marsh had descended further into criminality, from theft to assault and attempted rape, each time pleading to lesser charges that netted him little if any jail time. According to Kallik, Logan blamed Sam for his troubles, which was why Sam very much doubted that this meeting was an accident.

Bear continued to growl as the two men stared at each other, the sound filling the air with menace. The dog was gentle by nature, but he was fiercely protective. He wouldn't hesitate to attack anyone who tried to hurt Sam, something Logan must have realized as he weighed his odds of success. Even if he were able to land a blow, it wouldn't be worth being mauled by a hundred-and-fifty-pound animal. He gave Sam an oily smile and walked past, giving the two of them a wide berth.

"Well then," he said. "I'll see you around."

At Mollie's Café, Sam took a table in the far corner with enough room underneath for Bear to eat in peace. They each had two poached eggs over salmon hash, Sam washing his down with coffee so sweet it was almost syrup. Bear finished his quickly and started searching the floor for any scraps he might have missed. When Mollie came by to refill Sam's coffee cup, he asked her if she knew of any tenders for sale.

She squinched up her face thoughtfully.

"Can't think of any right off," she said. "I could ask around, if you want."

"That'd be great." Sam glanced toward the men at the next table. "But I'd prefer you didn't mention it was me asking."

Mollie gave him a sly wink.

"No problem. Lots of folks selling don't want their names broadcast, either. Sometimes I think this whole town is one big rumor mill."

"You may be right."

The bell in front rang as another customer walked in.

"I gotta go," Mollie said. She took out her order pad and handed him his ticket. "Here. Write your number down, I'll give you a call if I hear anything."

"Thanks, I appreciate it."

Sam left his cell number and a large tip and he and Bear headed out.

After that, they stopped by the union hall, which was crowded that day due to the fishing ban. There were no tenders posted on the board, and a few disgruntled seamen were saying that anyone betting his savings on the fishing industry was a fool, given the current conditions.

"Every year, the season gets shorter and the fish get smaller," one said. "Pretty soon, there'll be no fish left. Then where will we all be?"

Sam did his best to disregard their grumbling. He'd seen worse years than that one, and the fish had always come back. Governments were putting limits on the amount of stock they took each year, too, and there was still a lot of ocean out there. It might last forever and it might end tomorrow. Either way, he figured, there was no sense in worrying about it.

With breakfast time over, the cruise ships were disgorging their passengers onto the docks. Avid bargain-hunters swarmed onto Front Street and into the open arms of shopkeepers for whom every arrival was a windfall. Ketchikan was a magnet for all sorts of artists, and the promise of eager summer buyers made toiling through the dark months bearable. A few years back, Sam had let himself be talked into joining a musical theater group and ended up loving it. Once salmon season was over, they'd be starting rehearsals for their winter production.

Giving the tourist district a wide berth, Sam and Bear checked out a few more community bulletin boards, spreading the word to a couple of people whose discretion could be relied upon, but nothing new had been posted and no one he spoke to knew of a vessel like the one he was looking for. It was frustrating. He knew he'd have had better luck posting his own information and the type of ship he wanted, but the chances that word would get back to Travis or Jack were too great. As difficult as it was, Sam would just have to be patient. When they reached the last place they could think to look, they turned around and started back.

Having done everything he could to find himself a ship, Sam was feeling antsy. He'd never been good at killing time, especially during fishing season, and the last thing he needed was to go home and start pacing the floor like a caged animal. Maybe he'd just head down to the dock, see if his crew needed a hand. They might not be hauling fish, but that didn't mean there wasn't plenty of work to do. There was nothing like cleaning the bilge or scraping barnacles from the hull to distract you from your troubles.

"Come on, Bear," Sam said. "Let's go see how Ben and Oscar are doing."

Sam kept a sharp eye out for Logan Marsh as they crossed Washington, wondering where the man had slunk off to. Running into the guy so close to his own neighborhood had given him an uneasy feeling. What if Logan had been watching Sam's house, waiting for him to leave so he could break in? Coming home to find the place trashed—or, worse, being confronted by an armed and angry man—would be a nightmare. Sam might be a big guy, but hatred was a surprisingly effective tonic. If the two of them came face-to-face again, there was no telling what might happen.

The cannery was up ahead on their right. As Sam and Bear got closer, they slowed down to take a look. With no fish coming in that day, the enormous white building seemed abandoned. Gulls and crows that should have been feasting on the dock strutted around the empty parking lot, searching for scraps and fighting over anything they found. The doors that had been open just the day before were closed, the only workers inside doing cleaning and maintenance, glad to be making a few dollars while the place sat idle.

Sam had a fleeting recollection of running through those doors and seeing the girl—Emily—sprawled on the floor, facedown in fish guts, and smiled. When he first realized that it was a girl Bear had knocked over in the cannery, he'd been expecting hysterics. Instead, Emily had looked up with those amazing eyes and smiled. At the time, he assumed she was trying to tell him she was all right, but when he thought about it now, Sam wondered if what she was really doing was telling him that she got it. She knew how funny the whole thing must look and would have been laughing, too, if she'd been in his place. He wished he'd had a chance to ask her about it last night when she showed up at the bar, but with Kallik grinning at him like an idiot, there was no way.

They'd just stepped onto the dock when Sam's phone buzzed. He checked the caller. It was Mollie.

"Hey, what's up?"

"Guy came in here a little while ago, says he knows of a tender for sale. I got his number if you're still interested."

Sam felt his heart leap. Maybe this was the one!

"Of course I am. What's the number?"

She gave it to him and he repeated it twice to be sure he had it right.

"I'll give him a call right away. Thanks, Moll. You're the best."

Sam's hand shook as he dialed the number. As the line rang, he started pacing the dock, Bear watching him uncertainly. He was formulating a message to leave on the guy's voice mail when he finally picked up. Sam asked about the tender for sale and the man gave him the particulars, including the price he was asking for. It was a bit more than he wanted to spend, but if it was as clean as the man said it was, it could be worth it. They agreed to meet at the southern marina in an hour to look it over. By the time Sam hung up, he'd sweated through his flannel shirt.

He looked down and grabbed his dog around its neck.

"This could be it, Bear. Isn't it great?"

CHAPTER 7

Problems at the cannery had still been on Emily's mind when she went to work that day. The place might not have been processing fish, but that didn't mean the interns had the day off. Instead, Tim Garrett had decided it was the perfect opportunity to give them all a lesson on the federal regulations pertaining to fisheries. The goal, he said, was to give them a deeper understanding of how and why NOAA had developed rules for the taking of fish in Pacific waters. Unfortunately, Tim's idea of teaching was to spend the morning reading the rules verbatim over the hum of the cannery's generators, and by midmorning, eyelids were starting to droop. If Emily's mind hadn't been busy elsewhere, she was sure she'd have fallen asleep.

She tried not to let Tim see her as she sneaked another quick peek at the clock. It wasn't his fault that "Subpart H Regarding Deviations From the Allocation Schedule" was so boring, but it felt as if time were standing still. Emily had been rehearsing what to say to enlist Sam Reed's help since she woke up that morning, and the more time that passed, the less confident she felt. In the back of her mind, she kept hearing Noah's snide retort when she declared her determination to find the source of the problem: What was she going to do about it?

What she *wasn't* going to do, she told herself, was turn her back and pretend that things were fine. She could see how tightly wound Tim was, and on the drive to work, the other girls had told her how distracted he'd been, trying to deal with complaints while he worked with the interns. If there was an answer out there, she was determined to find it. First, however, she had to get Sam's buy-in, and as Tim droned on, Emily was losing her nerve.

At last, twelve o'clock rolled around and he let them out for lunch. As the others argued about which fast food joint to hit, Emily hung up her lab coat and grabbed her wallet. She'd get herself something to eat on the way back, she thought, right after she'd talked to Sam—if she talked to Sam. The fact was, she had no idea which of the many tenders tied up outside was his.

Emily hurried down the metal stairs that led from the catwalk to the factory floor, feeling the structure vibrate with every footfall. She was already at the bottom before the rest of them started to descend.

"Hey, Emily!" Rachel called out. "Aren't you coming with us?"

She shook her head. "Got an errand to run. I'll see you guys after lunch."

Through the row of windows that lined the southeast side of the building, she saw people out on the sidewalk making their way to their own lunchtime rendezvous. Then a blur of black caught her eye as it hurried past.

Bear!

She looked ahead and saw Sam a few feet in front of the dog. Head down, hands tucked into his jacket pockets, he seemed to be in a hurry. If she didn't get out there fast, she might miss him.

Emily ran to the big double doors and tried to push one open. It was surprisingly heavy, and she was only able to move it a few inches, just far enough to squeeze through the narrow opening. By the time she got out to the sidewalk, there was no sign of Sam or his dog. Nevertheless, she told herself, they couldn't have gotten far, and she knew which direction they'd been going. If she just headed that way, she'd run into them sooner or later.

The wind felt as if it were coming straight off an iceberg, numbing her cheeks as Emily headed up the road. She was glad she'd worn her fleece jacket that morning. She passed the cannery and the stacks of shipping containers outside its loading dock, searching for any sign of Sam and his dog. By a boat shelter big enough to house a couple of hundred-foot tenders, she saw a man in a pair of dusky overalls, and beyond that two small metal sheds with a sign out front that said DAVIS AND SON—still no Sam. Three large blue buildings took up the rest of the next block, and after that, Emily saw an open field that someone had been using as a makeshift dump. She turned her back to the wind and scanned the other side of the road. There were several small, derelict buildings that might or might not be businesses, but no indication that Sam and his dog were in any of them. As she realized that her quarry had gotten away, Emily felt her spirits flag. Short of knocking on every door she'd passed, there wasn't much else she could do to locate them.

What now?

As she started to retrace her steps, she saw a man coming toward her. Was it the same man she'd seen next to the boat shelter? She wasn't sure. He certainly looked like the sort of men she'd seen working on the dock: weather-beaten and slightly seedy, with a distinctive roll to his walk as if he were compensating for the swell of the ocean, even on dry land. When he got closer, Emily noticed a distinctive red birthmark on his left cheek that drew her eye.

"Afternoon, miss."

"Hello," she said.

She was trying not to stare. It must be hard to live with something like that on your face without having people gawking at it all the time. Emily willed herself to ignore it.

"Are you lost?" he said. "I only ask because I saw you looking around and now here you are coming back already."

"No," she said. "I'm not lost. Just looking for someone." She took a second to scour the area again. "Unfortunately, I think I lost him."

The man's smile made pleats across the birthmark.

"Well, he'll be sorry he missed you, I'm sure. I don't suppose there's anything I could help you with?"

Emily's first instinct was to say no. There was something about the man that she found disquieting, and she would have preferred to hurry back and join the others at lunch. But he'd done nothing to make her think he was a threat; on the contrary, he'd been concerned for her welfare. Was she just letting his disfigurement affect her judgment? Shamed by her own intolerant attitude, she decided to tell him who she was looking for and why. After all, if this man was a regular on the dock, he might also have useful information.

"Sam Reed?" he said. "Of course I know him. I used to be part of his crew. Good man, Captain Reed."

Emily was excited. Not only did this man know Sam, but he'd worked the same waters and probably knew the same people—both on the docks and in the cannery. Congratulating herself for ignoring her prejudices, she decided to take him into her confidence. Had he heard of anyone, she asked, who might have it in for Tim Garrett and his interns?

The man dipped his chin and made a discreet survey of their surroundings. The street was not well-traveled, but there were a couple of people on the other side of the street who might overhear if he said more than a few words. With a wordless jerk of the head, he directed her toward the spot where she'd first seen him and walked off with Emily right behind. When they got to the first small shed, he motioned for her to come around the far side, out of sight of the road.

Emily hesitated; the uneasiness she'd felt before was back. Martial arts training had given her the confidence to defend herself in a threatening situation, but it was always better—and easier—to avoid an attack than to fight one's way out of it. The man turned and beckoned her again.

"Come on," he said. "Do you want my help or don't you?"

"Yes, but—"

"I'm taking a risk here, you know. If anyone hears I've been a rat, I'll be blackballed. Might never get another job. Do you want that?"

She took a cautious step forward.

"No, of course not."

Emily hadn't expected him to be so quick. Before she could react, the man had grabbed her by the wrist and twisted it hard. She felt her knees buckle as she tried to relieve the pressure on her arm.

"Come along then," he snarled. "I'll give you what you're looking for."

As he pulled her toward the back of the shed, Emily fought the urge to panic. She felt foolish more than anything else. How many times had Sensei Doug warned her not to ignore her inner voice? She was in pain and she'd lost the upper hand, but she wasn't beaten—not yet, anyway. Whatever happened, though, she wouldn't be getting out of this unscathed.

Before she could make a move, though, Emily heard the

jangle of metal and scuffling on the asphalt behind her. The man holding her looked up and his face paled. She felt the brush of fur against her shoulder as Bear rushed forward, snarling. The man released her hand at the same moment she heard Sam's voice.

"Bear! Get back here!"

Sam rounded the corner and pulled up short as the man gave him a look of pure hatred. Emily was expecting Sam to tell the man to back off. Instead, he turned and gave her an admonishing look.

"Why didn't you wait for me? I told you I'd be right back."

Emily felt a flash of anger. Why was this *her* fault all of a sudden? Sam hadn't even known she was looking for him. She was about to tell him off when she saw the pleading look in his eyes asking her to play along.

"I didn't think you were coming back," she said through gritted teeth. "You certainly took long enough."

Sam laughed and looked at the other man.

"She didn't think I was coming back," he said. "Women, right?"

Emily could see that the man was still poised, ready to fight for his prize if given the chance, but the presence of the snarling dog slowly changed his mind. He turned and gave her a simpering smile.

"It seems you've found what you were after," he sneered. "I suppose you won't be needing any more from me."

As he slipped away, Emily shivered. Even though she was sure she'd have been able to spare herself the worst possible outcome, the thought of what he'd had in mind was chilling.

Sam turned on her in a fury.

"What are you doing," he hissed, "hanging out with a guy like Logan Marsh? The man's a pervert."

She reared back.

"I wasn't 'hanging out' with him. I didn't even know his name. Besides, he's your friend, not mine."

"Is that what he told you? That we were friends?"

"He said he was part of your crew."

Sam looked at her like she was addled-brained.

"The crewmen on my ship aren't my *friends*," he said. "I hire them to do a job; they either do it or they don't. If they do, I keep them on. If they don't, they're fired. That guy," he said, pointing, "is bad news, which is why I fired him."

"Well, how was I supposed to know that?"

"If you didn't, then you shouldn't have been wandering around down here by yourself. You're lucky Bear and I showed up when we did."

Emily felt her lips tighten. She wasn't some helpless naif who needed to be rescued. Logan Marsh might have gotten the drop on her—temporarily—but as far as she was concerned, she'd never been in any serious danger. It was time to straighten this guy out.

"For your information, I was doing just fine when you showed up."

"Oh, right." He chuckled. "And how 'fine' do you think you would have been once he dragged you behind that shed?"

"I wouldn't have let him."

Sam looked away for a second, shaking his head.

"Look," he said. "Just try not to be so trusting, okay? Or at least find someone who can clue you in to this place before you get yourself killed."

She smirked. "Oh. Someone like you, perhaps?"

"Sure." Sam shrugged. "Why not?"

"Well, thanks," she said. "But I think I've gotten enough 'help' for one day."

CHAPTER 8

Sam walked off in a huff, Bear trailing reluctantly behind him. Who did that girl think she was? He'd taken a risk confronting Logan Marsh, and she hadn't even bothered to thank him.

" 'I was doing just fine when you showed up,' " he sneered. "Yeah, right, sister. You just keep telling yourself that."

He'd already been in a bad mood when Bear took off, and getting grief from Emily hadn't helped. After hustling down to meet the man whose number Mollie had given him, Sam discovered that the guy wasn't actually selling a ship; he was a broker trying to add to his list of interested buyers. Guys like that were part of the reason commercial vessels cost so much. By raising sellers' expectations of what they could get for their ships, they guaranteed themselves a hefty finder's fee and made it all but impossible for buyers to negotiate a reasonable price. The second Sam realized who he was dealing with, he'd turned around and walked out the door. Whatever Bear had heard or sensed in the meantime had sent him sprinting off before Sam could stop him.

He looked down at the dog loping beside him.

"Who needs her?"

With a long afternoon still stretching out ahead of him,

Sam returned to his previous plan and headed to the wharf to give his crew a hand. Oscar was topside, checking the gear for wear, and Ben was in the water, cleaning the hull. Regular maintenance of the ship's bottom was crucial: it preserved the finish, made the boat easier to handle, and because it cut down on drag, it saved on fuel. Off-season was the time when extensive maintenance and repairs were carried out, but downtime anytime provided a good opportunity to catch problems early.

Sam went onboard and signaled for Ben to come join him. The crewman climbed up the side and pulled off his mask, smiling as water sluiced off his wet suit onto the deck.

"Hey, Skipper. Come to join the fun?"

"Thought I would," Sam said.

He stripped off his shirt and threw it aside, then took off his shorts and grabbed the wet suit he kept in his footlocker.

"How much have you done so far?"

Water was running into Ben's eyes. He shook his head and sent seawater flying.

"The foils are cleared and I'm working on the props. They're fouled pretty bad."

Sam looked up sharply. Fouled propellers could wreak havoc on a ship's handling.

"Barnacles?"

Ben nodded. "More than I'd expected this early in the season. Oscar just cleared them two weeks ago."

Barnacles were a constant headache on a ship, secreting a cement-like substance that held them fast to a ship's hull and making them all but impossible to remove. Even then, their adhesive remained, compromising the smoothness of whatever part of the underside they'd attached themselves to—in some cases, rendering it useless. An increase in barnacle formation could spell disaster if they didn't stay on top of it.

Sam threw a sponge and a light-duty 3M pad into a floating bucket and lowered it over the side.

"You keep working on the props and shaft. I'll start on the hull."

Even with his wet suit on, the shock of cold water made Sam gasp as he went in. He dipped his mask into the water, then slipped it on and cleared the snorkel. So far, the afternoon had left him feeling frustrated and angry. It felt good to have something physical to help work it off.

Unfortunately, though, the distraction didn't last long. Cleaning a ship's hull was a pretty dull job, and as he bobbed along the waterline, Sam began to obsess about the quarrel he'd had with Emily. Why had she come down on him so hard? All he'd been trying to do was help, and she'd acted like he was in the way. Was she really so naïve that she hadn't recognized the danger she was in? And then, when he'd suggested she find someone to clue her in about what parts of town were unsafe, it was like she thought he was making moves on her. Which maybe he was, but she didn't have to be such a . . .

He shook his head and grabbed another sponge out of the bucket.

Stop thinking about it. It's over. You'll probably never even see her again.

The hull was pretty clean—surprisingly so, considering how encrusted Ben had told him the props and rudder were. It made him wonder if Oscar's cleaning job had been as thorough as he'd said. Some ships' crews had underwater cameras to document the condition of the hull and metal instruments below the waterline, but Jack and Travis were too cheap to pay for anything they considered extras. They said it was because they trusted their crew members, but the truth was, they left it to Sam to verify that the work had been done well, and he couldn't sign off on what he couldn't see. Once he was finished at the waterline, he'd have to check out the bottom again to make sure.

The day was getting warmer, and by midafternoon Sam could feel the back of his neck starting to burn. He knew it wasn't good, knew it'd hurt later, but he'd spent a long winter and a cold, miserable spring dreaming of being out in the sun. Even if he had to pay for it later, it was worth it just to feel some heat on his bare skin again.

Bear was enjoying the warm afternoon as well. Lolling topside, stretched out along the deck, he'd been keeping track of Sam's movements in the water, opening one eye every so often and adjusting his position so the two of them remained close to each other. Bear would spend half his life in the ocean if Sam would let him—Newfoundlands loved the water—but getting salt water out of the dog's coat was a chore he didn't feel like tackling all that often. Once the season was over, the two of them would hike out to the river and go for a frolic. Until then, the dog would just have to be satisfied to watch.

Sam was doing a final check of the hull when he saw Bear sit up and go trotting off toward the far side of the ship. He heard Oscar talking to someone on the dock, and seconds later, the crewman was staring down over the side.

"Someone here to see the captain," he said. "You want to come up, or should I tell 'em you're busy?"

Sam glanced at the portion of the hull he'd been working on, satisfied that it was as clean as he could get it, and checked his watch: five-thirty. He'd been down there for over three hours; he figured he was due for a break.

"Tell them I'll be up in a second," he said.

He threw the sponges back into his bucket and started up the ladder.

★ ★ ★

Emily hadn't been able to get much work done that afternoon. When she got back to the cannery, she was still fuming over her encounter with Sam. How dare he treat her like she was helpless? She felt humiliated and belittled, convinced that he thought she couldn't take care of herself. It wasn't until she returned to the classroom and saw the rest of the interns that the seriousness of what had just happened to her sank in.

"What's wrong with your arm?" Kimberley demanded.

Emily shrugged. It had felt a bit sore on the walk back, but that wasn't surprising. It certainly didn't feel any worse than some of the injuries she'd gotten during her practice bouts with Sensei Doug.

"It's nothing," she said. "Just—"

She held up her wrist and gasped. Her entire lower arm was black and blue, the clear outline of Logan Marsh's fingers embedded in the flesh. A thin line of blood dribbled from a tear in her skin. Had he really done all that in such a short period of time? And how had she not felt it before now?

"Oh, my God," Rachel said. "You're bleeding!"

Tim Garrett came striding into the room.

"Who's bleeding? What happened?"

"I . . . I don't know," Emily said. "I didn't think it was that bad."

He walked over and took a look at her arm.

"It looks like someone grabbed you."

"He did," she said, bewildered.

"Who did?"

Tim's voice sounded urgent. Emily glanced at the others, hoping to find one who agreed that the damage to her arm wasn't serious, but none did. As she looked at their concerned faces, it dawned on her that the encounter she'd brushed off as trivial might indeed have been more dangerous than she'd realized.

"I'll get the first aid kit," Tim said. "You girls help Emily to the bathroom so she can clean that arm. If she passes out, call 911 immediately."

"I'm okay," Emily said, though, in fact, she was starting to feel woozy. "It was just . . . this man by the shed. He . . . he said he wanted to tell me something."

"That's it," Tim snapped. "I'm calling the cops. Would you recognize him if you saw him again?"

Emily felt a sudden urge to sit down. She collapsed onto a chair.

"His name is Logan. Logan Marsh."

Rachel and Kimberley helped her back onto her feet. By the time they got to the door, Tim was already on the phone to a dispatcher.

"Yes, that's right," he said. "Logan Marsh. He attacked one of my interns. . . ."

The two girls helped her clean up, and the EMTs arrived a few minutes after the police. Pictures of her injured arm were taken, after which the cut was disinfected and her entire forearm securely wrapped by a paramedic who quietly asked if Logan had hurt her "in any other way." At that, Emily started to shake; she'd finally realized just how badly she'd misjudged the situation. If Sam and his dog hadn't shown up when they did, she thought, she might have been raped—maybe even killed. She felt embarrassed and ashamed. More than that, she felt she owed Sam an apology.

Which was why she was standing on the dock that afternoon, waiting for him to come out and talk to her. It had taken Emily almost twenty minutes to find someone who would point out Sam Reed's tender, and by the time she got there, it seemed as if everyone around was staring at her. It made her feel shy. She hoped that Sam wouldn't make her wait too long.

She saw movement on deck and found Bear looking down at her, his tail wagging happily. He barked twice, and she waved her injured arm, the white bandage looking like a flag of truce.

Maybe it is, Emily thought.

Then Sam stepped up behind his dog, and Emily stopped breathing. He was dripping wet, standing there in the bottom half of a wet suit as the top half had been pulled down to his waist, his naked torso glistening in the sun as he dried his hair with a towel. The raw physicality of him made her heart race. She looked down and stared at her feet.

"What are you doing here?" he yelled.

"I, um . . ." Emily swallowed. "I—"

"What? Speak up. I can't hear you."

Stop being silly, she told herself. It wasn't as if she'd never seen a man without his shirt on before, and the poor guy would never hear her if she kept staring at the ground. Emily took a deep breath and lifted her chin. Sam had his head tilted to one side, trying to clear the water from his ears.

"I came to apologize," she said loudly. "And to thank you for helping me." She held up her arm. "You were right."

"You're welcome." He leaned over the railing and nodded. "How's it feel?"

Emily shrugged.

"It hurts. The EMTs fixed me up, and I gave the police a report. They said they'd keep an eye out for him. You said his name was Logan Marsh, right?"

"Yup."

He looped the towel over his shoulder and started drying his back. Emily's cheeks started to burn. She thought he might be the sexiest man she'd ever seen.

"Anything else I can help you with?" Sam said.

"Yes," she yelled. "Can I take you out to dinner?"

CHAPTER 9

They ate at a fish and chowder shop near the wharf. Ketchikan was a pretty laid-back town, and even dressed as they were, Emily was sure they could have gotten into someplace nicer, but Sam seemed uncomfortable letting her pay at all, much less for something more expensive. As she watched him polish off a double helping of cod fillets, though, she thought he might have a point. The man could put away a lot of food.

"So," Sam said. "Tell me why you were wandering around in no-man's-land this afternoon."

Emily shrugged. When she thought about it now, her crusade to find the source of Tim's problems at the cannery seemed pretty childish. He hadn't asked her to, and besides, what made her think she had a better chance of figuring it out than he did? Sam would probably laugh when she told him, but she supposed she owed him an explanation. She'd already had to apologize; a little more humiliation couldn't hurt.

"I wanted to ask if you could help me with a . . . Well, not a problem, exactly. More of a mystery I'm trying to solve."

"What sort of mystery?" He reached for his beer. "I have to warn you, I'm not much of a detective."

"I'm not, either," she said. "To tell you the truth, I'm not even sure I should be trying to solve it. It's just that—" She shook her head. "I don't know. "

Emily looked down at her plate. How could she explain why this seemed so important?

"I guess I hate to see people get blamed for something they didn't do. Even when I was a kid, I was always trying to fight back against injustice."

Sam picked up a french fry and pointed it at her.

"Nobody likes a buttinsky."

She grinned. "Yeah, I know, but aren't there times when people need to get involved? I mean, if somebody is getting hurt, don't you have a responsibility to try and help?"

He put the fry in his mouth and chewed thoughtfully.

"Maybe," Sam said. "As long as you're sure that what you're doing is really going to help. As often as not, it seems to me that helping only makes the situation worse."

Emily rested her chin in her hand, picked up her fork, and started pushing the uneaten portion of her dinner around her plate. Maybe Sam was right, she thought. Maybe she should just leave well enough alone. But were things at the cannery really going "well enough"? Not if the others were right and someone was trying to get rid of the internship program.

"Why don't you just tell me what the mystery is?" Sam said. "If I can't help you, then it doesn't matter whether helping is a good idea or not, right? And if I can, then you can decide if you want to pursue it."

She stabbed at a cold piece of cod.

"Yeah, I guess."

"Oh, come on," he said. "I saw you take on Logan Marsh this afternoon. You can't be that easily discouraged."

"Right," she said. "And look where it got me."

Emily held up her bandaged arm.

"Yeah, that is disappointing," he said. "And here I thought you were some kind of kung fu master."

Sam grinned at her and took another sip of beer.

Her mouth fell open. She hadn't said anything to him about the incident with Bear in the cannery. Did someone tell him, or had he actually seen her divert his dog away from the slime line?

"How did you know about that?"

"Are you kidding? You've been *the* topic of conversation on the dock since it happened. If anyone had thought to get their smartphone out, you and Bear would be Internet stars by now. I'm sorry I missed it."

So Sam *hadn't* seen what happened, Emily thought. Did it really matter? No, probably not, but still.

"For the record," she said, "it wasn't kung fu, it was aikido, and I was just trying to keep Bear from running into the slime line."

"So, he didn't knock you down?"

"Not exactly." Emily smirked. "And don't look so disappointed."

Sam finished off the last of his fries.

"Aikido, huh? Where'd you learn that?"

"There's a dojo near my house."

"And you took it for self-defense?"

She laughed. "Not really. When I was a kid, my mother signed me up for every kind of lesson there was: horseback riding, tennis, swimming, kung fu, surfing, you name it. Aikido's the only thing I ever enjoyed enough to keep at it."

"Sounds like fun."

"It was, for a while, but when every spare minute of your life is spoken for, it doesn't leave you much time for anything else. I started feeling as if I was always preparing for life instead of living it. What's the point?"

"You certainly made good use of your aikido." Sam reached down and stroked the dog's head. "And I know Bear appreciated it."

"Yeah, at the time, I was feeling pretty critical of myself, thinking that I shouldn't have fallen. Now, though, it makes me happy. All those hours of practice finally paid off in the real world."

He looked up at her and smiled.

"First, Bear runs into you at the cannery, then this afternoon he gets between you and Logan Marsh. Don't look now, but I think my dog has a crush on you."

"Well, I doubt that," she said, glancing at the dog lying quietly under their table. "But if he does, I'm flattered."

"Speaking of Bear," he said, "we need to get home. I think I hear his stomach growling."

"Oh."

Emily couldn't help feeling disappointed. In spite of any second thoughts she might have had, she'd still been hoping to ask Sam if he could help her with the problem at the cannery. Now, it looked as if she'd missed her chance.

He wiped his mouth with a napkin, then wadded it up and dropped it on the table.

"Come on," he said, standing. "You can tell me about your mystery on the way."

Sam's house was a four-bedroom split-level with a view of the harbor and a backyard big enough for a dog Bear's size to stretch his legs. While the Newfoundland waited impatiently for his dinner, Emily gave herself a tour of the upper floor. In the living room, she saw two comfortable couches facing each other in front of a brick fireplace. An old harpoon was mounted over the mantelpiece, and bookshelves lined the wall on either side. She wandered over to take a closer look. In addition to the predictable—Melville, London, Poe—she found novels by Llosa, Proust, and Conrad, and nonfiction titles on celestial mechanics and physics, including one of her personal favorites, *What Do You Care What Other People Think?* by Richard Feynman. When Sam walked into the room, she turned to him and smiled.

"I'm trying to decide what your major was in college. Literature or physics?"

He glanced at the bookcase and frowned.

"Neither," he said. "I'm just one of those dummies who reads what he likes."

Emily felt herself flush. She hadn't meant to insult him.

"Sorry. I mean, not everybody goes to college. I know plenty of smart people who—"

"Don't worry about it," he said. "Can I get you a glass of water?"

"Yeah, sure," she said, relieved. "That'd be nice, thank you."

While Sam went back to the kitchen, Emily took a seat. As nice as the house was, it felt as if something was missing. Parts of the interior were well-furnished, but others were completely bare, with only faint outlines on the wall to indicate that something had been removed and not replaced.

Someone's left him, she thought, *and not that long ago, either.* His wife? Or a girlfriend, perhaps? Not that she'd ever ask. Even a buttinsky had her limits.

Sam, however, must have been watching her and guessed what she was thinking. As he handed Emily her water, he said: "Last month."

She took a sip. "*Hmm?*"

"Tiffany, my ex-girlfriend. She moved out at the beginning of May. Isn't that what you were wondering?"

Once again, she felt her face redden.

"Was I that obvious? I'm sorry. It's none of my business."

"No, it's okay. I thought it would last, but then she started using. It's not easy when you realize that someone loves their addiction more than they love you."

"I'm sorry," she said again. "I know a lot of people are dealing with the same thing."

He shrugged. "It's okay. We're both better off now."

The two of them sat there for a few seconds more, lost in their own thoughts. As sorry as Emily was for Sam's situation, there was a part of her that felt glad he was unattached even as she felt guilty for feeling that way. It reminded her that she hadn't thought of Carter all day—not even when the EMTs were bandaging her arm. In three months, she'd be home and Sam would be moving on with his life. She had no business having any feelings for him at all.

Time to get down to business.

"So," she said. "The mystery."

Sam nodded. "Let's hear it."

For the next few minutes, Emily detailed everything she knew about what had been going on at the cannery. Some was firsthand, but for most of it, she was passing along things that the other interns had seen or heard about, including their surmise that the ultimate aim was the elimination of the internship program. Sam listened attentively, interrupting her only to clarify something he wasn't sure about. Even if it turned out that he had no more clue how to fix the problem than she did, Emily appreciated his taking the whole thing seriously. If she'd been in his shoes, she wasn't sure she'd have done the same.

"So," he said, when she was finished. "You want to find out who might or might not be trying to embarrass Tim and/or sabotage the interns, is that correct?"

"Yes."

"And do you just want my opinion, or are you asking if I can help?"

"Well . . . both, I guess."

He took a deep breath and leaned back, staring at the ceiling.

"I can see why you're upset. Tim sounds like a good guy, and the program gives experience to people who might not be able to get it anywhere else."

"Right, and if NOAA shuts it down—"

"Hold on. The problem is, you have no way of knowing if what's going on is being done deliberately or is just coincidental."

"Yeah, I suppose."

"You're also taking the word of the other interns as gospel," he said. "Something I'd be very careful about if I were you. People often exaggerate, even when they don't mean to. Unless Tim Garrett tells you that he needs your help, my advice would be to let this go—"

"But—"

"—*for now.* In the meantime, keep your eyes open, write down anything concrete that you find, but don't jump to any conclusions. This could be something real or it might just be someone's overactive imagination. At this point, I don't think you know enough to tell the difference."

Sam pointed toward a book on the shelf behind her.

"Remember what Richard Feynman said: 'The first principle is that you must not fool yourself—and you are the easiest person to fool.' "

Emily thought about that for a moment. *Had* she been fooling herself? The fact was, she had very little actual evidence that some larger conspiracy was behind the problems at the cannery. What if they were just normal, everyday issues that had nothing to do with Tim or the interns at all? If that was the case, then trying to solve the "mystery" would be a waste of time. Emily had come to Ketchikan to get experience and, with luck, a glowing recommendation from her supervisor. She couldn't afford to waste her time chasing after a chimera.

"You're right," she said. "I need to remember that. Thanks for listening."

"No problem; you're good company. And, hey, if you see or hear something that convinces you there's more going on, I'll be happy to help. Now come on," he said. "I'll give you a ride home."

Emily got up and grabbed her purse.

"Oh, no. That's okay. I can walk."

Sam gave her injured arm a pointed look, and Emily chuckled.

"On second thought," she said, "that would be nice. Thanks."

Emily stood by her front door and waved as Sam drove away. It had been a good evening; she was glad she'd asked him to dinner, happier still that she'd shared her suspicions about the cannery. He might not have a college degree, but Sam was a deep thinker. He'd been able to see through the complicated scenario she'd presented him with and point out the essential truth she'd been missing. In the future, she would try to re-member Occam's razor: the simplest explanation is most likely the right one.

Kimberley was waiting for her when she stepped inside.

"Where have you been? We were all worried about you."

Emily looked around. There was no one else in the room.

"Who was worried?"

"Everybody. After work, you just ran off and nobody knew if you were okay. We had to go to dinner without you."

"I'm sorry if you were worried," she said, setting her purse on the floor. "But I had someone I needed to talk to."

Kimberley crossed her arms, tossing her head toward the door.

"You mean Sam Reed."

Emily gave a grunt of confusion.

"Yes, if you must know. Why? What do you care?"

The girl hesitated, looking momentarily flustered before recovering her nerve.

"I thought I told you—"

"What, that you saw him first? And now he's your personal property?"

The girl's cheeks flushed. "I didn't say that."

"Good. Because I'm not trying to take him away, all right? When this"—Emily held up her bandaged arm—"happened, Sam and his dog chased the guy off. I thought I'd buy him dinner as a thank-you. That's *all*."

This declaration seemed to mollify Kimberley somewhat. She uncrossed her arms.

"How's it feel?"

Emily hadn't thought about her injuries the entire time she was with Sam. Now, her whole arm was starting to throb.

"It hurts like hell. So if you don't mind, I think I'll get ready for bed."

She opened the hall closet and took out a towel.

"But we were all going out for karaoke," Kimberley said. "I was just waiting for you to show up. Don't you want to come?"

"No thanks."

"Whatever." She snatched her wallet off the table. "Don't bother waiting up. We'll be back late."

"Fine," Emily said as she headed down the hall. "Maybe I'll take another pain pill, too, so I can get some sleep. Which isn't easy, by the way, with you guys walking in and out of my 'bedroom' all the time."

She walked into the bathroom and slammed the door.

CHAPTER 10

Sam kept a sharp eye out for Logan Marsh as he drove home. Emily had heard nothing from the police about an arrest, and the uneasiness he'd felt seeing the guy near his neighborhood that morning still lingered. He did a quick swing around the block before turning up his driveway and into the garage. The last thing he needed was to be caught unawares.

Bear shot past him into the kitchen when he opened the door, nosing his food bowl aside and checking the floor for any overlooked morsels. Sam set his keys on the counter, then went to check the doors and windows before hanging up his jacket. It was probably more vigilance than the situation warranted, but then, no one ever died from an excess of caution.

There was cold beer in the refrigerator. He took one out and popped it open. Now that the fishing ban had been lifted, he'd be back out on the water in the morning, but he still wasn't sure whether Bear would be with him. Sam glanced at the time—even for a work night, it was too early to go to bed. He wandered into the living room and turned on the television.

He stood there flipping through channels, hoping to find something halfway interesting to fill the time, then turned it off and tossed the remote back onto the couch. Since Tiffany's departure, his life had changed in a lot of ways, but evenings were the hardest. Bear was good company, but it wasn't the same as having another human being in the house. Maybe that's why he'd been so willing to hear about Emily's mystery. It meant he could hold back the loneliness a little while longer.

He heard the phone ring and walked back into the kitchen to see who it was.

"Hey, Kallik. What's up?"

"Me and Marilyn are going down to Jojo's for some karaoke. You wanna come?"

Sam looked around. Bear was crashed on his dog bed and the house was secure. Other than playing solitaire or rereading one of the books on his shelves, there wasn't much to do.

"Sure," he said. "Why not?"

Jojo's Bar was surprisingly busy for a Sunday night. Sam spotted Kallik at a table about halfway toward the front. He gave his order at the bar and started wading through the crowd. Marilyn was up at the stage with the KJ, karaoke jockey, looking through the song list. Before Sam could join Kallik at the table, she waved him over.

"They've got 'I Got You, Babe' in here. Will you do it with me?"

"Why? Won't Kallik do it?"

She made a face.

"My husband might look like Sonny Bono," she said, "but he sings like Bob Dylan."

Sam laughed. "I don't know, Mar."

"Come on," she wheedled. "It'll be a great warmup for *Phantom*."

He raised an eyebrow.

"Who told you we were doing *Phantom?*"

"Junie. She says the part's yours if you want it." She took his arm. "You really should, you know. You have a gorgeous voice."

Sam shrugged. Rehearsals for the winter musical—whatever it was—were still a long way off. In the meantime, he had an entire salmon season to get through, with all the problems that entailed. He couldn't afford to get distracted.

"Well, think about it," she said. "In the meantime, sing this duet with me. If you don't, I'll be stuck with Sonny 'Oh no!'"

"Oh, come on. He's not that bad. Give the guy a chance."

"Okay, but remember: you asked for it."

Sam's drink arrived at the table just as he did. Kallik smiled and lifted his glass.

"Thanks for coming. Marilyn's been wanting to sing a duet, and I needed a ringer to take my place."

"Really?" Sam deadpanned. "She just told me she was looking forward to singing it with you."

Kallik looked at his drink.

"In that case," he said, signaling for the waitress, "I'd better have a few more of these."

As he sipped his beer, Sam took a look around. Two tables over, he saw the NOAA interns doing shots and raising hell. He wasn't surprised that Emily wasn't with them. After what she'd been through that afternoon, he figured she was holed up at home, hiding under a blanket. One of the girls—a bosomy blonde—raised her glass to him. Without thinking, he returned the gesture before turning back toward Kallik.

"I saw Logan Marsh today—twice, as a matter of fact."

"What's that rat up to?"

"No good, as usual. He gave me a start on my way to breakfast. Said he was just out for a stroll, but it bothered me seeing him so close to the house. Then, this afternoon, I caught him trying to drag a girl off behind those sheds near Davis and Son."

"What was she doing down there, hooking?"

"As it happens, she was looking for me. She saw Bear walk past the cannery and tried to follow us. I'd already ducked through a doorway by the time she made it out to the sidewalk. She must have walked right into him."

"Wait a minute. The cannery was closed today."

"She's one of the interns."

The engineer smiled slyly.

"Is this, by any chance, the green-eyed lady we saw at the bar?"

Sam felt his face flush.

"Oh ho," Kallik said, lifting his glass in acknowledgement. "This is getting interesting."

"What is?" Marilyn demanded as she took her seat.

"Lonely boy here has an admirer."

"No surprise there." She leaned forward. "Who's the lucky girl?"

Sam took another long sip of beer. He hated being put on the spot, especially since he knew next to nothing about Emily. Was she even single? Nevertheless, when he thought back to the time they'd spent at his place, there'd definitely been some mutual attraction going on. He set his glass down and grinned thoughtfully.

"Her name's Emily. She works at the cannery."

Marilyn pulled her chin back.

"The cannery! You going after jail bait now?"

It was a fair assumption; cannery work was the preferred summer job for high school kids in the area. Nevertheless, Sam felt a bit miffed at the accusation.

"For your information," he said, "she's interning with NOAA. I don't know how old she is, exactly, but she's got to be at least college age."

Kallik, who'd once had a job guessing people's ages at a

carnival, weighed in with his expert opinion: "I'd say some-where between eighteen and twenty-five."

His wife rolled her eyes.

"Well, that's comforting."

"Don't get too excited about it," Sam told her. "I doubt she'll be sticking around after the season's over."

"That could be a good thing, man," Kallik said. "Give you a chance to dip your toe in before jumping into the deep water."

As the lights dimmed, Marilyn looked at Sam and shook her head.

"Where did I find him?"

On stage, the spotlight went on. The KJ introduced him-self to a smattering of applause, then checked the sign-up list and announced the first singer, a bright-eyed woman who'd come with a table full of girlfriends. As she got up on stage, her cheering section went wild.

"Divorcées," Marilyn whispered.

Kallik nodded. "Late thirties to mid-forties."

Sam sat back as the woman on stage belted out "When Will I Be Loved." She wasn't terrible, but she wasn't that good, either. Her voice was weak and she held the mic like it was going to bite her. Most people, he thought, had no idea how to sing into a microphone.

The next person up was a friend of Marilyn's.

"I gotta get a video of this," she said, reaching for her phone. "You guys stay here. I'll be back in a mo'."

As his wife made her way closer to the stage, Kallik looked at Sam.

"How's the search going?"

"Nothing yet," he said. "Mollie gave me a lead on some guy who came in for breakfast, but he turned out to be a bro-ker trawling for buyers."

"Damn."

He nodded. "That's how I ran into Logan the second time," Sam said. "I went down there to talk to the guy, and as I was leaving his office, Bear took off. By the time I chased him down, Logan had turned the girl loose, but her arm was pretty badly bruised. She made a police report, so the cops are out looking for him. I just hope they find him before he breaks into my house."

"You think he would?"

"You said yourself that he blames me for ruining his life. If he thought he could even the score, why not?"

Kallik took another sip of beer and shook his head. "You never know about people, do you?"

"Nope. You never do."

Marilyn hustled back to the table just in time for the KJ to call her name. She gave Sam a last pleading look before turning to Kallik and taking his hand.

"Come on, baby. Let's go knock 'em dead."

Kallik downed the last of his beer and leaned toward Sam.

"Thanks for nothing," he muttered as his wife dragged him away.

As his friends took the stage, Sam saw movement off to his right. A few seconds later, the blond intern who'd been eying him came staggering over. She plopped down in Kallik's chair and gave him a sloppy smile.

"Hey there, handsome."

As opening lines went, it was pretty artless, but then, it looked like she was pretty drunk. Sam took another sip of beer, trying to figure out a way to get rid of her without being cruel. He nodded toward the stage.

"This is a short song. My friends will be needing that chair back."

She leaned closer.

"I'm Kim," she said, blowing whiskey fumes in his face. "You don't remember me, do you?"

He shook his head. He couldn't remember meeting any of the interns besides Emily, but if Kim was a local, she might have been in the audience at one of his performances. People who stopped by after the final curtain sometimes imagined that a brief interaction with one of the actors constituted a meaningful connection.

" 'Fraid not," he said. "Sorry."

Up on stage, Marilyn had just sung the opening lines of their duet while Kallik hammed it up, trying to compensate for his lack of talent. Ordinarily, Sam would have contributed a few hoots and whistles to the show, but Kim's continued presence made him self-conscious. As the girl lingered at his table, his irritation grew. Couldn't she take a hint?

"Look, Kim, no offense—"

"What's the matter, don't you like girls?"

Sam felt his lips tighten. He'd tried to be nice, but this was too much. Whatever her problem was, he wasn't in the mood to deal with it.

"Oh, but that can't be true," she added. "I mean, you like Miss Emily just fine, don't you?"

Hearing her invoke Emily's name put an end to any attempts Sam might have made to spare the girl's feelings. He set down his drink, determined to get rid of her. Instead, Kim leaned in closer, putting her cleavage on display.

"Wouldn't you rather have yourself a local girl?"

On stage, Kallik and Marilyn were singing the last line of "I Got You, Babe," their arms cradling the child in Marilyn's belly. People all around them were on their feet, cheering in support. Sam nodded toward the other interns.

"I think you need to go back to your friends now."

"Fine." Kim pushed her chair back hard enough to topple it over. "Go ahead and make a fool of yourself with that spoiled little rich girl. What do I care?"

Sam set the chair back in place as Marilyn and Kallik returned to the table, still acknowledging the cheers from the audience. As she plopped down in her chair, Marilyn took her husband's arm.

"Be sweet and get me a glass of water," she said, fanning her face. "I'm hotter'n a bear's tail."

"Will do."

She cast a glance toward the interns' table. "What was that all about?"

"Nothing."

Sam watched Kallik make his way to the bar. "I envy you guys, you know? Finding love's not that easy."

"What about that honey who was keeping my seat warm?"

"No," he said, hunkering over his glass. "Not by a long shot."

"So, that's not the green-eyed girl?"

He shook his head. In spite of himself, Kimberley's words had stung. Was he making a fool of himself?

Marilyn lifted her hair and started fanning the back of her neck.

"I know things with Tiffany didn't work out, but that doesn't mean you shouldn't try again, you know."

"Maybe, but not with Emily."

"Why? She not your type, either?"

Sam regarded his glass.

"You know me, Mar. I'm not the kind of guy who goes in for short-term relationships, and she's only here for the summer. If I'm going to put myself through all that again, it'll have to be for something that can last."

Marilyn laughed. "Oh, Sam. You can't possibly know that from the outset."

"Maybe not," he said. "But as far as Emily goes, I do. Once her internship's over, she won't be sticking around."

She put a hand on his arm. "If you give her a reason to, maybe she will."

Kallik came back and handed her a bottle of Dasani. Marilyn unscrewed the lid and started guzzling it down.

"She's been like this for the last couple of weeks," he told Sam. "With all that water she drinks, I'm thinking there might be an orca in there."

Sam pretended to take the comment seriously.

"Well, it makes sense. Don't orcas symbolize motherhood?"

Marilyn set down her empty bottle and took a swipe at her husband.

"He just means I'm getting fat."

As Kallik kissed his wife's cheek, Sam looked away. Their playful banter just pointed out how empty his own life was—not that he and Tiffany had ever had the kind of relationship the two of them had. Looking back, it seemed as if there'd always been something reserved about Tiff, some part of her that was hidden—maybe even from herself. Still, he thought, it had been better than nothing.

"So," Kallik said. "You found a sitter for the dog yet?"

"Nope. You guys hear of anyone?"

"I asked around," Marilyn said. "No luck so far."

"Maybe they just need time to think about it," Kallik said.

"What'll you do in the meantime?" Marilyn asked.

Sam shrugged. "Leave him at home, I guess. Not sure what else I can do."

"He's a good dog. He'll be fine on his own," Kallik said.

"Yeah. You're probably right," Sam answered.

"Tell you what," Marilyn said. "I'll try and check on him if I'm in town. I can't really take him out in my condition—"

"I wouldn't expect you to."

"—but I can at least make sure he's got food and water."

Sam smiled. "Thanks, Mar. That'd be great."

CHAPTER 11

By Wednesday, Ketchikan's fishing season was back to normal. Salmon were being caught, tenders were bringing them in, and the cannery was humming. Unfortunately, the same couldn't be said of Emily's relationship with her roommates.

The argument on Sunday night had escalated to the point where Emily now found herself accused of "toying" with Sam, who'd apparently been "crushed" by his breakup with Tiffany. Even worse, Rachel had taken Kimberley's side, and although Uki hadn't weighed in one way or the other, she was doing her best to avoid all three of them. Aside from the absurdity of casting Sam as some sort of fragile, broken-hearted wretch, Emily was insulted that anyone would call her a tease.

As if the whispered comments and cold shoulders weren't bad enough, the interns were working in pairs that morning and Tim had decided to put Emily and Kimberley together. Whether it was just a coincidence or an attempt on his part to put an end to their feud, it wasn't working. By noon, they were no closer to a rapprochement than when they'd arrived. Nevertheless, as the two of them walked along the filleting station, any thoughts Emily might have had about their quarrel had been temporarily banished. Instead, she was brooding about her mom.

It had started the night before. In addition to her work at the cannery, Emily was hoping to spend part of her time in Ketchikan as a fisheries observer, and between working the line during the day and reviewing fishing regulations at night, she could truthfully say there hadn't been time for her to call home. She knew there'd be hell to pay once she did, but the relief from the never-ending drama that was her mother's life had been worth it.

Then last night, while the others were out at a movie, she'd finally given her mom a ring. It didn't take long for her to regret the decision.

"Sorry I haven't called," Emily said. "I've been super busy. Got a lot on my plate up here."

"Well, how good of you to find the time."

Emily had known that something like this might happen when she called; her mother wasn't the type to come right out and say she was upset, after all. Luckily, though, the sulking rarely lasted long. She'd just have to find a way to jolly her mother out of it.

"How've you been?" she said.

"Oh, like you: busy. Too busy, really. I got stuck running the holiday gala at the club *again* this year and the whole thing is just overwhelming."

Yeah, right.

As much as her mother complained, the woman loved being in charge of the gala. It was the perfect combination of shameless theatrics and conspicuous self-sacrifice, and woe betide anyone who suggested someone else take the job.

"How are things up *there?* No more dog attacks, I hope."

Emily glanced at the angry purple bruises on her arm.

"Nope. No more problems with the dog."

"I mentioned that whole incident to Judge Dorset when I ran into him at church on Sunday. I thought we might have a legal case against the owner."

Emily was mortified. It was just like her mother to harangue a family friend—a judge, no less!—about some minor personal matter.

"And what did he say? Did he think we should sue the dog?"

There were several seconds of silence on the line.

"Is that supposed to be funny? Because I don't happen to consider my daughter's welfare a joke."

"I'm sorry, but it just wasn't that big of a deal—honestly. Certainly not big enough to bother Judge Dorset about."

"Oh, please. He understood; he and I are old friends."

Her mother did have a point there, Emily thought. If anyone could understand the workings of an unstable mind, it was a judge in the juvenile court system.

"Speaking of people at church," her mother continued, "Sheila Trescott and I had a word with Reverend Taylor after the service. He says if you and Carter are planning a June wedding next year, you need to contact his secretary and get yourselves on their calendar as soon as possible."

"Are you kidding?"

"I know, dear. I could hardly believe it myself, but apparently these places book up very quickly."

"No, I mean, why did you guys tell Reverend Taylor that we were getting married?"

"Why not? You are, aren't you?"

Emily was aghast. Their mothers had been dropping hints for months, but this was the first time they'd said anything explicit about marriage. Yes, she and Carter had been dating each other exclusively for a while, and yes, there'd even been some casual banter about "maybe someday," but that hardly amounted to a commitment. The last thing she wanted was for either of them to feel as if they had to marry just to please their families.

"Mom, please. Carter and I both have a lot of things to do before we're ready to get married."

"Like what?"

"He still has to finish his residency, for one thing, and I've got to get a job."

"Don't be silly. Once Carter is in practice, you won't need a job."

"I didn't say I'd *need* one, but I'd like to have a career of some sort."

"Well, I don't think you need to get so upset about it. I was only trying to help."

She was right, Emily told herself, there was no reason to be upset. If anything, she should be happy to have a boyfriend her mother liked well enough to want as a son-in-law. Heaven knows, she had friends whose mothers would kill to have their daughters dating someone like Carter. Nevertheless, it didn't mean she wanted to encourage this kind of thing. Better to just try to change the subject.

"How's Uncle Danny doing?"

"Oh, you know your uncle. The man is indestructible."

Emily wasn't so sure about that.

"Did he get the test results yet?"

"*Hmm?* No, nothing definite."

"But you'll let me know right away if it's anything bad, right?"

"Of course. Now, listen, you just take care of yourself, all right? And don't worry about us. Everything's fine."

As she hung up, Emily had felt relieved about her uncle and proud of herself for making it clear—firmly, but gently—that her mother's meddling was unwelcome. It was only afterward that she began to have second thoughts. Not because her own mother had tried to interfere, but because she knew that Carter's mother would be doing the same thing to him, and she wasn't sure that he'd be as resolute.

Emily knew it was unfair and even sexist, but it bothered her that Carter never seemed to stand up to his mother. Whenever Sheila insisted he do something, he always went along with whatever it was, even when Emily knew he didn't want to. Not only did it seem unmanly for him to just accede to his mother's wishes, but the implications for any future they might have together were troubling. After the two of them were married—if they got married—would his mother try to run *both* their lives? And if so, would Carter simply expect Emily to go along?

"How are you guys doing over here?"

Emily gave a start, roused from her musings. As Tim Garrett approached, she felt embarrassed and wrong-footed.

"Everything getting checked off your list?"

Kimberley nodded, turning the clipboard around to show him their checklist. With Emily's arm still recovering, Tim had asked her to act as their scribe.

"So far, so good," she said.

"Glad to hear it." He looked at Emily. "How's the arm?"

"Much better, thanks. I go in to have it checked tomorrow."

"I hear you're looking for experience as a fisheries observer."

"I'm hoping to, yes."

"You've already completed your new observer training?"

"I did, yeah. At Scripps."

"Catch shares or non?"

"Catch shares, of course."

Catch sharing was a management tool that divided the total allowable catch, or catch limit, among the fishery participants. By sharing catch limits among themselves, fishermen could optimize the time they spent at sea while guaranteeing their take wouldn't exceed the area's overall catch limits. Before choosing her training class, Emily had been careful to check the rules for Alaskan waters.

"Excellent! Why don't I get you signed up for catch monitoring training, then? It'll be three days, sometime in the next couple of weeks, nothing too strenuous. Once you're finished, we'll slot you onto a ship. I'm thinking middle to late July. Sound good?"

"Sounds great."

"Good. In the meantime, why don't you two break for lunch? We'll meet back here at one-thirty."

As Tim walked away, Emily beamed. This was exactly the sort of thing she'd been hoping for when she came to Ketchikan. As an intern *and* an observer, she'd have even more of the kind of hands-on experience that would move her resume to the top of anyone's pile.

Kimberley seemed perplexed.

"I thought you just wanted experience at the cannery," she said. "Why go out as an observer, too?"

"More experience is always good. Plus, my interest is in biodiversity and conservation. If I'm out there monitoring what's being caught, I can see firsthand how well fisheries management is working."

"My dad says that if the government had its way, there wouldn't be any more fishing in Alaska. Ketchikan would just be one big tourist trap."

Emily was surprised that anyone in the intern program would be foolish enough to believe that, but she wasn't about to contradict the girl's father. The two of them were barely getting along as it was. Why make things worse?

"Well, I'm sure he has his reasons," she said. "Don't forget to take that stuff to Tim."

Kimberley nodded vaguely.

"Yeah," she said. "See ya."

As Emily left the cannery, she took a deep breath, relieved to be free of Kimberley's unspoken hostility and grateful for a chance to warm up after a morning spent in the refrigerated air. She was glad there'd been no mention of having lunch together. Not that she'd expected it, but the two of them had had a relatively peaceful morning, and the alternative meant eating alone. Until Kimberley got over her obsession with Sam, Emily was determined to spend as little one-on-one time with her as possible.

The whole situation was just ridiculous. For one thing, Emily had a perfectly good—no, make that a *great*—boyfriend back home, and even if she and Carter weren't engaged, neither one of them had ever expressed an interest in seeing other people. Sure, there were times when it felt as if her choices had been a bit limited, but that was only because she'd been too busy with school to do a lot of dating. It wasn't as if she were being forced into an arranged marriage; Emily loved Carter, full stop.

So, no, she thought as she headed up First Street, she had not been flirting with Sam Reed, and even if she had been, so what? He knew perfectly well that Emily's job in Ketchikan was only temporary, and it wasn't Kimberley's business who either one of them spent time with. If she didn't like their hanging out together, she could take it up with Sam.

At McDonald's, Emily stood in a long line of cruise ship passengers for a Big Mac and fries, then took her bag outside to find a table, eager for a chance to enjoy the sunshine. The sky in Ketchikan was more intensely blue that time of year than it was at home, the brilliant sun a striking contrast to the interior mountains still overspread with snow. Between the snowcaps and the harbor lay a swathe of dense forest that enfolded the island's foothills like a blanket of phthalo green. To someone who'd grown up in a semiarid climate, like she had, the whole place seemed magical.

As she took a seat on the warm concrete bench, Emily sighed contentedly. It was good to be away from the noise and the smell of the cannery for a while. Even with a checklist, everything moved so fast that it was hard to ensure that each fish had been processed carefully, and the workers still seemed resentful of their presence. With Kimberley being catty, too, it made the job that much harder. It was amazing how tiring dealing with other people's attitudes could be.

She unwrapped her burger and had just taken a bite when she saw Bear, up on his hind legs, rooting through one of the heavy trash cans by the side door. Emily looked around, but did not see Sam.

"Bear? What are you doing here?"

The dog pulled back, a discarded carton of fries in his mouth. When he saw her, he got down, trotted over, then jumped onto the seat beside her and set his prize on the table. Emily smiled.

"Well, hello. Fancy meeting you here."

She thought she'd be eating alone that day. Now, it looked as if she'd found some company.

Two little boys at the next table nudged each other and giggled as Emily and Bear ate their meals. Their mother smiled hesitantly, probably unsure whether or not she approved of dogs eating at the table, but seemed to soften when she saw Bear return the empty carton to the trash bin when he was done. As if on cue, the boys followed suit and were rewarded with licks of approval.

"He's very polite," the woman said as her boys returned to their seats. "You've trained him well."

"He's not mine," she said. "But I'll tell his owner you said so."

While she ate her meal, Emily kept an eye out for anyone who might be there with Sam's dog. It occurred to her that whoever it was might have left him outside while they went in and ate lunch, but she'd been paying close attention to everyone who came and went through the doors and none had shown anything more than a fleeting interest in the dog. Bear, she decided, must have gotten out on his own.

What should she do?

She couldn't just go back to work and leave Bear wandering the streets. Sam would be out on the tender all day and she was sure he wouldn't want his dog to be running loose. Plus, animal control would pick him up sooner or later, if he didn't get himself killed or injured in the meantime.

She petted Bear's head, digging her fingers into the thick coat on his neck.

"What am I going to do with you, huh?"

Emily wished she had Sam's number so she could tell him what had happened and ask if there was anyone who could keep an eye on the dog, but even if she did, she wasn't sure his cell phone would work while he was at sea. She did know where his house was, though. It seemed as if the best thing to do would be to take Bear home and hope he didn't escape again before Sam got back.

She wadded up her bag and stuffed it into the trash can.

"Come on, Bear. Let's take you home."

The big dog seemed excited to have company. As the two of them headed down the street, he did a few lumbering pirouettes and small half-leaps that sent his ears and heavy coat flapping. Emily had wondered if the weight of so much fur was a strain on Bear's joints, but other than making his movements a bit ungainly, it didn't seem to hamper him a bit. Perhaps when it got hotter, she thought, it would be a different story.

They left downtown and passed through an industrial district not far from where Logan Marsh had accosted her. Emily set her hand lightly on Bear's back, reassured that if anything like that happened again, the dog would protect her. It still puzzled her how Bear had known to come running when she was in trouble before. Were all Newfies as sensitive to human distress as he was, or was Sam's dog just a special case? She grinned, remembering Sam's comment.

Don't look now, but I think my dog has a crush on you.

Maybe she and Bear did have a special connection, she thought. If so, she was glad of it.

As they turned down Sam's street, Bear hurried ahead. When Emily finally caught up, she found him waiting for her at the front door.

"Sorry, Bear. I can't let you in." She patted her pockets. "No key."

It didn't take long to find the open gate at the side of the house through which Bear had escaped, though. As she walked back around to retrieve him, Emily hoped the dog was as anxious to get back into his yard as he'd been to get out. If not, she'd just have to find some way to persuade him; Bear was simply too big and too heavy to be dragged unwillingly.

As she headed up the walkway, Emily could see that the dog had decided to make a game of it, going down on his forelegs and sticking his bottom in the air, ready to dart away if she got too close. She was creeping forward, hoping to grab onto his collar before he bolted, when the front door opened and a lovely—very pregnant—woman stepped out.

Tiffany.

The name flashed through Emily's mind, followed quickly by disappointment and dread. Sam had told her almost nothing about his ex-girlfriend, but it was obvious how much he missed her. They must have made up, she thought, and for a good reason, too.

No wonder Kimberley had been so insistent that she leave Sam alone.

She was about to make her excuses and go when the woman at the door gave her a warm smile.

"Hi there! You must be Emily."

CHAPTER 12

It had been a long day on the water, but the weather had held and the fisheries were packed. When their count was tallied, the tender and its crew had made enough to compensate for the missed days and most of the one before. As Sam drove up to his house that evening, it looked like this season would be as good as or better than any he'd ever seen. There was nothing like the promise of a big payday to keep both his crew and the ship's owners happy.

Bear was inside the house, so eager to greet him that Sam had to shove his way through the door. Marilyn must have come by and let him in, he thought as he stroked the dog's back. He'd have to remember to call and thank her.

Right after dinner.

Sam opened the freezer, took out that night's meal—beef rib tips with mashed potatoes and gravy—and stuck it in the microwave. While it cooked, he poured some kibble into Bear's bowl and took out his phone, checking for messages. There'd been a notice about a ship for sale down at the dock that morning and Sam had discreetly given the guy a call and left a message, hoping to get his foot in the door before anyone else. No asking price was mentioned, but the size and type of ship sounded like exactly what he was looking for. With luck, the owner would be reasonable and willing to bargain.

He scrolled through the screens: no message, no e-mail, and no voice mail, either. Sam shrugged and set the phone aside. If he didn't hear something in a couple of hours, he'd try again. In the meantime, dinner was ready. He took the container out of the microwave and set it on the table, singeing his fingers in the process, then poured himself a drink, grabbed a loaf of bread and a stick of butter, and sat down. He'd just taken his first bite when he saw the note propped up against the salt and pepper shakers.

He didn't recognize the handwriting. In fact, it wasn't until he'd snatched it up that Sam realized it had been written by two different people. The main message was from Emily, followed by a PS from Marilyn. He stuffed a piece of bread in his mouth and started to read.

> *Hi, Sam!*
> *I saw Bear running loose down at McDonald's today*
> *and brought him home. Marilyn was here and she said*
> *it would be better to put him inside. He ate some fries*
> *for lunch. Hope that's okay.*
> *Emily*
> *PS—I like her.   ~ M.*

Sam set the note aside and took another bite. Just as he'd feared, with no one there to watch him, Bear had gotten out; heaven knows what would have happened if Emily hadn't found him when she did. And thank goodness Marilyn had been there when she brought him home, too, or he might have gotten right back out again.

He glanced over at Bear. "Hanging out at Mickey D's, huh?"

Then Sam reached for the note and read it a second time.

So, Marilyn had met Emily and liked her, huh? That was big. Marilyn didn't usually take to people that quickly. As outgoing and friendly as she seemed, she was careful about who she allowed to get close, and she could be critical of people she considered phonies, not bothering to hold back when someone rubbed her the wrong way. For all the time they'd known each other, he knew she'd never warmed up to Tiffany. Kallik had never told him why, just that his wife didn't trust her.

But she did like Emily.

The phone rang and Sam snatched it up. He was hoping it was about the ship for sale, but seeing Emily's name was even better.

"Hey, there," he said. "I just read your note. Thanks for returning my dog."

"No problem. He's a good lunch companion."

"Yeah, he is. Still, I owe you one."

"I agree. Have you had dinner yet?"

Sam looked at the half-eaten beef tips.

"Uh . . . nope."

"Good," she said. "How soon can you pick me up?"

He gave his shirt a sniff: fish, sweat, and diesel fumes.

"I don't know," he said. "Maybe half an hour?"

"Perfect. I'll see you then."

They sat across from each other, eating Mongolian beef while watching the seaplanes take off and land outside their window. Sam's hair was still damp from the shower, but at least he was clean—he'd even found some fresh clothes to wear. Which was a good thing because Emily looked and smelled terrific.

"I really can't thank you enough for getting me out of that house," she said. "If I'd had to spend another minute there, I think I would have lost my mind."

Sam put down his glass.

"What's the problem? If you don't mind my asking."

"Oh, you know," she said, stabbing at her plate. "Girl stuff. My friends back home warned me, but I'd never had room-mates before. I thought it'd be fun."

She chewed thoughtfully and shrugged. "Maybe it's just me."

He shook his head. "I doubt that."

"I suppose I should look on the bright side. At least I'm not obsessing about my mother anymore."

"There, you see?" he said. "It was good for something."

Sam reached for a deep-fried shrimp and ran it through the sweet and sour sauce. Sitting there, the two of them talking about their day, he was struck by how natural it felt. Emily was easy to talk to and easy to like. Perhaps that was what Marilyn had sensed about her, too.

"So," he said. "I hear you met my friend Marilyn."

"Yes! And she was so nice. The two of us got to talking so long I was almost late getting back to work."

"Yeah, Marilyn's a great gal. She and Kallik have been waiting a long time for this baby."

Emily stared at her plate.

"To tell you the truth, when I first saw her, I thought she was Tiffany." She shrugged. "And then when I saw she was pregnant—"

"You thought, 'What kind of a scumbag ditches his pregnant girlfriend?'"

"Something like that."

"Well, just for the record, I'm not that guy."

She looked up. "I didn't think you were."

For just a moment, Sam felt breathless. Emily's green eyes were striking, but when she smiled the effect was exhilarating. He wondered if she realized how lovely she was.

"So," he said. "You two were talking."

"Right. And she offered to take me out to Totem Park on

Saturday. Members of their tribe are carving totems and she says I can watch them as long as I don't act like a *atk'átsk'u*." She grinned. "That's *child* in Tlingit."

"I'm impressed."

"Don't be. She says my pronunciation is horrible."

The waiter came by and asked if they'd like to see a dessert menu.

"Oh, no thanks," she said. "I don't think I could eat another bite."

As the man walked off to get their check, Emily looked at Sam.

"Thank you again for bringing me here. I really appreciate it."

"Anytime," he said. "It beat the heck out of another heat-and-eat dinner from the microwave."

"Maybe so," she said, "but it was awfully short notice. At least let me pay for dinner."

"No way. If it wasn't for you, I'd be out looking for Bear right now."

"Well, if it happens again, you might try McDonald's. You should have seen him eying those kids' Happy Meals."

The check came and Sam paid. He hated to see the evening end. He couldn't remember when he'd enjoyed talking to someone as much.

"This has been a lot of fun," he said. "I'm glad you called."

"Me, too. And not just because I needed to get out of the house, either."

They looked at each other.

"You ready to go home?"

Emily looked down and shook her head.

"Me neither. Why don't we go for a walk?"

"Now? It's almost nine o'clock."

Sam glanced out the window.

"Still light out. Why not?"

"I'd feel like a kid staying up past her bedtime."

"So . . . ?"

Emily hesitated a moment.

"Sure," she said. "A walk sounds good."

Out in the harbor, the sun was crawling slowly across the horizon, its golden light spreading outward across the inky water and illuminating the bottoms of the violet clouds. Overhead, gray-winged gulls wheeled hopefully, still on the lookout for an easy meal. As Emily took it all in, Sam could tell she was moved. He'd always felt proud of Ketchikan and the life he'd made for himself there, but it was fun to experience it through the eyes of someone seeing it for the first time.

"It's beautiful," she said.

He nodded. "It is, isn't it?"

"Where should we go?"

"Have you been to Creek Street?"

"That's the one built over the water, isn't it?"

"It is, and it's not too far from here. Can you walk in those shoes?"

"Oh, yeah. I didn't bring any fancy shoes with me."

"All right, then."

Neither of them said a word as they headed down Water Street, just one of several couples out enjoying a few extra hours of daylight. A light breeze was coming off the water. Sam saw Emily zip up her jacket and wondered if he should offer his arm, then thought better of it. Whatever there was between them felt fragile; he didn't want to ruin it by doing something that might be misconstrued.

Emily glanced over at him.

"Can I ask you something without seeming rude?"

"Sure."

"What do people *do* in Ketchikan? I mean, I know that fishing is big and the Coast Guard is here and probably other maritime industries, but, I mean, if you don't have any connection to those, what is there?"

The question surprised him.

"Well, we have everything most other cities have: schools, a local government, post office, grocery stores . . ."

"Yes, but what do you *do*, you know, when it's dark all the time? For fun, I mean?"

"You mean besides watch TV and make babies?"

Emily blushed. "That's not what I meant."

"No, but that's what a lot of people think."

"I'm sorry. I didn't mean—"

"It's okay. If I were in your shoes, I'd probably wonder the same thing. As it happens, Ketchikan is probably one of the best places for the arts that I know of. When the fishing season is over, we pour that same energy into art and music and theater."

He pointed to the spot a quarter mile ahead where Creek Street started.

"I've got a couple of friends who sell their artwork in there. You can see for yourself."

"I'd like that," she said. "And I'm sorry if I hurt your feelings."

They reverted to silence then, their footsteps matching right-left-right, and when Emily shivered and crossed her arms, Sam silently offered his elbow—an offer of peace as well as warmth. When she slipped her arm through his and hugged it to her, he smiled. Maybe this was what Kimberley had meant when she said what she did about Emily. If so, he thought, she was mistaken. Emily might be a bit too candid, but there was nothing about her that seemed the least bit spoiled.

"So," he said. "What is it about your mother that you've been obsessing about?"

She waved a hand in front of her face.

"You don't want to hear about that."

"Why not? I've been told I'm a pretty good listener."

"You are," she said. "You helped me a lot with that problem at the cannery. I just don't want to bore you with all of my mother's melodrama."

He jostled her with his elbow.

"Try me."

Emily narrowed her eyes.

"What are you, a glutton for punishment?"

"Absolutely. Plus, I'm curious. I've never heard of anyone who could literally drive a person insane."

"Oh, so I'm crazy now?"

"Hey, you said it, I didn't."

She sighed and looked away.

"No, that's okay. I don't want to get all worked up again."

"Eh, fair enough. The offer's still good, though, if you change your mind."

Emily squeezed his arm. "What about you?"

"Me?"

"Yeah, what's your family like? Do they drive you crazy, too?"

"Sometimes. Not so much since I moved out."

"What are they like? Do they live around here?"

"No, my parents live in Juneau, which is where I grew up. My dad's a retired college professor. Mom's a nurse."

"Any brothers? Sisters?"

"One brother: Gabe."

"Older? Younger?"

"Older."

"What does Gabe do?"

"He's a biomechanics engineer."

"Sounds impressive."

"It is. At the moment, he's refining an artificial hand he designed as a science project in high school."

"Real underachiever, huh?"

"Yeah. The rest of the family's so embarrassed."

"So, how did you get into fishing?"

"Same as everyone else: it was a way to make a lot of money during summer break. If I wanted a car, wanted gas for the car, plus registration and insurance, I had to earn it."

"You worked in the cannery?"

"A couple of them, yeah. Started on the slime line, then moved on once I knew how things worked."

"They really throw you into the deep end there, don't they?"

"Why not? It's good pay for a kid."

"I'm not sure I could do it, honestly," she said. "The first time I walked in there, seeing all that blood? It turned my stomach."

"It turns everyone's stomach. You just get used to it."

"That's what Tim told me the first day."

"And . . . ?"

"It's true. I hardly notice it now. Funny, the things you just don't see after a while."

The lights of Creek Street were on, casting a warm glow on the faces of the shoppers peering into the windows. Sam and Emily paused as they approached the boardwalk, taking in the spectacle of an entire shopping area built over a fast-flowing creek. The two of them leaned over the railing, still arm in arm, and watched the water trip over the rocks below them. It occurred to Sam that if he turned his face, Emily would be close enough to kiss.

"It's like something out of a storybook," she said, peering down into the water. "Whoever thought of making something like this?"

Sam suppressed a smile.

"Actually, this used to be the red light district."

"So it is like a fairy tale," she said, her eyes twinkling. "Don't they all have happy endings?"

Now it was his turn to blush.

"Yes, I suppose they do."

Emily turned and looked at him.

"Have you figured out what you're going to do about Bear yet?"

"Not really. For now, I guess I'll just leave him in the house and hope he doesn't destroy the place by the time I get back. I hate to do it. We work long days in the summer, but I can't take the chance that he'll get out again. We were lucky today, but I don't expect lightning to strike twice."

"I've been thinking," Emily said. "Why don't I take him for walks on my lunch hour? That way, you can leave him in the house, but he won't be stuck there with nothing to do all day. The two of us can run around or play Frisbee or whatever and when I get off work, I can go by the house and keep an eye on him until you get home."

Sam was so shocked, it took a second for him to speak.

"Are you sure?"

"Of course," she said. "I'm normally a pretty active person, and being stuck inside all day is torture. Plus, frankly, it would give me an excuse to get away from the idiots I live with."

Sam was flabbergasted. Emily's offer was more than he ever would, or even could, have asked for.

"Wow. That would be, I mean, it would make things so much better for both of us." He laughed and spun her around. "Thank you."

There was a moment's hesitation as their eyes met. Sam felt his heart pounding, unsure what to do. Then Emily smiled softly, leaned forward, and, as her eyelids closed, they kissed.

CHAPTER 13

Time seemed to crawl by the next day at the cannery. After a morning spent out on the floor, the interns were herded back into the classroom for lessons on species identification and sampling methodologies—all of which was review for Emily. As Tim Garrett stood at the whiteboard explaining the subtle differences between coho and sockeye salmon, she rested her chin in her hand and thought about Sam.

Emily bit her lip, remembering the kiss they'd shared the night before. Neither of them had said or done anything to make her think it would happen, but when it did, it just seemed like the most natural thing in the world. The memory of it—the clean, soapy scent of his skin, the light prickle of his hastily shaven face, the warm press of his lips against hers—still thrilled her. As they'd stood there on the boardwalk, the water below them rushing past, it felt as if something inside her had suddenly come alive. It was only later that the reality of what had happened hit her.

Her first reaction had been an overwhelming sense of guilt. Emily and Carter had gotten very serious over the past few months, and their families certainly expected they would marry at some point. It seemed wrong to be kissing someone else while the two of them were still more or less committed. Emily was sure she'd be upset if she found out that Carter had been kissing someone else.

Then she'd remembered how irked she was about their mothers' interference, the feeling that she was just a passenger in a car being driven by someone else, and wondered if kissing Sam had somehow been an act of rebellion, a way to reassert control over her own life.

Kimberley's accusation had preyed on her mind, as well. The idea that, since Emily was only there for the summer, any involvement she had with Sam amounted to "toying" with him had bothered her more than it should have. It was true that when she took the job in Ketchikan, Emily had had no intention of staying past the three-month commitment of the internship, but the more time she spent there and the more she learned about it, the more she appreciated the town and its people. Yes, it was different from where she'd grown up, and if she moved there, the cold and the rain would be something she'd have to get used to, but the hectic pace and high cost of living in Southern California had already made staying there an open question.

Despite those conflicting factors, however, Emily was sure that none of them had anything to do with what had happened on Creek Street. What she'd felt for Sam at that moment—what she still felt—wasn't about interfering mothers or rebellion or even Kimberley. The fact was, from the first time she saw him, Emily had felt an attraction to Sam that she'd never felt for anyone else.

For starters, he was funnier and less inhibited than Carter was. There was a sexiness about him, too, that took her breath away—something she could not, in all honesty, say about Carter. Even the fact that Sam worked in a fishery was appealing. He understood the kind of issues marine biologists dealt with in a way that Carter had shown neither an interest in nor a desire to learn about. There'd been times, in fact, when he'd seemed annoyed that Emily had any interests at all other than his own.

Bear, too, was a big reason that Emily had grown so fond of Sam. The big dog had a way about him that had captured her heart from the very first, and rather than being intimidated, Emily found his size endearing. He seemed to know instinctively that his size made him formidable and went out of his way to compensate, showing a gentleness that was both touching and unexpected. She was glad Sam had agreed to let her watch him while he was at work. It gave her something to look forward to in the middle of the day and made a seamless place for her in both their lives. Anyone who owned a dog like that, she thought, was worth getting to know better.

Not liking dogs was another thing about Carter that being around Bear had pointed out to her. He'd always told her it was because dogs were unpredictable and he needed to protect his hands—which, for the most part, Emily understood. After all, a surgeon's hands were, as he liked to say, his fortune. Carter was also obsessed with keeping his hands clean, though, something that loomed large when she imagined what it would be like to marry him and have children together.

Emily's fondest moments with her own father were of building sandcastles and digging in the garden together. Even if Carter didn't want a dog, would he be willing to make an exception to his clean hands rule for things like that? What about changing diapers or cleaning up after a sick child? The fact was, he had no problem sticking his hands into a bloody wound. Was keeping his hands clean really that important, or was it just an excuse for him to avoid doing things he thought were beneath him? It was only at this remove that Emily had even asked herself those questions, and the implications bothered her. It didn't mean she didn't love Carter or that she didn't still think she might marry him, but seeing him in contrast to someone like Sam had opened her eyes in a way that nothing else had before. She didn't know what she was going to do about Carter, or Sam, for that matter, but last night had given her a lot to think about.

A buzzer signaling the end of class sounded, and Emily hastily gathered her things. She'd offered to make dinner for the two of them that night, and there were a few things she needed to pick up at the store. If she hurried, she could get everything in the oven before Sam got home.

Emily kept her head down as she headed out the open doors. Getting in late last night had spared her from any further criticism at the hands of Rachel and Kimberley, and Tim had decided not to have them working in pairs again. She'd thought briefly about finding an Airbnb for the rest of the summer to be done with the whole roommate situation, but had decided as a matter of principle not to give them the satisfaction of running her off. She hadn't done anything wrong. Why should she be the one to leave?

She was almost to the sidewalk when she heard someone calling her.

"Hey, Emily! Wait up."

It was Uki, hurrying toward her with her lab coat flapping behind her like a cape.

"Don't worry," she said, pausing to catch her breath. "They're not coming. How've you been? I haven't seen you at the house in a while."

Emily hesitated, wondering what this was about. She doubted Uki had stopped her just to ask about her general health.

"I'm fine," she said. "Just, you know, busy."

"How's the arm doing?"

"Pretty good." Emily held it out, displaying the still-fading bruises as she flexed her fingers. "Not pretty, but it works okay."

Uki looked down, running a hand through her hair.

"Listen, I'm sorry for the way things have been at the house. I thought it was just some stupid white girl crap at first, but it's pretty obvious now what's going on. I talked to Tim about it this morning and he said he'd get it sorted out." She grinned and threw a thumb over her shoulder, indicating the cannery. "That's where they are now—getting sorted."

Emily shook her head. "You didn't have to do that."

"Hey, man, I didn't want to deal with it, either. Like being back in high school, you know? No thanks."

"Well, I appreciate it," she said. "But for now, I think I'll probably just make myself scarce."

"Oh. Yeah, sure, that's cool."

Emily turned and saw a man walk out of the quartermaster's office with a black pennant in his arms. He unfurled it and started hoisting it up a flagpole by the gangway.

Uki groaned. "Aw, hell. Not again."

"Why? What's wrong?"

"That." She pointed at the pennant moving listlessly in the breeze. "It means someone's died at sea."

"*Anywhere* at sea?"

"Here in our waters. Someone sailing out of Ketchikan."

Emily shivered.

"They flew it for my cousin last year," Uki said. "My dad two years before that. He was on a seiner; went over the side and got caught in the net."

Emily was only half-listening. She'd known that Sam's work was hazardous, but it hadn't occurred to her that he was in any real danger until just then.

Uki frowned. "You okay?"

"Yeah. Just c-cold. I should have put on a jacket," she said. "I'd better go."

"Okay, sure. Just wanted you to know how things were hanging, that's all. I'll see you around."

"Yeah. Thanks."

Emily gave the black pennant another quick glance and hurried away.

By the time she got to Sam's house, Emily had managed to calm down. As tragic as it was, there was no reason to think that the black pennant had anything to do with Sam. If she'd never seen it, in fact, she would have spent the rest of the day in blissful ignorance.

Bear was still inside, greeting her as warmly as he had when she'd gotten there at lunchtime. He snuffled her hands and did his little half leaps and pirouettes as she made her way haltingly into the kitchen. Emily set the bag of groceries on the kitchen counter and put her arms around the dog's neck, burying her face in his coat.

"Hello, you big, fluffy boy. Did you miss me?"

He lumbered over to the back door and whined to be let out. Emily followed him into the backyard and double-checked that the gates were shut before going back in. Sam had been surprised when she told him she'd found one open the day before, and she wanted to make sure the latches were secure before she let him out unsupervised. The last thing she needed was for Bear to make a break for it while she was getting dinner ready.

Emily hummed as she chopped the ingredients for the meal she was preparing. Thanks to the Junior Chef Program for Kids, she was a pretty decent cook, but the only times she ever got to practice her skills back home were when Maria was either sick or visiting her grandkids in Mexico. She noticed that Sam had a pretty well-stocked kitchen for a bachelor, and wondered if it might actually be Tiffany who'd filled it with all the staples, Wüsthof knives, and high-end cookware at her disposal. Then again, Emily thought, anyone who'd take the knickknacks off the shelves when she left would probably have taken anything of hers from the kitchen, as well.

As Emily slid the Pyrex dish into the oven, she glanced at the time. It had taken longer than she'd anticipated to get everything prepped, and she was surprised Sam wasn't home yet. Still, she'd been hoping to take Bear out for a quick walk before they ate, and she sort of liked the idea that Sam would walk into the house and smell dinner cooking. She wrote him a quick note saying they'd be back soon, grabbed Bear's leash off the wall, and opened the back door.

"Who wants to go for a walk?"

The sun was nearing the horizon as they headed out, stretching their shadows clear across the road. Bear made a beeline for one of his favorite spots, sniffing it thoroughly before marking it and moving on to the next. The neighborhood was on a knoll overlooking the harbor, and as Bear checked out a particularly intriguing spot, Emily scanned the ships below, hoping to spot Sam's. A cold gust of wind blew up with a suddenness that startled her, and Emily was reminded of the pennant flying down on the dock. Death, too, could be swift and startling, she thought. Somewhere in the town that night a family would be grieving a loved one just as she had grieved the loss of her father eleven years before.

Back then, a black car had been the harbinger of misfortune. A knock at the door, a policeman telling her mother that their private plane had gone down with no survivors, then her mother's scream of anguish while Emily stood frozen in the shadows, trying to convince herself that she was still in her bed asleep. It seemed impossible that her father could be dead—as unlikely as gravity suddenly shutting off—and for her mother, at least, the effect had been very much the same.

Without her husband's steadying influence, Veronica Prentice became emotionally untethered, at times barely able to function. She insisted that the crash had been her brother-in-law's fault, that as the last person to fly the plane, Emily's uncle Danny had done something to compromise its airworthiness. And when the plane's logs showed that it had been overdue for maintenance, she doubled down, publicly accusing him of negligence. In the end, the NTSB found that adverse weather conditions had caused the crash, but her accusation had convinced at least one person, and that was Uncle Danny himself, who quietly accepted both the blame and the responsibility for his brother's family. He never flew again.

Emily, though, had never blamed her uncle. Instead, with a twelve-year-old's cynical view of the world, she placed the blame squarely where she thought it belonged: on her father. She had loved him, yes, and he'd meant the world to her, but he had his faults, and in his absence, they loomed large. He was impulsive, a gambler and risk-taker whose luck had finally run out. When she heard he'd died instantly, she refused to be comforted. He may not have suffered, but she and her mother would for the rest of their lives. She wondered if her father had ever even considered them when he'd stepped into that plane.

That was why Emily had vowed never to marry a man like her father, a man who would needlessly put himself in harm's way. And as she watched her mother try to fill the void in her life with shopping, Emily had thanked her lucky stars that at least her own trust fund was beyond her mother's reach.

By the time Bear completed his rounds, it was even later than Emily had anticipated. As she opened the front door, she was all ready with an apology for keeping Sam from his dinner.

"Hi there!" she called as they walked into the house. "Sorry we're late. Bear had some serious marking to do tonight."

She looked around.

"Sam? Where are you?"

Emily walked into the kitchen and opened the door to the garage. Sam's Jeep wasn't there. She checked the time. He should have been home long before then. A whisper of fear sent a chill down her spine.

So, he was a little late, she told herself. No big deal. But a small voice inside her head wouldn't listen.

What if the pennant was for Sam?

The reality hit Emily like an ice bath. She shivered; her teeth began to chatter; her knees felt like rubber. As she slowly slid to the floor, Bear circled her, whining his concern.

This was her fault, she told herself. She'd betrayed Carter— a safe, practical man—to pursue someone exciting, and look what had happened. Like her father, Sam had taken a risk, and now she was paying for it.

How could she have let herself fall for a man like that?

CHAPTER 14

Sam was beginning to worry. Halfway back to port, the tender's rudder had fouled, and it had taken almost an hour to clear it. All the while, the ship had drifted farther out to sea. He'd tried calling Emily from the ship's satellite telephone to tell her he'd be late, but she hadn't picked up, and he had no way of knowing whether she'd gotten his message. By the time the ship limped into port, he was on edge, snapping at the buyers to settle on a price and chivying his crew to hurry and empty the hold. He hoped her silence meant nothing, that Emily either had not gotten his message or had been too busy to return his call, but until he heard her voice again, he couldn't be sure.

As long as she hadn't changed her mind, he thought, everything would be okay.

The night before had been a revelation. Even before the two of them had kissed, he'd been amazed at how good it felt to be with her. He'd been captivated by Emily's green eyes since the first time he saw her, but the more he got to know her, the more they fascinated him. They seemed to change with her moods, from a happy apple green to thoughtful emerald, to a sultry jade just before their lips met. When the evening was over, he'd driven home in a daze, wondering how he'd ever gotten so lucky.

And now, he couldn't reach her.

It didn't help that there'd been bad news waiting when they finally made it to shore. Seeing the black pennant flapping on the dock had put the whole crew on edge. The men who worked those waters were a small fraternity, and the loss of any one of them sent ripples of alarm through all the rest. Making a living on the water required a certain amount of magical thinking, denying the possibility of disaster even as you did everything you could to prepare for it. When the inevitable finally happened, it was like being wakened from a pleasant dream by a slap in the face.

When the fish were finally sold and off-loaded, Sam had checked in with each of his men, making sure the tender was secure before taking off. No doubt he was worried about nothing, but the superstitious sailor in him couldn't help thinking that bad news came in threes. As he got in his car, he called Emily one more time, frustrated when it went to her voice mail. Why wasn't she answering? He told himself to be patient. He'd be there soon enough.

The house was dark when Sam drove up, the same single light he'd left on that morning the only sign of life. As he pulled into the garage, his stomach clenched. Emily said she'd be there for dinner. Had something happened to her, too?

The first thing Sam noticed when he opened the door was the smell of dinner cooking. So, he thought, she hadn't changed her mind after all. But if Emily had made dinner, where was she? And for that matter, where was Bear?

"Anybody home?"

He walked into the living room and switched on the light. Emily and Bear were on the sofa, the dog's head resting on her lap. As Sam stepped into the room, Bear lifted his head and thumped his tail in greeting but remained where he was. Emily turned to look at him and he saw that her eyes were red. Had something happened?

"Hey," he said. "Are you okay?"

She blinked at him uncertainly.

"You're alive."

Sam smiled and patted his chest.

"You're right, I am. Why? Did you think I wouldn't be?"

Emily wiped her nose on her sleeve.

"I saw the pennant. Someone died. I thought—" She sobbed, tears welling. "I thought it was you."

"Hey, hey," he said. "Don't cry. It's okay. I'm fine, see?"

He reached out to comfort her, and she shied away.

"What is it, Em? You're not sorry I'm back, are you?"

She shook her head. "What happened? Why are you late?"

"On our last run in, the rudder got fouled. The ship drifted quite a ways before we could get it free."

Her eyes flashed. "Why didn't you call me?"

"I *did!* I called a couple of times to tell you I'd be late, but you never answered. Didn't you get my messages?"

"My phone," she said. "The battery must have died."

"Look, I'm sorry if you were upset, but I was a little concerned myself. When you didn't answer, I wasn't sure what to think." He bent down, trying to catch her eye. "You're not sorry I'm here, are you?"

"Of course not. I'm glad you're okay. It's just that, when I left the cannery, I saw them putting out that black pennant, and Uki told me that someone at sea was dead. All I could think was that I might never see you again."

Emily covered her face.

"It reminded me of the day my dad died: seeing the police car drive up to the house, hearing my mother sobbing when she heard the news. I just couldn't bear the thought that that might be me, you know?"

Sam sat back on his haunches, wondering what he could say to reassure her. He supposed he could tell her it was silly, that nothing could ever happen to him at work, but that would be a lie. What he did was risky; refusing to acknowledge that would be both foolish and unkind. But if Emily was going to become distraught every time he was a little late coming home, then maybe it was better to call things off before the two of them got more involved.

He grabbed a box of tissues and handed it to her.

"Look, I know you're upset, but can we talk about this rationally for a minute?"

She blew her nose and nodded.

"First of all—and I'm not blaming anyone—the man who died was on a different kind of ship in deeper waters and he was younger and less seasoned than anyone working with me, okay?"

"Okay, but—"

"No, hold on a second. I'm not saying that what I do isn't risky—it is—but I want to reassure you that I am very careful with my ship and my crew *and* myself. I have the best safety record in these waters and I intend to keep it that way."

Emily sniffed. "I didn't know that."

"Well, now you do," he said. "It's true that accidents can and do happen in my line of work, but they happen everywhere in every line of work. I don't know how your dad died and I don't need to know, but I'll tell you this: There are no guarantees in this life. If that's what you're looking for, then I'm not the only guy in the world who's going to disappoint you."

She looked down at Bear and began stroking the huge head. The dog's gaze switched between the two of them, his eyes full of questions.

"Look," Sam said. "I don't have a crystal ball. I don't know what's going to happen in the future. I don't even know yet if *we* are going to happen—"

"I didn't say that."

"I know you didn't. I'm just trying to reassure you that every day when I get on that ship, I do everything possible to make sure that every man aboard makes it home safely. Fate may have other ideas, but there's nothing I or anyone else can do about that. And if I had to guess, there was nothing your father could have done about it, either."

"Maybe. I guess."

"Not all captains are like that, I admit. Some are too greedy or too impatient; they cut corners, ignore weather warnings, hire unreliable people, but that's not me, and that's not who I'll ever be." He paused and took a breath. "It's also why I'm trying to buy a tender of my own."

She looked up. "You are?"

Sam nodded; saying it aloud made him feel shy. He hadn't been planning to tell her about it until he'd secured a ship, but they'd shared a lot in the last few days, and her concern for his welfare was touching.

"So," he said. "Now that you know, what do you think? I'm crazy, right?"

"No, I think it's great. When will you get it?"

"I don't know yet. I've got some feelers out, but finding the right ship at the right price could take a while, and in the meantime, I have to be careful not to tip my hand. If my bosses find out I'm looking, I could be out of a job with no ship at all."

"And until then, you promise you'll be careful?"

"I promise I will be as careful as I always am."

A smile teased the corners of her mouth.

"Thank you."

"No problem. Feel better now?"

The smile widened. The green eyes shone.

"Yes."

"Good. Then can we please eat dinner? Whatever you made smells wonderful."

The first thing Emily did when she got home that night was to plug in her phone and check her voice mail. Sure enough, Sam had left three increasingly frantic messages telling her he'd be late and asking her to call. Hearing them, she felt heartsick, remembering her own mounting anxiety as she'd waited for him to get home and knowing now how Sam, too, had worried about her. She wished she could go back in time and reassure them both that everything was going to be fine.

If only she'd let her mother buy her a new phone like she wanted to, it never would have happened. The irony was not lost on Emily.

Speaking of her mother, Emily noticed that she'd missed a call from her, too. Her finger hovered over the PLAY button. Did she really want to listen to it now? Whatever the message was, it would no doubt be preceded by a complaint about Emily's lack of contact, something she was in no mood for, and her mother had always been adamant that calling after nine o'clock was something one did only in case of an emergency. Maybe, she told herself, it would be better to wait and call back in the morning.

Then Emily noticed the time stamp on her mother's message: nine fifty-one. Was there an emergency back at home? The same constriction she'd felt in her chest when she believed that Sam had been killed gripped her anew. Without pausing to listen to her mother's message, Emily hit the CALL BACK button. Whether or not the message was important, she knew she'd never be able to sleep if she didn't find out.

Her mother's voice sounded thick, as if she'd woken from a

dream, and Emily immediately felt a pang of guilt. Perhaps being without power so long had reset the phone's internal clock, she thought. Maybe the message hadn't been made after nine o'clock after all. Then her mother burst into tears.

"Mom, what's wrong? What's happened?"

"It's Uncle Danny. The tests came back and . . ."

Her sobs made the rest of her words unintelligible. Emily gripped the phone harder.

"What happened? Is he okay?"

Interminable seconds passed while her mother struggled to regain her composure.

"I'm sorry, Em. It's just been such an awful day, and then when you didn't call back, I thought—"

"You thought something had happened to me, I know. I'm sorry I didn't call back sooner. I forgot to charge my phone, and it ran out of juice before I could get back here."

She pressed her lips together, trying to be patient while her mother calmed down.

"Are you okay?" she asked.

"Yes. Yes, I'm fine now."

"So tell me about Uncle Danny. What happened?"

"They'd found a spot on his lung. I didn't tell you because we hoped it was nothing serious, but . . ."

Emily nodded, fighting the urge to cry. She was afraid this would happen, had suspected as much, in fact, when Carter mentioned the oncology department. Lung cancer had killed both of her paternal grandparents; had he lived, it probably would have killed her father, too. Knowing it was inevitable, though, didn't make the news any easier to hear.

". . . now the doctors want him to have surgery."

"When?"

"Tuesday morning."

"Should I come home?"

"No. Not now. The doctor says they'll know more after they've opened him up. Once that's done and we have a prognosis, you can decide what you want to do. The good news is, your uncle's in good spirits, and for the moment, at least, he's not in any pain. If you were to come home now, I'm afraid it would only upset him."

Her mother was right. Uncle Danny's first concern had always been their well-being rather than his own. As anxious as she was to be with him, for now it was probably best just to send her prayers and good wishes.

"All right," she said. "But call me as soon as the doctor tells you what the prognosis is, okay? In the meantime, I promise I'll have my phone charged the next time I leave the house."

"Oh, are you and your roommates getting along better these days?"

"Not really," Emily said. "I was at Sam's."

"Sam?" her mother said, an undeniable edge creeping into her voice.

"He's just a guy I met. He needed someone to watch his dog while he's at work and I said I'd help out. It's no big deal," she added, hoping her mother would drop the subject.

She should have known better, of course. Emily's mother had a keen ear for half truths, and this evasion had not gone unnoticed.

"Emily, dear, are you sure that's wise?"

"Why not? He's a good dog."

"No. Don't you try and jolly me out of this. You know what I mean. Why are you getting involved with another man when you have someone like Carter back home?"

"At home, yes, but I've barely spoken to him since I got here. I've called and left messages and all I've gotten back is a couple of texts telling me he's busy."

"Well, of course he's busy, dear. He's busy working hard so he can make a good life for you. You can't blame him for that."

Emily could feel her temper rise. It was bad enough being told how to live her life when she was living under her mother's roof. She wasn't going to be bossed around from a thousand miles away.

"That's funny," she said. "Because he hasn't called me once since I got here."

"Darling, you must know that Carter adores you. Every time I see him, you're all we ever talk about."

Emily pursed her lips. There were times when she wondered if it was her or her mother that Carter adored.

"Look, I'm not involved with Sam, okay? I'm just watching his dog. And yes, we've struck up a friendship, but I don't see how that's any of your business or Carter's."

"How can you say that? Our families have always thought you two would get married someday."

"And maybe we will," Emily said. "But unless and until Carter actually proposes, I'm still a free agent."

CHAPTER 15

On Saturday morning, Emily loaded Bear into the back of Sam's Jeep and headed over to Marilyn's to take her to Totem Park, where friends of hers were putting on a carving demonstration. Sam had loaned her the vehicle the night before so she could take Bear along and give Marilyn a break from driving. Her original plan had been to give the dog a walk around the park, but Sam insisted she take Bear's cart, as well.

"His *cart?*"

"He gives the Tlingit kids rides in it," he'd said. "Believe me, if you show up anywhere in Saxman with Bear and no cart, you're going to be sorry."

Emily had eyed the homemade dog cart—a cross between a sulky and a buckboard—and had shaken her head.

"I never heard of a dog pulling a cart. How do you attach it?"

"Marilyn can show you. The important thing is to get the pulling harness on correctly. Once you do that, attaching the shafts is pretty simple. Stick a couple of kids on the seats and away you go."

"I don't know. . . ."

Sam laughed at her skepticism.

"You'll see," he said. "Just think of him as a pony that drools."

Marilyn was standing by her front door nursing a travel mug of coffee when Emily drove up. When she saw the Jeep, she locked the door behind her and started waddling toward the street.

"Man," she said when Emily got out to give her a hand. "This kid is getting heavy."

She looked into the back seat, where Bear had been watching her progress through a foggy, drool-streaked window.

"Hey, big guy. Ready to do some pulling today?"

Bear barked once, his tail thrashing the interior of the car as she slid into the front passenger seat.

"*Oof!*" Marilyn winced and rubbed her belly.

"You okay?"

"Yeah, yeah. Just Braxton-Hicks contractions. I've been getting a lot of them lately."

"Would you rather stay home and take it easy? We don't have to do this today."

"No," she said. "I'd rather get out of the house. Nothing to do in there but sit and watch my belly grow. Besides, the kids know we're coming; they'd never forgive me if we didn't show up."

Emily put the Jeep in gear and started down the road, doing her best to avoid any bumps along the way. Sam had told her that Marilyn and Kallik had waited a long time for this baby. She figured it was the least she could do to keep from jostling it around.

"So," Marilyn said. "You and Sandy still hanging out, huh?"

"Sandy?"

"Sandy Sam. That hair, that skin? The man looks like he's made from a big ol' pile of sand."

Emily laughed. "I hadn't thought of that, but you're right."

"Yeah," Marilyn said, glancing out the window. "You can

pound that pile with your fist and it don't move an inch, but if you start picking at it—pick, pick, pick—it can start to crumble. Pretty soon, it's so weak even a little thing like the wind can blow it all away."

The comment, coming out of nowhere as it had, left Emily feeling uneasy. Was this a warning of some sort? Perhaps Marilyn, like Kimberley, thought that a relationship with her wouldn't be good for Sam.

"So, you think I'm picking at Sam's weak spot?"

"I'm saying it's already been picked at. The man's still strong, but not like he once was. He doesn't need anyone to be messing him around just for fun."

"I understand what you're saying," Emily said. "But I'm not the sort of person who'd do that."

"You sure?"

"As sure as I can be. I don't know where things are going right now, but I didn't come here looking for a summer romance. For now, I think we're both just keeping an open mind about the future."

"That's fair." Marilyn shrugged. "I meant no offense."

"No offense taken," Emily told her. "As far as I'm concerned, Sam's lucky to have friends like you and Kallik."

Marilyn grimaced and set her hand on her growing girth, stroking it gently. Emily was tempted to ask again if they should postpone their outing, but a quick frown told her the suggestion would not be welcome. Instead, Marilyn changed the subject.

"You like being an intern?"

Emily hesitated. Was she enjoying it? It was hard to tell sometimes, especially since she was living and working with the same people—two of whom had been going out of their way to make her life miserable.

"It's all right. I'm learning a lot about how the fish are

processed and managed, which was the main reason I signed up, but it would be nice if the workers themselves were a little friendlier."

"Why should they be? They've got work to do, and it's not like you're going to stick around."

"I know," she said. "I just hope it's not more than that."

"Meaning what?"

"Meaning a couple of the other interns think someone's trying to make our boss look bad so they can sabotage the internship program."

Marilyn pulled a face.

"Nah, I don't believe that. Interns, no interns, who cares?"

"Good question. When *I* first heard about the problems at the cannery, I thought maybe someone had it in for our supervisor, but the other interns told me they thought the real target was the internship program. Then Sam pointed out that we were all just guessing and that it might be nothing at all. I mean, stuff happens, right? It doesn't mean anyone's out to get you."

"It also doesn't mean that somebody *isn't* trying to cause problems for the guy, just maybe not for the reason you think."

Emily glanced at her. "You mean someone might be trying to get rid of Tim?"

"Maybe. Either him or someone he answers to. I guarantee you'll find plenty of bad stuff going on down there if you look hard enough. I love Ketchikan, but it has problems just like any other place: smuggling, drug running, human trafficking. It's just a fact of life."

"Yeah, there's plenty of that in San Diego, too," Emily said. "I think a lot of it has to do with being a port city. Strangers coming in and out all the time, it's easy to miss something that's out of the ordinary."

"Exactly."

Now that the ice had been broken, it occurred to Emily

that Marilyn might just be the person to answer some of the questions she had about the work that Sam did and how to keep from worrying about it.

"Can I ask you something?"

"Sure."

"Does it ever scare you that Kallik's job is so dangerous?"

Marilyn laughed. "Only every minute of every day. Why?"

"So, what do you do about it?"

"Do about it? What can I do? Being scared won't help; worrying won't help. All that does is make you miserable."

"I know, but—"

"Look, what happens in this life happens. If you make yourself unhappy thinking about all the bad stuff, you'll miss the good that's right in front of you."

"Easier said than done."

"Yeah, I know, but think of it this way. If you worry yourself sick feeling all that pain and nothing bad happens, then you've suffered for nothing. And if something bad does happen, then you will have suffered over the same thing *twice.*"

Emily thought about that for a second. Isn't that what she'd done the night Sam had come home late, filled herself with unnecessary pain and suffering?

"You're right," she said. "I'll have to remember that."

Marilyn stroked her belly again and looked out the window.

"Don't invite sorrow into your life. When the time comes, believe me, it'll open the door on its own."

When Emily drove into Totem Park, she saw a woman standing near the entrance who looked like a tougher version of Marilyn.

"That's my sister, Jane," Marilyn said, pointing. "She'll take Bear and his cart while the two of us watch the totem makers."

Emily hesitated. While Sam was at work, she considered

Bear her responsibility. He hadn't said anything about some-one else watching his dog.

"Has she done this before?"

"Oh, yeah," Marilyn said. "Lots of times. Believe me, the kids will behave better with a clan mother in charge than they will with you."

Emily took Bear out of the back, and the three of them walked over to say hello. Her apprehension disappeared as soon as Bear and Jane greeted each other.

"Are you sure you're ready for this?" Emily asked.

"Oh, yeah," Jane said. "Me and Bear make a good team."

"Okay," Emily said, handing her the dog's lead. "Let me get the cart out for you."

Marilyn and Jane chatted away in Tlingit as Emily wrestled the cart from the Jeep. Just as Sam had said, it took only a few minutes to get the dog hitched up and ready to go. It was a good thing, too. Already, word had spread and a crowd of children was gathering nearby.

"Now you see why I asked Jane to come," Marilyn said. "Once the kids saw Bear and his cart, we wouldn't have had a moment's peace."

"Thanks for thinking of it." Emily turned and smiled at Jane. "And thank you, too."

As Jane led Bear away, Emily and Marilyn took the opportunity to walk through the park.

"Might as well," Marilyn said. "The demonstration won't start for another few minutes, and the doc says walking is better for me than just sitting around."

The totem poles were spread out across a wide, grassy area. In front of each was a number and a short description of the figures it represented.

"These are incredible," Emily said, staring at the colorful poles looming over them. "How old are they?"

"Most of them were made during the Depression. The Civilian Conservation Corps commissioned Tlingit carvers to copy them from the original poles found around the island, most of which were in bad shape. If it hadn't been for the New Deal, this part of our history might have been lost forever."

Emily marveled at the smoothness of the wood as well as the details and the expressions on the human and animal faces.

"And these were all made by hand?"

"No other way to make them. Totems are sacred to us. The tools and the techniques we use came to us from the Creator. The figures on the poles are our family members." Marilyn pointed. "Bear, Beaver, Eagle, Raven—they all have stories to tell."

"So the totem poles are their stories?"

Marilyn waggled her head.

"Yes, and no. The stories themselves are passed down orally or through song. The totem poles are more about a clan's deeds and the interaction between animals and humans that we can learn from."

Emily found a pole that particularly interested her. Pole number eleven was the only one without a solid base. Instead, it looked as if it were standing on two legs. As Marilyn lumbered over, Emily stepped closer and read the title: Kats and His Bear Wife.

"Why is it cut out at the bottom?"

"It's a door—or it was. Something like this would have been set up in front of the entrance to the tribal house. On special occasions, the people would pass through it on their way inside. The rest of the time, they went in the other entrance."

"What was the significance of that?"

Marilyn shrugged. "Who knows? You gotta remember, a lot of our culture was wiped out when white folks came."

Emily let her eyes travel to the top of the pole.

"How do you read these things?"

"You don't read them, per se; every part relates to every other part."

Marilyn pointed to the large human face that dominated the pole.

"That's Kats. The thing on top of his head is a she bear."

"His wife?"

"Right. See the faces in Kats's ears and nose?"

Emily squinted. "Sort of."

"Those symbolize his keen sense of smell and hearing. Kats was the greatest of all bear hunters. He used his superhuman powers to find and kill them."

"Wait a minute. I thought his wife was a bear."

"What's your point?"

"I don't know. I just thought that, you know, if he was killing bears and she was a bear . . ."

"Tlingit don't view death the way you white folks do. When we kill a bear, we thank it for its life and promise to use its body for the benefit of all. Kats's bear wife would have understood that her husband was honoring the bears he killed."

"I guess I'll have to take your word for it."

"By the way, in the context of the story, the opening between the legs symbolizes the entrance to a bear's den—not something you do lightly."

Emily pointed at the smaller human figures at the bottom. "Who are those people supposed to be?"

"Those are their descendants. We have several people in my tribe who trace their lineage back to Kats and his bear wife."

Emily wasn't sure she believed that, but she wasn't about to argue with someone about their religious beliefs. If it helped to think that one was descended from a bear, where was the harm?

"So, whatever happened to Kats and his wife?"

"Kats was killed."

"How?"

"The stories don't tell us. Probably by a bear. After he died, though, his wife left their village and went into the hill country, where she sang her songs of mourning."

"That's sad."

"Yes, it's sad," Marilyn said. "But sadness is just part of life."

"So what's the point of the story? To explain why bears live in the mountains?"

"Could be. Remember, though, totems and totem carving are very spiritual. Trying to distill their meaning into one simple lesson ignores their sacred purpose."

"Oh, sorry."

"No, it's all right. To me, it's a lesson about learning to accept what life offers. Just like Kats's bear wife, we all know sorrow. It's how we honor those we've lost that's important."

Marilyn stroked her distended belly as she spoke, and Emily wondered if she was thinking of the miscarriages she'd suffered. At least it looked like this one would make it, she thought. Marilyn and Kallik didn't deserve any more sorrow.

CHAPTER 16

Monday morning was the day Emily had been dreading: she'd be working in the freezer. Not all day, thank goodness, but even half a day was misery. As the heavy metal door shut behind her, she shuddered. In spite of her heavy coat and gloves, the cold was seeping through her clothes, chilling her to the bone. How people who worked there withstood it every day was a mystery.

She looked down at her checklist, her frozen fingers fumbling with the pencil. At least there wasn't any liquid blood in the freezer, she thought, trying to look on the bright side. And the smell wasn't quite so bad, either.

Or maybe my nose is just frozen.

There were two workers in the freezer with her: a man and a woman who checked the boxes of processed fish as they were brought in and put them in neat stacks against the wall. As Emily watched them work, the man ignored her, but the woman flashed her a friendly smile, for which Emily felt pathetically grateful. She hadn't realized until she mentioned it to Marilyn just how upsetting it was to have people glaring at her every day. It was hard being treated as an enemy when you were just doing your job.

At least the tension back at the house had eased up a little; whatever Tim had said to Rachel and Kimberley must have gotten through to them. Things might not be as friendly as they'd been at first, but at least the two of them had stopped whispering and giving her dirty looks whenever she walked into a room. Uki, too, was making a point of talking to her more often, which made the house feel a lot less lonely. Still, Emily was glad she still had an excuse to get away and be with Bear for a while, and seeing Sam most days was a huge bonus.

The man who'd been stacking boxes went out for a cigarette break, and Emily took the opportunity to have a closer look at the work he'd been doing. As she made a count of what was already there, the woman sidled over.

"You're one of the interns, huh?"

"Yes," Emily said. "I'm with NOAA."

The woman glanced furtively at the closed door.

"How are things going? Still a lot of problems?"

"Some, yes. Why?"

"I thought so." She gave Emily a pleading look. "Why doesn't anyone do something?"

"About what?"

Another quick glance at the door.

"Him. He's the one causing the problems, not us."

Emily felt as if she'd been jerked awake. Was this woman saying there really was someone behind the problems at the cannery? Someone deliberately causing snafus to happen? She glanced at the door.

"You mean the guy who just left?"

"No, the other one."

The woman's wariness was understandable, but maddening under the circumstances. If she knew who the troublemaker was, why didn't she just come out and say it?

"Who are you talking about?" she said. "Do you know his name?"

The woman nodded.

"Then tell me. Please. I promise I won't let anyone know who told me."

She heard the latch on the metal door click, and the man walked back inside. The woman shook her head and shuffled quickly back to where she'd been working. Emily could have screamed. She'd finally found someone who'd talk to her about the problems at the cannery, and she was too scared to tell her who was behind them. Over the next couple of hours, she tried repeatedly to start up their conversation again, but the woman avoided even making eye contact with her. Unless the man left again, it looked like her chance to find out more was gone.

Still, Emily thought, it was confirmation that something was going on. She'd have to talk to the others and see if they'd been approached as well.

"Okay, tell us again. What exactly did she say?"

The six of them were all together at dinner that night—the first time the interns had dined as a group since the night Emily had arrived. The day's catch limit had been met by midday, and Sam hadn't needed her to take Bear out for a walk, so Emily had been free to spend some time sharing her concerns with her coworkers. Huddled around a table in the back of the restaurant, they were discussing the conversation she'd had that morning with the woman in the freezer.

"First, she asked how things were going, were there still problems?"

"Which means she knew there'd been problems in the past," Dak said.

"Right. Then she asked why no one was doing anything about it."

"Like what?"

Everyone turned and looked at Noah. Pushed back from the table, his chair balancing on two legs, he'd been checking his fingernails in an exaggerated show of skepticism.

Emily scowled. "What do you mean, 'like what?'"

"Just what I said." He looked around. "Come on. We're interns—we're only here a couple of months. What the hell are we supposed to do about it?"

"Oh, I don't know," she said. "How about telling someone?"

"Like who?"

"Tim, of course."

"Really?" Noah sneered. "You're sure about that?"

The way he'd said it brought Emily up short.

"What do you mean?"

"I mean," he said, letting his chair fall back onto all four legs, "did it ever occur to you that Mr. Tim Garrett might just *be* the problem?"

"Oh, please. He's the one who's been getting into trouble over all this stuff. Why would he be causing it?"

"Is he, really? In trouble, I mean."

"Sure. I mean, I think so." Emily looked around. "I know he's gotten calls where he has to go running off afterward, and you guys all said there'd been problems before I got here."

Embarrassed glances darted around the table.

"We've seen him get phone calls," Dak said. "And he's always upset when he comes back."

"And I heard him tell one of the managers a couple times that there was a problem," Uki added.

"So did I." Rachel nodded. "But other than that . . ."

Emily couldn't help feeling let down. She'd been so excited by the prospect of solving a mystery at the cannery that she hadn't considered the possibility that there was no mystery there to solve. Thank goodness she'd listened to Sam or she might have done something drastic. It was looking as if this whole thing was nothing more than make-believe.

"But why would the woman in the freezer tell me there was something going on if there isn't?" she said. "I mean, okay. I guess we all might have made too much of a few phone calls and overheard conversations, but I didn't tell anyone about it but you guys. Did any of you say something?"

"Not me," Dak said.

"I didn't," Uki added as the others shook their heads.

"So, we're right back where we started," Emily said. "If there's someone trying to cause problems at the cannery—and I'm not saying there is—then the only thing we can do is keep our eyes open and hope that more evidence comes to light."

"Not me." Noah looked around at the others. "Personally, I've got better things to do."

"Me, too," said Kimberley. "I signed up to be an intern, not Sherlock Holmes."

Emily nodded toward the other three.

"What about you guys?"

"I'm fine with keeping a lookout," Uki said. "As long as it doesn't take a lot of time."

Dak and Rachel both nodded.

"Same here."

"All right. In the meantime, I'll hold off saying anything to Tim about it," Emily said. "Noah's right. If there's a chance that he's part of the problem, we don't want him to know we suspect anything."

When Emily had interviewed for the intern position, Tim Garrett had warned her that it rained a lot in Ketchikan, but she hadn't really believed it until she got there. How could she? The place got as much rain in the month of August as San Diego did in an entire year. It sounded like a lot—and it was—but from day to day it wasn't really that bad. The rain tended to be intermittent, and most days had at least some period of time when the sun was out and the people there could get outside and exercise or stretch their legs. She imagined it might not be as easy once the days got shorter, but so far, she'd actually been enjoying the change from constant heat and sunshine.

However, as she and the others stepped outside after dinner that night, the rain was coming down hard, and as luck would have it, Emily had forgotten to bring her umbrella. By the time she made it from the restaurant to the car and then into the house, she was drenched. All she wanted was a nice, hot shower.

Unfortunately, Kimberley and Rachel had made plans to go clubbing that night and begged to be allowed to use both bathrooms at once, which meant that Emily and Uki would have to wait until they were done to freshen up.

"No biggie," Uki said, before she went to her room and shut the door. "I'm not going anywhere."

Emily, who was reluctant to spoil the detente they'd been enjoying the last couple of days, agreed.

"Yeah, you guys go ahead," she told them. "I'm staying in, too."

As the other two disappeared down the hallway, she walked out to the garage, took off her wet shoes and socks, and set them on the drying rack, then stripped off her wet jacket, hung it on a hook by the door, and went back into the house to think. In spite of the others' doubts, she still believed that the woman who'd approached her in the freezer that day had honestly been trying to pass along some important information. The only question was, who was the man she'd been referring to?

Before Noah brought it up, Emily hadn't even considered

that it might be Tim. She'd seen him after one of the calls he'd gotten, and the man seemed genuinely upset. Once his name was mentioned, though, she noticed that none of the others had come to his defense. She'd always thought of herself as a pretty good judge of character, but their silence was unnerving. Could she have so badly misread the man? If nothing else, she thought, it argued against telling him about the woman's comments—at least until she had more information.

Rachel and Kimberley took off again a little after eight, saying they'd be home late and promising not to wake her when they came in. Emily nodded and waved them off. Though she appreciated the sentiment, the chances were they'd forget by the time they got back. Her only hope was that she'd be so soundly asleep by then that she'd be able to drift back off once they went to bed.

Emily walked into the bathroom and ran a hand through her hair. The rain had increased its natural wave, separating it into ringlets that hung down around her face like the strands of an old-fashioned string mop. Definitely not a good look. She was about to turn on the shower when she heard her phone ring. It was Carter—on FaceTime. Thinking of how she must look, her finger hovered over the DECLINE button.

Then Emily felt a stab of guilt. She couldn't just send the call to her voice mail; it was Carter's birthday. She'd sent him a text that morning, thinking she'd call him later, but she'd gotten so caught up in the discussion at dinner that she'd forgotten. With a sigh, Emily realized she'd have to answer. If he was calling now, it probably meant he was at the hospital and might not be free to talk later.

He doesn't need to see me like this, though.

She switched the output to AUDIO ONLY and picked up. "Hi there, birthday boy. How's it going?"

"Great," he said. "I got your text this morning. It really made my day."

Emily pulled a wry face. Carter wasn't usually so jolly when the two of them talked on the phone, and he certainly wasn't in the habit of saying things like *it really made my day*. Nevertheless, she was touched that he'd enjoyed getting her text, even if she did suspect he'd had a few celebratory drinks.

"Well, I'm glad," she said. "I've been thinking about you all day."

"I've been thinking about you, too," he said. "Uh, Em? I can't see you. Something wrong with your phone?"

"No," she said. "I switched it to audio. I just got in out of the rain and I look awful. I was going to call you as soon as I took my shower."

"Yeah, but it's been a whole week now, and I really miss seeing you. Couldn't you just turn the video back on?"

She reached up and fingered one of the dried ringlets of hair. It was like touching a curly piece of straw.

"Maybe another time. Like I said, I was about to take a shower and I'm not at my best."

"Aw, come on. I don't care about that. I'll bet you look a lot better than you think."

She smiled. Whether or not it was true, it was a sweet thing to say.

"Oh, okay," she said. "But only because it's your birthday. Don't say I didn't warn you."

As she turned on the video feed, Carter's face filled the screen.

"Hey there," he said, the edges of his grin expanding beyond the phone's limits.

Emily grinned back. His silly, too-close face confirmed her suspicion that Carter had been drinking.

"Hey yourself."

"I got you a present," he said.

"Nooo. It's *your* birthday. You're the one who's supposed to get the presents, not me."

"Well, maybe if I give you my present, you'll give me one, too."

A premonition of disaster touched Emily's neck, sending chills down her spine. She shook her head, hoping to stop him from saying anything else. Instead, he held the phone farther from his face, revealing that, far from it being a private conversation, their phone call was being witnessed by dozens of their friends and family. As the partiers waved and called to her, Emily was mortified. They were all in party attire while she stood there looking like a bedraggled street urchin. If it hadn't been Carter's birthday, she'd have hung up.

No, she told herself, *he means well. He just wanted to include me in the party. They're our friends and family members; they'll understand.*

Then Carter reached into his pocket, took out a small, velvet box, and went down on one knee. He held the open box up to the screen so that she could see the contents: an enormous emerald surrounded by ten tiny diamonds. She gasped. It was the most beautiful ring she'd ever seen.

"Do you like it?" he said.

"I love it, but Carter—"

"The emerald made me think of your eyes."

"That's so sweet."

"So will you do it, Em? Will you marry me?"

Emily looked from the ring to the expectant faces in the room. What should she say? Did she love Carter enough to marry him? Before leaving for Ketchikan, she would have said yes, but now? She didn't know. In some ways, what she felt for Sam seemed more like love than what she and Carter had, but maybe that was because it was new and hadn't been tested. Was it possible to love two men at the same time?

Seconds ticked by as she stood staring at her phone. If she didn't answer soon, the embarrassed looks would start and Carter would be humiliated. She couldn't do that to him, Emily thought. Even if she had to break the engagement later, she couldn't embarrass him in front of all those people.

"Of course," Emily said. "Of course I'll marry you, Carter."

"Thanks," he said, getting back on his feet. "I knew you would."

CHAPTER 17

Emily stared at her feet as water coursed down her back and swirled down the drain. She'd been standing in the shower so long that the water had turned cold, yet she found it impossible to get out. *I must be in shock,* she thought. It was the only excuse that made sense.

Why had she answered the phone when Carter called? She knew it was a bad time, that she was still distracted about the woman in the freezer and the other interns' reactions to what she'd said. It had been a long day, too. She'd been tired and wet, mentally and physically exhausted. Why couldn't she have just let it go to voice mail and called him back when she was ready? At least then, people might have left the party and the two of them could have talked about it without a bunch of witnesses waiting for her answer.

She slammed her hand down on the knob to stop the flow of water, her anger switching from herself to Carter.

Who proposed like that, anyway? When Emily had pictured his proposal—which she had, she admitted, several times—it had always been in some quiet, romantic spot, just the two of them making a commitment together. Instead, Carter had not only turned it into a public spectacle, but he'd made a spectacle of her, too. Darn it, she'd *told* him she needed to take a shower. Did he really have to put her on display like that? It was almost as if he'd wanted everyone to see what a sacrifice he was making, reminding everyone that she should feel grateful to be marrying so well.

I knew you would.

And she *had* felt grateful. Emily was well aware that the Trescotts were much better off than she and her mother were. In spite of all the money her father had made during his lifetime, his estate had been quite a bit smaller than her mother had expected. They'd both known he was a risk-taker in his business dealings, but neither one had suspected just how much and how often he'd gambled, nor had they realized how risky some of his investments had been. It wasn't as if they'd been left with nothing, but it did make her mother's lavish spending habits worrisome. Thank goodness Emily's own trust fund was in Uncle Danny's capable hands or she might have had nothing to pay for college, much less something to give her a good start in life.

If she and Carter did marry, of course, money would never be an issue. Surgery was a well-paid profession, and he and his sister Chelsea stood to inherit their parents' considerable fortune. There was no doubt in Emily's mind that the life he was offering her was one of ease and comfort. So why wasn't she happier?

And accepting Carter's proposal didn't just mean they'd be getting married someday, it meant she'd have to tell Sam she was engaged—now. They could still be friends, she supposed, and she'd be happy to keep watching his dog, but there'd be no more private dinners and lingering looks, much less any stolen kisses. She felt a pang, realizing how happy she'd been lately, playing with Bear on her lunch hour and taking him for walks, then talking things over with Sam when he got home. The thought that she'd have to give up all of that was distressing. She'd need time to find the best way to break it to him.

Emily had just gotten dressed and was drying her hair when the doorbell rang. She heard Uki answer it, then the murmur of voices. Probably Dak, she thought. He'd been mooning over Uki for weeks. Emily set down the dryer and shook out her hair. It wasn't perfect, but it looked a heck of a lot better than it had when she and Carter were on the phone.

There was a knock on the bathroom door.

"Somebody here to see you."

At this hour?

She opened the door a crack. "Who is it?"

"That Sam guy. Says it's important."

Emily felt a flash of annoyance. Hadn't this day been tough enough without having him come over, unannounced? When she'd finally told him about the tensions with Kimberley and Rachel, Sam had agreed not to just drop by without checking with her first. Sure, it was a moot point at the moment, but she was still dealing with the repercussions of Carter's proposal. She needed time to get her thoughts in order, to be sure that she was doing the right thing before she broke the news to him. Ready or not, however, it looked as if she was going to have to just suck it up and get out there.

Sam was slumped on the couch when she walked out, looking so troubled that Emily's first thought was that he already knew about the engagement. But how could he have found out so quickly? Had Uki overheard Carter's call and contacted him? Or—the thought horrified her—had her mother somehow gotten hold of him?

"Hey," she said. "What brings you here?"

He lifted his head, his eyes welling.

"Marilyn's in the hospital."

★ ★ ★

Neither of them said a word on the drive there. Back at the house, Sam had told her what the situation was—the increasing contractions, the blood, the panicked rush to the doctor—but once they were in the car, any thoughts they might have had about the situation remained private. Emily had volunteered to stay at Sam's and watch Bear while he returned to the hospital, but he said Kallik had asked specially for her to come along. Marilyn, he said, had been asking for her.

At the emergency room, they found out that Marilyn had not been taken to the maternity ward, and Emily started to cry. Carter had told her once that women in danger of losing their babies were sometimes kept away from the new mothers in hopes of minimizing the pain of their impending loss; the situation must be worse than she'd thought. Then Kallik came out with a cautious smile on his face, and her heart lifted. Maybe it wasn't so bad after all, she told herself. Maybe Marilyn and the baby would be all right.

The two men embraced, then Kallik gave Emily a hug.

"Thanks for coming."

"Of course," she said. "I'm flattered you'd ask."

"How is she?" Sam said.

"Better," Kallik told them. "They gave her a transfusion and the bleeding has stopped."

"Do they know what caused it?" Emily said.

"Placenta previa—we lost the last one that way. This time, though, they say it's in a different place. After they gave her a transfusion, the doctor suggested starting her on steroids in case the baby comes early. Once she's stable, they'll move her into a room so they can monitor her overnight. The doc says she should be able to go home tomorrow."

"Oh, thank goodness."

Kallik looked at Sam. "Jane can watch her once she's home,

but I'm going to have to stay here at least until tomorrow afternoon."

"Don't worry about it. I'll make some calls. We'll have you covered."

"What about Jack?"

"I'll take care of Jack. You just take care of your wife."

"Thanks, man." Kallik smiled. "You guys ready to say hi?"

Emily looked at Sam. "You go ahead."

"No, you go," he said. "I drove them here. Besides, she asked for you, remember?"

"I know she'd like to have another lady to talk to," Kallik said. "Jane couldn't make it."

"Oh. Okay."

"You have to check in at the desk first. She's in the second room on the right."

At the desk, Emily was given a visitor's badge and a gown. She put them on, grabbed some hand sanitizer, and headed down the hall. Marilyn was propped up in bed, staring at the silent television screen. Emily knocked on the partition, and she waved her over.

"Come in; have a seat."

She walked over to the bed and pulled up the visitor's chair.

"How're you feeling?"

"Eh, could be better. You?"

"The same." Emily shrugged. "At least I'm not in the hospital."

"Good point." Marilyn glanced at the needle taped to the back of her hand. "This sucks, but at least the little tyke's hanging in there this time."

Emily felt a sudden rush of emotion, tears filling her eyes.

"I'm sorry I made you walk around the totem park. You

were already having contractions. Maybe if you'd stayed off your feet—"

"Hey, hey. Stop it. That had nothing to do with this. The problem didn't even show up on the ultrasound. It happens; it's nobody's fault."

Emily nodded but couldn't stop the flow of tears. All the way to the hospital, she'd been thinking about death—not just that Marilyn or her baby might die, but that her relationship with Sam was also going to die and it would be all her fault. How was she going to live with that?

Marilyn leaned over, trying to catch her eye.

"You okay? You look like you lost your best friend."

"Yeah, I'm fine," Emily said. "Just got myself worked up, worried about you and . . . other things. Sorry."

"Anything you want to talk about?"

"No, that's okay."

"You sure?"

"Yeah." Emily laughed, embarrassed. "Here I am, blubbering away when I'm supposed to be helping you feel better."

Marilyn waved away her concern.

"Eh, that's all right. Gives me something else to think about for a while."

A nurse walked in and looked at Emily, tapping her watch.

"Looks like I'd better let you get some rest."

"Thanks for coming," Marilyn said. "Tell that man of yours I appreciate his bringing you."

"Sure thing."

Emily turned and walked away quickly before another cascade of tears started to fall.

Emily seemed unusually quiet on the way back to the house. Sam cast several sidelong glances in her direction as he drove, hoping for a chance to talk, but it was clear she wasn't in the mood. On the way to the hospital, he'd chalked it up to concern for Marilyn and the baby, but now he wasn't so sure. Whatever was bothering her, he hoped she'd tell him soon. He had something he wanted to tell her.

Even before Kallik had called him, Sam had been anxious to talk to Emily. He'd gotten a call that afternoon from a man with a tender for sale, and the ship sounded like exactly what he was looking for. They'd haggled a bit over the price and the guy said he'd think about it, but even if he didn't agree to bring it down, Sam would still be able to cover the amount. It was great news, something he was eager to share with Emily, but if the time wasn't right, he didn't want to push it. Unless and until the seller accepted his offer, he thought, the deal wasn't really done anyway. Maybe it would be better just to wait until they'd agreed on a price before he told her. Nevertheless, the closer they got to the house, the more her silence worried him. If something was wrong, why wouldn't she tell him?

"You want to stop and get a coffee or something?"

She shook her head. "Too late. It'll keep me up."

"There's always decaf."

He grinned, hoping she'd realize that there was something on his mind, but Emily just shrugged and stared out the window.

"If you want something, that's fine," she said, "but drop me off first. I really need to get home."

Her dismissive tone put an end to any hope Sam might have had for discussing the ship that night.

"Yeah, I'd probably better get home, too. I still need to find someone to take over for Kallik tomorrow."

As he pulled up in front of her house, he leaned over to give her a hug, but Emily had already thrown open the door.

"Thanks for the ride."

"No problem," Sam said as he watched her walk away. "I'll talk to you tomorrow."

CHAPTER 18

Sam would never have told Kallik, but his engineer couldn't have picked a worse day to miss work. From the second he woke up and saw the blood-red sky, Sam had known it was going to be a bad day on the water, and the news from the weather service only confirmed his fears. Back-to-back storms were coming at them from the Sea of Japan, and the Radiofax from Kodiak warned of heavy swells arriving midday and lasting at least until Friday, with the worst getting there sometime midweek. Bob Crenshaw, a retired engineer Sam knew from years past, had agreed to take Kallik's place that day, but if the storms intensified or—God forbid—Marilyn took a turn for the worse, Sam would be scrambling to find someone else to take his place. If that happened, he'd have no choice but to tell Travis and Jack, and there was no telling what they'd do.

Bob was already onboard with the rest of the crew when Sam got to the ship with coffee and donuts. While Oscar and Ben had theirs below decks, captain and engineer went into the wheelhouse to go over the map and make plans for the day ahead, including how to handle any storm-related issues. Bob might not be a young man anymore, but what he lacked in stamina and strength, he more than made up for in experience and good sense. If Sam couldn't have Kallik aboard under the current conditions, he figured Bob was the next best thing.

"I double-checked the levels and made sure the equipment is secure," the older man said. "As I expected, your engine room was in good condition."

Sam flashed him a quick grin. "Well, he learned from the best."

Back when Kallik was newly licensed, his first job had been on a factory ship working under Bob Crenshaw's careful supervision. To hear him tell it, the old man had been something of a taskmaster, but his lessons had proved invaluable. When Kallik returned to work, Sam would have to tell him that Bob Crenshaw had given his domain a thumbs-up.

"Your crew tells me you had a fouled propeller a few weeks ago. I take it everything's been cleared since then."

"It has," Sam told him. "Went down there myself to make sure."

"Don't you guys have cameras for that?"

"I've asked, but so far the owners haven't seen the need. It's fine, though. There's really no substitute for checking things up close."

Bob reached up and stroked his upper lip. Since retiring the year before, he'd grown a beard and an impressively long mustache, trimmed and well-waxed, that he twirled whenever he was thinking.

"When was the last time you'd inspected it?"

"Couple of months." Sam shrugged. "I know what you're going to say, and I agree: somebody didn't do his job properly. I've already spoken to Oscar about it, though, and I'm sure he got the message."

The older man, however, was not to be put off so easily.

"You know, in my day, something like that would have

been a firing offense. You can't have people onboard who're too lazy to do their work. It puts everyone onboard in danger."

Sam took a second before answering. Bob was a good man—one he couldn't afford to offend, under the circumstances—and he felt an obligation to give him the respect due a senior mariner, but there could be only one captain onboard the ship, and it wasn't Bob.

"I agree," he said. "But in this case, I think it was an honest mistake. He simply didn't notice the problem."

"Well, I hope you're right," Bob said. "I'm not going to put my life into the hands of someone who can't be bothered to maintain his ship. Look at what happened on the *Skippy Lou.*"

Sam gritted his teeth. The captain of the *Skippy Lou,* Ray Hollander, was exactly the sort of guy he had in mind when he'd told Emily that some captains cared more for money and speed than the lives of their crew. The fact that Bob would mention an unforeseen fouling of his tender's propeller in the same breath as the kind of sloppy maintenance that went unchecked on the *Skippy Lou* felt dangerously close to an indictment of Sam's character.

"There's no comparison between a fouled prop and what happened on the *Skippy Lou.* A man would have to be desperate to sign on with Hollander."

"You bet he would. Ray called me up right after it happened and asked if I'd come aboard. I told him I'd rather play Russian roulette. All the money in the world isn't worth risking my life on an unsafe ship."

"I agree," Sam said. "Believe me, I'd never ask you to."

Bob nodded, seemingly mollified, and took a bite out of his donut. He'd said his piece. For the time being, anyway, that seemed to have been enough.

The day, however, had not improved much after that. Whether

in anticipation of heavy weather or a chastening caused by the death on the *Skippy Lou,* Bob felt the need to recheck every system he'd already given the green light to before they left port. Once again, Sam and his crew lagged behind the rest of the tenders with the predictable result that the fish took longer to acquire and commanded lower prices when they brought them in. When Bob insisted on taking a half-hour break before setting off again, Oscar and Ben looked mutinous.

"Sorry," the engineer said as he returned. "Had a couple of calls to make. We can go now."

Their second run was quicker and the fish more plentiful. Even better, the black clouds that had been gathering on the horizon seemed to have stalled for the time being. In spite of Bob's continued grumbling, both Sam and his crew were beginning to feel as if the day's haul might actually be pretty decent. Their optimism, however, was short-lived.

As the tender pulled up to the dock, Travis and Jack were waiting for them. When Sam saw the co-owners, their arms crossed, their faces grim, it felt as if a knife had been stuck in his gut. It was rare for even one of them to show up during work hours, much less both at once. What on earth was going on?

Then he remembered that Kallik was not onboard, and the knife in his gut twisted. It was hard to believe that either of them would begrudge the man a day off with his hospitalized wife, but Jack had already been looking for an excuse to fire him. Nevertheless, Sam told himself, it wasn't anything he couldn't handle. The ship was ready for the incoming weather, and they had an experienced and licensed engineer aboard. The tender might have gotten a late start that day, but this second haul had nearly made up for the shortfall. There was nothing for either one of them to complain about.

Travis's smile was friendly enough, if a bit constrained. As the ship docked, he stepped forward.

"Could we have a word, Captain?"

Sam jumped down, and they shook hands.

"Would you mind if I get my catch sold first? Want to get the best price."

The co-owners exchanged a look.

"Sure. We can talk when you're done."

As Sam haggled over the price of fish, he wondered what had brought the tender's owners down to the dock. If it had been an emergency, he was sure they'd have said something right away, which made the fact that they were willing to wait seem even more ominous. It was as if whatever was on their minds was already as bad as it could get and waiting a bit longer to talk about it wouldn't really matter.

When he'd finally settled on a price and his crew was off-loading the fish, Sam headed back to where Travis and Jack were waiting. He was surprised to find Bob standing there, conversing with the other two. Sam frowned, thinking about the calls the engineer had made after their first run. Had Bob asked the two of them to come down to the docks? And if so, why?

This time, there were no smiles as he approached, in spite of a concerted effort on Sam's part to seem open and friendly.

"So, what brings you two down here?" he said. "Whatever it is, I hope it won't take long. I'd like to make another couple of runs before those clouds move in."

"Where's Kallik?" Jack snarled.

"At the hospital, with his wife. As you know, she's pregnant again, and there was a problem that needed medical attention. The doctors wanted to keep her overnight."

The look on the man's face made it clear that he had no interest in hearing any more details about women and their problems.

"This is the third time he's missed work."

"That's right. Three times in three seasons, counting this one."

"He's had other problems, too."

"One or two, but they were minor and easily remedied. Kallik and I discussed them, and they've been taken care of." He glanced at Travis. "I reported all of this at the time."

But Jack refused to back down.

"You *discussed* them."

"I did."

"And you thought that was enough?"

Sam stood a little straighter, emphasizing the height difference between them.

"As the captain, it's my prerogative to determine corrective action aboard my ship. Are you saying there have been other problems that I'm not aware of?"

"I don't know," Jack said. "But it sounds as if there are problems that *I* haven't been made aware of."

Sam glanced at Bob, who quickly looked away.

So, he did call them.

Travis, who until then had been reluctant to join the conversation, cleared his throat.

"Bob tells us you've allowed the ship's maintenance to slip."

"He did? Well, that's interesting. When he came aboard this morning, he told me the engine room was in good condition."

"He mentioned a fouled propeller."

"That was weeks ago," Sam said. "We snagged a net that had fallen off another ship. I went in the water personally to make sure there was no damage, but it did take quite a bit of time. You can check the log; it's all in there."

Travis turned and gave his co-owner a stern look. "I told you we should get those cameras."

Jack looked at Bob. "You're the senior mariner here. What do you think?"

The man shrugged dramatically.

"Gadgets are all well and good," he said. "But an experienced captain knows it's better to trust his own eyes. All things considered, it wasn't a bad call."

Wasn't a bad call?

Sam stared. A few hours ago, it was Bob who'd been saying the ship should have had cameras. Now, here he was arguing just the opposite. What the hell was going on?

"I'm glad Mr. Crenshaw approves of my actions," he said, trying to keep the bitterness from his voice. "The fact is, props get fouled all the time. Cameras might have reduced the amount of time we lost, but the ship and her crew were never in any danger. We took care of things—as we always do."

Travis nodded thoughtfully. "So, you're satisfied that the ship's maintenance has been completely satisfactory?"

"I am."

Sam glared at Bob, daring him to contradict a senior officer. The fact was, the man had no evidence other than Sam's word that there had been any lapse in maintenance on the tender.

"Nevertheless, it doesn't excuse Kallik's absence," Travis continued. "I told you before that if there was another problem, he'd have to go."

"But his wife—"

"Is having a hard time, I know. But this isn't the first time he's used her as an excuse."

Sam felt his lips tighten.

"An *excuse?* They've lost three babies, Trav. This could be their last shot."

Jack shook his head. "We're not a social agency."

Sam rounded on him.

"No, you're a hard-hearted SOB who's trying to make me do your dirty work. Well, I've got news for you. This isn't the *Caine* and I'm not Commander Queeg."

Travis stepped quickly between the two men, holding his hands in a placating gesture.

"I'm sorry, Sam. I know you like the guy, but we've already talked it over. Kallik needs to go."

"No," he said calmly. "I will not fire him. He's an excellent engineer, and the time he's missed has had no effect on the safety of this ship or our ability to do our jobs. There's no good reason to fire him."

"Fire him," Jack said. "That's an order."

Sam looked down, determined not to lose his temper a second time. He might be young, but he was as qualified as any other captain in port and a darned sight better than most; replacing him at this point in the season would be close to impossible. Whether they realized it or not, these guys needed him a lot more than he needed them.

"If you fire Kallik," he said, "then you'll have to fire me, too."

The co-owners looked at each other, a silent message passing between them. If they had any brains at all, Sam thought, they'd forget the whole thing and let him and his crew get back to work. The longer they made him wait, the more money they were losing. He knew it and they had to know it.

As the seconds ticked by, he felt a smile playing on his lips. He looked up and gave Bob a triumphant look. *Whatever your little game is,* he thought, *you won't beat me that easily.*

"Fine," Travis said at last. "You're both fired."

CHAPTER 19

Emily had not slept well. When she wasn't worrying about Marilyn, she was worrying about her uncle Danny, and when she wasn't worrying about either of them, she was worrying about what to tell Sam. Dealing with any one of those things would have been difficult enough, but having all three hit her at once was like being caught in an emotional tsunami. No matter how hard she tried, she couldn't stop herself from being swept along; she could only pray she'd reach safety before the waters pulled her under. By the time her alarm went off, she was exhausted.

Unfortunately, Tim Garrett had noticed that something was wrong as soon as she'd arrived at the cannery, and he was waiting for her outside of the locker room. As Emily rushed out to start work, she ran right into him.

"Sorry," she said absently. "Didn't see you."

He frowned at her puffy eyes and reddened nose.

"You okay?"

"Yeah, fine. Just didn't sleep well, that's all."

He gave her a searching look.

"Is it the girls again? I told them if they didn't cut it out—"

"No. No, everything's fine at the house, really. They got the message."

Emily kept her eyes on the ground as they spoke. She made it a point never to discuss personal problems at work, and Noah's comment the night before was making her especially wary of confiding in Tim. If he was really the source of the problems at the cannery, then he wasn't to be trusted. Nevertheless, when she finally looked up, the expression on Tim's face sent a stab of guilt through her heart. He seemed genuinely concerned, and she had no one else she could talk to. It would be such a relief, Emily thought, to tell someone what was going on, even if there was nothing he could do. She felt her lips start to tremble and put a hand over her mouth.

"Emily, what is it? What's wrong?"

"M-my friend is in the hospital and my uncle is h-having surgery this m-m-morning and I—"

Emily felt her face flush as tears began coursing down her cheeks. She felt embarrassed and stupid for being so weak, and yet it felt so good to finally uncork at least some of the feelings she'd been bottling up that she simply couldn't stop herself. Even if Tim had been causing problems, she was too desperate to care.

He hesitated, gingerly setting a hand on her shoulder.

"I'm so sorry. That must be awful."

She nodded, afraid that if she tried to say anything more she'd howl like some strange, demented creature.

"Come on," he said. "Have a seat in my office. When you've calmed down a bit, I'll give you a ride home."

Emily shook her head. She didn't want him to think she was too emotionally fragile to work hard.

"I'm okay, really. I j-just need a minute."

Tim shook his head. "It's not a problem, really. I'll just tell the others you weren't feeling well."

"No," she said angrily. "I'm not sick, I'm just . . . sad."

Again, she broke down in sobs, her body heaving with every breath.

"Of course you are."

He sighed and looked around.

"Tell you what. If you don't want to go home right now, that's fine. We're having class time this afternoon, though, and it's all going to be stuff you've had before. Why don't you go to my office and take a few minutes to pull yourself together, then go out on the floor until lunch break? After that, you can either walk home or I'll take you."

"I don't know," she said. "Maybe."

"Come on," Tim said, smiling. "The others already know you're ahead of them on classwork. They'll be glad you're not there to wreck the curve—for once."

Emily forced a smile even as the tears continued to flow.

"That sounds good," she said. "Thanks."

The house was quiet when Emily got home. She unlocked the front door, then turned and waved to Tim before stepping inside. She'd be heading over to Sam's in a little while to check on Bear, but first she needed a few minutes to think. While she was out on the floor that morning, she'd heard one of the workers repeat a phrase her father used to tell her whenever she'd get discouraged—a bit of nonsense from Yogi Berra that had never failed to lighten her mood. Hearing it again, especially under the circumstances, had given her an eerie feeling. It was almost as if her dad were trying to tell her something.

It ain't over till it's over.

Hearing those words, Emily had suddenly realized that none of the things she'd been worried about was over yet. Marilyn and her baby were still alive, and so was Uncle Danny. And though she and Carter might be engaged, they were still a long way from being married. Until the day she said *I do,* Emily had every right to change her mind.

It wasn't over till it was over.

Seen in the light of that phrase, the world no longer seemed so bleak. She wasn't the girl who'd hidden in the shadows while a policeman delivered the news that would send her life spinning out of control. Things in the past could not be changed, but the future wasn't written yet. Emily was a grown woman now, with power over her life and its direction, if only she'd accept it. No matter what happened from here on out, she told herself, she would not give in to despair. Marilyn was right: there was no sense suffering twice over the same misfortune.

Once she recognized the options still open to her, Emily had decided to talk to Sam. Not about her engagement— since, for the moment, at least, she considered it on hold—but about the two of them. When she'd searched her own feelings, she realized just how fond she was of Sam and how much he meant to her. The way he listened patiently to her without trying to steer the conversation around to himself; the way she could share her problems with him knowing he wouldn't simply jump in and try to solve them for her; the way he treated her as if what she thought and felt was every bit as important as his thoughts and feelings—all of that, and more, had won a place for Sam in her heart. The only question was: did she occupy a similar place in his? Until Emily knew the answer to that question, she wouldn't know what to do about Carter.

Emily took a quick shower and put on a fresh change of clothes. Even if she'd become accustomed to the smell of the cannery, she knew her hair and clothing still reeked of fish guts and blood. If she was going to talk to Sam about what was on her mind, she needed to maintain her sense of strength and purpose—something she knew would be hard if her clothes stank. When she was ready to go, she put on her rain slicker and grabbed the bag from the pet store that she'd hidden in the closet. Then she locked up the house and headed out to visit Bear.

The big dog was watching out the window when Emily arrived, a halo of fog framing his anxious face. When he saw her, Bear gave a series of sharp barks that, to her ears at least, sounded like a rebuke. She was late, he was telling her. He'd been worried.

"I know, I know," Emily said as she opened the door. "I'm sorry, Bear. You're right. I should have gotten here sooner."

All was forgiven, though, as she'd known it would be, and Bear's leaps of joy and sloppy kisses were offered up like champagne on New Year's Eve. Emily lifted the bag in her hand and gave it a shake.

"I brought you a present, too. Want to see?"

Emily opened the bag, but before she could retrieve its contents, Bear thrust his entire head inside. Emily had to struggle to wrest it away.

"Hold on there, buddy. Give me a second."

She put her hand into the bag and took out a brush and comb, holding them out for his inspection.

"What do you think?" she said. "Ready to get gorgeous?"

One of the few advantages of being shunned by her roommates had been the amount of alone time it afforded her, and Emily had been determined not to waste it. Since she would be in charge of Bear at least part of every day, she'd decided to learn as much about the Newfoundland breed as possible, and to call it an education was an understatement.

The dogs' enormous size, sweet disposition, and love of children were not surprising, but their reputation for rescuing people from the water was a revelation. Stories about tens and even hundreds of people being pulled from shipwrecks by Newfoundland dogs—even those with no training in water retrieval—were fairly common. She could see why Sam had wanted to have his dog along at work; he and his crew had actually been safer with Bear onboard.

Among the dogs' many wonderful traits, however, was a potential problem that Emily thought she might be able to help with. Newfies, as they were affectionately called, had thick double coats that insulated their bodies and kept them warm in the harsh winter months. When the weather was warm, though—as it was then—that same double coat quickly became a burden, threatening them with heat-related complications. With summer already underway, Emily figured that Bear might just appreciate having both the weight and the heat of his thick, insulating coat thinned out a little. As the dog sniffed his new grooming implements warily, she grinned.

"Just think of this as a spa day."

It took a while to convince Bear that the brush and comb were not, in fact, toys for him to play with, but after a brief game of keep-away and a tug-of-war that left some impressive tooth marks in the brush's handle, Bear decided that being groomed while taking a nap was a perfectly acceptable way to spend the afternoon. When Emily had finished brushing out the fur on his left side, he'd rolled onto his right without even seeming to wake. As the pile of discarded fur grew, Bear's coat became darker and glossier. Emily smiled. She hoped Sam would be pleased.

Sam.

A smile played on her lips as she contemplated what a future with him might be like. Emily already knew what her future held if she married Carter, because it wouldn't be all that different from the way their parents had lived: a beautiful home near the beach, nice cars, dinners out, a maid and possibly a cook, plus a nanny once their children were born. Whether she worked or not would be up to her, of course, but Carter's work commitments would determine how much she did outside the home and when. Because he was a doctor, their friends would be other doctors, with whom they'd attend medical society functions, charity balls, and cocktail parties with drug company reps. All things considered, it wouldn't be a bad life, Emily thought, but was it what she wanted?

On the other hand, life with Sam would be less secure, at least as far as money went. His house was good-sized, but it was older, and even with extensive remodeling it would never be the sort of palatial house the Trescotts owned. But the place was homey, and Emily liked the fact that all of the rooms were functional, too, none of them set aside merely to make an impression. She could still remember the shock she'd felt when Carter told her that the couches in their main living room had never been sat upon, nor were they intended to be. Instead, he told her, they were there merely "to show others," whoever they were. She'd never have told him, but the lavishly appointed space had struck Emily as almost criminally wasteful.

None of that, of course, was an indictment of Carter himself nor of the values he held. People didn't go into medicine because it was an easy way to make money, after all, and he'd proved his concern for other people many times over the years. But she also knew that he took for granted the advantages he'd been given in a way that Emily never had. She and her mother might be better off than most people, but their finances were much more precarious than either their neighborhood or her mother's spending habits might suggest. Emily's father had been a good provider, but since his death, the family's day-to-day circumstances had been uncertain.

She heard a car drive up and the sound of the garage door

opening—Sam was home early! Bear reared up and started for the kitchen, a patch of discarded fur waving from his tail like a flag. Emily's heart raced as she gathered up the excess fur and stuffed it into the pet store bag. This was her chance, she thought. She knew now which future her heart had decided on. She could only hope that Sam wanted it, too.

CHAPTER 20

Emily knew something was wrong the second Sam walked through the door. His face was drawn, his eyes downcast, his normally pink-cheeked complexion was wan and sallow. When he saw her, he shook his head and looked away. She felt a stab of fear. Had something happened to Marilyn, or was this about the two of them?

"Are you okay?" she said.

He shrugged, absently stroking Bear's head as he stared out the window.

"Not really."

Emily took a cautious step closer.

"What happened?" she said. "Is it Marilyn?"

Sam shook his head and took a deep, shuddering breath.

"I lost my job."

"You lost your—" She frowned. "You mean they *fired* you?"

He leaned against the counter and hung his head. It looked as if he was literally falling into despair. Emily felt like weeping. She wished there was something she could do to help.

"But why? I don't under—"

"They wanted me to fire Kallik," he said. "He's had some

issues in the past—nothing big, but I think Jack had it in for him. When Kallik didn't show up today—"

"But that was because of Marilyn. Didn't you tell him that?"

Sam nodded. "It didn't matter. He was waiting for an opportunity, and he took it."

Emily clenched her fists. The whole situation just made her blood boil. A man takes a day off to care for his pregnant wife while she's in the hospital and he loses his job? *He ought to sue those guys.*

"So, what happened? You didn't fire him, did you?"

"Of course not. I told them they'd have to fire both of us if they wanted him gone. They said that was fine and they let me go."

"Oh, Sam. I'm so sorry."

He turned and looked at her.

"Doesn't matter. I was sick of those guys."

"They'll change their minds," she said. "I mean, they don't even know how to run the ship, right? Isn't that what you said?"

"They don't need to," he told her. "They found another captain."

Sam leaned his back against the cabinets and ran his hands through his hair, laughing ruefully.

"I hired Bob Crenshaw to take Kallik's place today. I'd heard he was having a hard time since he retired and thought I'd do the guy a favor. Instead, he tells my bosses I've been letting things slide and then gives them the name of a buddy of his who can take my place. Bingo. Kallik and I are out and Bob and his buddy are in."

The unfairness of the whole situation hit Emily like a weight. Sam had been trying to do a good turn and been stabbed in the back. She felt like punching that other guy.

"What are you going to do?"

"I wasn't worried about myself. I could miss the entire season if I had to," he said. "But Kallik was in a panic when I told him. Without a job, he can't pay for his medical insurance."

"And with the baby on the way, he can't afford to lose that." Emily nodded. "So, what's he going to do?"

Sam looked at her.

"He got another job."

"Already? That's great!" She hesitated. "Isn't it?"

He looked away.

"It's on Ray Hollander's ship."

Emily frowned. "Wait a minute. Isn't that the one that just lost a crewman?"

"One and the same."

"But that was just an accident. I mean, accidents happen, right? That's what you said."

Sam took a deep breath.

"On most ships, yes. On the *Skippy Lou,* I'm not so sure."

Emily put a hand over her mouth. No wonder Sam was so stricken. Not only had Kallik been fired without good cause, but in his eagerness to find employment, he'd signed on to a ship with a dangerous captain. Her mind immediately flew to Marilyn. In her condition, how would she take the news?

"Wasn't there any way you could talk him out of it?"

"Nope. The guy needs the money—I knew that—so, I did what I had to do." He looked at her. "I hope you understand."

He'd given Kallik the money. Sam knew his friend was hurting, and he'd parted with some of what he needed to buy his own ship. Emily smiled and nodded. Of course she understood. It was a kind and generous thing to do.

"I'm sure he appreciated it. Who knows? You might even find a ship that's a little less expensive."

Sam frowned. "What?"

"That's what you did, isn't it? Lent him the money so he wouldn't have to take the job?"

"No. I knew Kallik wouldn't take it—he's too proud—but the man's forty-two, Em. Working as a crew member on a seiner is hard work. I couldn't let him go alone."

"Wait a minute. You're not—" She shook her head. "You're not going *with* him, are you?"

"It's only for ten days," he said. "After that—"

"No! You can't."

"Em, I have to. If I go, I can keep an eye on the guy and—"

"And what? Get *yourself* killed?"

"C'mon, Em. Don't exaggerate."

Sam reached for her, and she pulled away.

"You promised. You told me you'd never go to sea on a dangerous ship—*ever!*"

Tears sprang to her eyes. How could he have broken his promise to her? Sam knew how scared she was for him, knew that she'd lost her own father in an accident. How could he even think of taking a risk like that, knowing that if anything happened it would destroy her?

She thought of all the reasons why she'd wanted to put her engagement on hold—Sam's kindness and honesty, his willingness to listen, the other traits that would make him a good father someday—and pushed them away. She would not live out her mother's nightmare, ending up a young widow because of her husband's recklessness. Carter might be a bit pedantic, he might not give her chills when their eyes met, he might even be finicky about keeping his hands clean, but he had a nice, safe job. He wasn't going to throw his life away needlessly. Better, she thought, to have a finicky, dull husband than a dead one.

Sam ran a hand down Bear's back and smiled.

"You've been grooming him. Thank you."

Emily's body felt stiff and awkward. Sam's betrayal, coming

on the heels of the last twenty-four hours' trauma, had left her numb. Opening her mouth to speak felt like a monumental effort.

"I took the afternoon off."

As he looked up, his brow wrinkled.

"Are you okay?"

"I'm fine," she said. "I just . . . have to go."

She walked to the door and put on her jacket.

"Wait," he said. "I'll give you a ride."

"No, thanks. I'd rather walk."

Bear whimpered, nuzzling her hand, and Emily almost lost it. She stroked the velvety fur of his ear.

I think I'll miss you most of all.

"I'm going home," she said. "My uncle had surgery today, and I want to be with him."

Tim would understand, she thought, and if he didn't, her mother was right: with Carter for a husband, she wouldn't really need a job.

"Oh, Em," Sam said. "I'm so sorry. Why didn't you tell me?"

He stepped toward her, and she stepped away. She would not allow him to comfort her. If she did, Emily thought, she might lose her nerve.

"You'll have to find someone else to watch Bear," she said, her throat tight.

Sam's face buckled.

"Yeah, sure," he said. "I'll call Tiff, see if she can take him."

Emily hesitated, wondering if her departure would drive Sam back into his ex-girlfriend's arms, then shook her head.

It wasn't her problem, she told herself. Better to just get this over with.

"I don't think I'll be coming back," she said, forcing a smile she didn't feel. "You see, I'm getting married."

CHAPTER 21

Tiffany's new place was at the end of a gravel road on the farthest edge of town. As Sam drove toward his ex-girlfriend's house, his tires seemed to find every pothole, jouncing the SUV and setting off explosions of muddy water while Bear clung like a limpet to the back seat. If he'd had any choice at all, Sam would never have asked his ex-girlfriend to watch his dog, but Bear couldn't go ten days without someone to take care of him, and the *Skippy Lou* sailed in the morning. With Emily leaving, there was no time to find anyone else.

She's getting married. I'm never going to see her again.

Sam gripped the wheel harder and pushed the thought away.

The shabby little house at the end of the road was a depressing sight. Years of deferred maintenance had left the roofline sagging, the paint shattered and peeling. A stack of moss-covered bricks—the sad remnant of a long-abandoned project—lay forgotten in the front yard, and a lopsided gate on the side fence swung idly from a single hinge. For a moment, Sam considered turning around and forgetting the whole thing, but the thought of leaving Kallik to his fate strengthened his resolve. Tiffany might have her issues, but being cruel to animals wasn't one of them. Besides, Sam told himself, it was only ten days. With luck, he'd have his own ship by the time they got back, and Bear could be with him every day. Until then, he just had to believe that the dog would be fine.

Tiffany was waiting for them when they drove up. Leaning against the front door frame and smoking a cigarette, her slim build made gaunt by drug use, Tiffany didn't look like she'd once been a beauty. As Bear ran to greet her, she squatted down and held out a bony hand for him to sniff, then gave his neck a hug.

"Hey there, big boy. You gonna keep me company while Daddy's at work?"

"Sorry to do this to you at the last minute," Sam said. "If I hadn't been stuck—"

"No problemo," she said, steadying herself on the dog's back as she stood. "Me and Bear always had a good time together, didn't we, boy?"

Sam and Bear exchanged a worried glance.

"And you're sure that, um . . ."

"Seth." She nodded. "Yeah, he's cool with it. Don't worry. We'll be fine."

He grabbed his wallet and took out five twenties and a ten.

"This is all I've got on me."

"You don't have to pay me."

"Just take it. We were out of kibble; you'll need to buy him some food. If he damages anything, let me know and I'll pay for it when I get back."

"Yeah, sure," she said, stuffing the bills into the waistband of her shorts. "We'll be here whenever."

Tiffany took Bear's collar and turned him toward the open door.

"Come on, Bubba. Judge Judy's on."

Sam had just gotten back into his Jeep when he heard an

engine roar and saw a black Toyota Land Cruiser charging up the road, catching air and sending mud and gravel flying. For a few agonizing seconds, he was sure the guy was going to plow right into him. Then the driver slammed on his brakes and skidded to a halt, stopping within inches of Sam's back fender.

If the thought of imminent disaster had ever crossed the other man's mind, however, he didn't show it. He leaped out of the front seat and strode over to the Jeep, a fiercely confident smile on his face.

"D'I scare ya?" He laughed.

"A little. You must be Seth."

Sam stepped out and offered his hand.

"Well, if I must be, then I guess I am."

The handshake Seth gave him was painful—aggression disguised as civility. Sam had seen guys like him before. Not so old or so far gone that the drugs had destroyed them physically, they saw every human interaction as a chance to show how powerful and in control they still were, all the while knowing that time was running out. Addicts before the fall, he called them—hale, hearty, and unpredictable. For a fleeting moment, he considered going back inside and snatching Bear away. Instead, he got back into the Jeep and started it up.

It'll be okay, he told himself. *Tiff won't let anything happen to him.*

He slammed his door and started back down the road. The *Skippy Lou* wouldn't be leaving until the next morning, but Sam wanted to stop by the ship and take a look around. The Coast Guard conducted an investigation of every fatality at sea, and he was curious to see what, if anything, they'd pinpointed as the cause of this latest misfortune. Official results could take months, but that didn't mean there weren't early indications, and he knew a couple of the investigators. He hoped he might be able to wangle some information out of one or both of them.

Tiffany was already back on the couch when she heard Seth drive up. Bear had his head in her lap and she was petting him absently, enjoying the warmth that radiated off his large body. It was good to have the big black dog to cuddle with again, she thought. Tiffany hadn't been warm a single day since moving out of Sam's place.

She heard Seth's too-loud voice outside and frowned. Why did he have to yell all the time? Tiffany grabbed the remote and turned up the volume, smiling as the woman on the television drowned him out. If she turned it up loud enough, it was almost as if he weren't there.

The door flew open and Seth strode into the room. Bear startled, but Tiffany patted his back to reassure him.

"It's okay," she whispered

"Turn that thing down!"

Tiffany reached for the remote, but Seth beat her to it. Judge Judy disappeared.

"Hey," she said. "We were watching that."

He pointed the remote at Bear.

"What's that thing doing here?"

"This is Bear," she said brightly. "Bear, say hello to—"

"I don't care what its name is. What's it doing here?"

"I'm watching him for Sam," she said. "Remember?"

"Remember what? You didn't tell me you were watching a dog."

Tiffany hesitated. She knew she'd thought about telling him, but when she tried to remember actually doing it, things got sort of fuzzy.

"Well, he's here now," she said. "So it doesn't matter."

"Fine, but it can't stay inside. I don't want its hair all over my furniture."

Seth threw the remote in her lap and stalked into the kitchen. "What's for dinner?"

"I thought we'd have pizza. I've got a coupon for God-father's." She turned the TV back on. "And we need to get dog food."

"You mean we gotta feed that thing, too?"

Seth walked back into the room and stopped between the couch and the television. Doing it on purpose so she couldn't see the screen. Tiffany pursed her lips. Just because she didn't have a job at the moment, that didn't mean he could be a jerk about everything.

"Don't worry about it," she said. "I've got money."

She pulled the bills from her waistband and fanned them in the air.

"Where'd you get that?" He snatched them out of her hand.

"Sam gave them to me."

As he counted the bills, Seth's face hardened.

"How long was he here?"

Tiffany shrugged.

"A few minutes. Why?"

"This is more than a hundred bucks. Dog food don't cost that much. What'd you do for this, huh?"

She felt a flash of anger.

"Nothing. Sam gave me that for watching his dog."

He grabbed a handful of her hair and pulled. "You sure?"

Bear lifted his head and growled. Seth let go.

"It's okay, boy," she said.

Tiffany held out her hand.

"Give it back. The money. It's mine."

Seth took out his wallet and slipped the bills inside.

"Dog's in my house. That makes it my money."

She sagged, rubbing her head as the anger drained away. Why bother arguing with him? Seth always won.

He went back into the kitchen to get the number for Godfather's Pizza.

"What kind you want?" he said, taking out his phone.

"Don't care," she said, staring at the screen. "Whatever."

While Seth made the call, Tiffany sighed and patted her lap. Bear put his head back down.

"They said fifteen minutes," he said as he put the phone away. "I'll stop and get more beer on the way."

She nodded. "Don't forget the dog food."

He walked back into the living room.

"When I get back, I want that thing"—pointing at Bear—"out in the garage."

Seth grabbed his keys and headed for the door.

"Hey," she said. "Don't you want the coupon?"

"Nah." He grinned, patting his pocket. "Don't need it now."

CHAPTER 22

Fishing marinas are squalid, grubby places against which the crisp blue shirt and navy slacks of a summer-weight Coast Guard uniform stand out like a beacon. Warren Taylor, officer in charge of marine inspection, was standing on the dock, making notes on his clipboard while Ray Hollander ranted incoherently. Whatever the inspection of the *Skippy Lou* had uncovered, Sam thought, it must not have been good.

Maybe he'll pull its license, he thought hopefully. Even a week's suspension might give Sam enough time to close the deal on the tender. With a sure thing to offer his engineer, he could put Kallik on his payroll, find a crew, and still have enough of the season left to make them all some money. It'd be tight, but it beat the hell out of sailing with Ray Hollander.

He saw Taylor look up and say a few words to Hollander, who turned on his heel and stalked off to the harbormaster's office. Curious, Sam stepped onto the dock and gave the inspector a friendly nod.

"You out here on official business?"

Taylor gave him a cool look.

"You know I am," he said. "What do you want?"

"Just thought I'd see how the inspection's going. Find any-thing interesting?"

"Plenty—as always. Nothing serious enough to keep the *Skippy Lou* in port, though."

Sam glanced over at the harbormaster's office, trying to hide his disappointment. So, he thought, they'd be sailing after all.

Taylor clicked his pen and stuck it back in his breast pocket.

"I heard you signed on with this guy. You want to tell me what in the hell you were thinking?"

"Easy for you to say; you've still got a job."

"And I happen to know you don't need one."

Sam stuck his hands in his pockets and shrugged. He hated being put on the spot, especially like this.

"My engineer's got a baby on the way. Without his pay, he can't afford medical insurance and he's too stiff-necked to let me cover it."

"Okay, that explains *his* bad decision. What about yours?"

Sam ducked his head, glancing up and down the dock to make sure no one was listening.

"The guy's getting old. Ten days crewing on a seiner would kill him without someone there to pick up the slack."

"So, you're going along as backup?" Taylor blew a soft whistle and shook his head. "Well, it's your funeral."

"Come on, it can't be that bad."

Taylor looked at his clipboard again and made a face. It seemed that he was struggling to find an answer to some un-spoken question. After a few more seconds of indecision, the man nodded.

"You know the stuff in here is confidential."

"Of course."

"There'll be an official report in a couple of weeks, but until then I'm not allowed to talk about my findings."

"Sure. I get that."

Taylor shot his own quick glance up and down the dock.

"If I were you, I'd keep an eye on the position of the winch, especially during the third and final pulls. Power blocks are expensive and that one's had some issues. If someone's trying to save themselves the expense of a new one by playing with the weight of the seine, the men on deck might be paying the price."

Sam was shocked. Purse seining became more dangerous as the net was drawn up and the fish were brought onboard. Even as the number of the fish it held decreased, the net grew heavier, its waterlogged corks combining with the lead weights at the bottom to put extraordinary pressure on the winch and power block. To keep the men on deck safe, tension on the net had to be kept steady and strong. Even a slight decrease could catch a man in the net, leaving him vulnerable to being crushed, swept over the side, or dumped into the hold under tons of thrashing fish.

He nodded grimly.

"Thanks for letting me know. I'll keep my eyes open."

"You do that," Taylor said. "And if you see anything else I should know about, radio me at once. I'll get our ship out there, pronto."

"I will. Thanks."

As Taylor walked off, Sam went aboard the *Skippy Lou*. It looked as if winches and power blocks weren't the seiner's only problems. The deck was littered with equipment: a poorly stacked net, its corks lying helter-skelter, and a tangle of lines that looked like an obstacle course. He stepped through to the bridge and found the engineer sitting glassy-eyed in the galley, nursing a cup of coffee. Sam introduced himself and threw a thumb in the direction of the harbormaster's.

"I saw the captain outside. What's got his knickers in a twist?"

The man frowned briefly, as if trying to translate Sam's words into some other language.

"Crewman broke his leg on the way in. Can't sail until we find another hand."

Sam nodded. No wonder Hollander was ranting. Taylor must have threatened to keep the *Skippy Lou* in port until she had a full crew count. Once again, he thought, Ray Hollander was staying in business by the skin of his teeth.

"Mind if I take a look around?"

"Suit yourself."

Sam went down to the crew quarters—a dank hovel with a ceiling so low he couldn't stand upright. Forming an L along two sides were four plywood bunks, each with a single foam rubber pad, a threadbare blanket, and about eighteen inches of headroom. The rest of the space held an assortment of instruments and equipment for which there'd apparently been no room elsewhere onboard: a fire extinguisher, spare hoses, a twelve-volt bilge pump, grinder blades, and power tools. A chunk of loose insulation hung from the far corner. It was bad, but not surprising; Hollander had a reputation as a cheap SOB.

It was only ten days, Sam told himself as he turned around. He could put up with anything for that long.

He heard a familiar voice hailing the ship and hurried back topside. Kallik was on deck, duffel bag in hand, staring at the tangle of lines that coiled around his ankles like vipers.

"This is the sorriest, most lubberly looking place I have ever seen."

Kallik had spent ten years in the navy before returning to

Ketchikan. The habits of neatness and order were deeply ingrained.

"Where's the rest of the crew?" he asked.

"Engineer's in the galley, Hollander's out looking for another hand to replace a guy who broke his leg on the return trip."

"That must have been where he was going when I got here. He came out of the harbormaster's hut looking like a wet cat."

Sam grabbed a line and started separating it from the rest of the tangle on deck.

"Go stow your gear and give me a hand with this, will you?"

While Kallik headed down to the crew's quarters, Sam did a quick inspection of the winch, looking for any obvious signs of weakness in the power block. Whatever Warren Taylor had noted in his report, it wasn't anything that a casual observer could see. Maybe it wasn't as bad as he thought.

Kallik emerged from the wheelhouse and looked around. "Where'd you stow your gear?"

"At home," Sam said. "I just came by to check things out, see what time we're taking off in the morning."

The two of them set to work, separating the lines and coiling them in neat stacks.

"Heard any more about that tender?"

Sam shrugged, not wanting to jinx the deal before the details were finalized.

"The paperwork's with the broker. I should hear back from the seller before we ship out."

"I hope it comes through. I wouldn't mind making this cruise a one-off."

"That makes two of us."

They worked another half hour in silence. As the sun started its slow passage across the horizon, Sam kept a wary eye on Kallik. He hadn't complained, but the man was sweating a lot and Sam could tell he was pushing himself pretty hard. When the lines had all been coiled on deck and the corks stacked neatly on the net, Sam suggested they take a break.

"I'm starved. Let's go get some grub."

The sky was darkening as they walked into the fish and chips shop around the corner. As he reached for the door, Sam felt the first drops of rain hit his face. They placed their order and took a seat at one of the tables.

"Is Emily watching Bear while you're out?"

Sam felt a twist in his gut. He'd been trying so hard to put their breakup out of his mind that he'd forgotten to tell anyone else about it. He glanced at his watch: seven forty. It had been three hours since Emily had told him she was leaving Ketchikan to get married. Three hours that felt like a lifetime. He shook his head.

"We broke up," he said. "Turns out she's got someone waiting for her back home."

"Oh, man. That sucks."

"It's fine. I knew it was only temporary."

Kallik nodded.

"Yeah, sure. Summer lovers, right?"

Bile rose up, burning Sam's throat. Was that all it had meant to her, just a last fling before settling down with Mr. Right? He swallowed hard.

"Tiff's watching Bear till we get back."

"What about that dude she lives with? He okay with it?"

"She said he was cool." Sam paused. "Why?"

"No reason, just—" He shook his head. "Marilyn saw her a couple of weeks ago. Looked like she'd been knocked around some. Tiff told her it was an accident, she'd walked into a door or something, but you know."

Sam shook his head in disgust. He wasn't surprised; Seth looked like he had a hair trigger. Maybe that was why Tiffany had been so eager to watch his dog. She knew how protective Bear was. Perhaps she thought that having the big guy there would give her a way to keep her boyfriend in line. He just wasn't sure if that was a good thing or not.

Kallik shifted in his seat, wincing as he rubbed his back, and Sam felt a prick of anxiety. If the guy was hurting already, what would happen once they were pulling fish? He wished he'd been able to talk the guy out of signing up with Hollander. Failing that, though, he was glad he'd be going along. He'd never have forgiven himself if something happened.

Their number was called and the two men attacked their food with single-minded purpose. By the time they were finished, they could hear the rain coming down hard outside.

"You think Hollander's found another hand by now?"

Sam wiped his mouth and dropped the paper napkin in his bag.

"Most likely. You can always find someone on the docks if your standards are low enough. Chances are, he grabbed the first guy who'd work for peanuts and frog-marched him back to the ship before he changed his mind."

They finished their beer and got up from the table. The rain had intensified—the heavy drops looked like bullets shooting down from the sky. As Sam put his hand on the door, he felt a brief premonition of disaster. Like all mariners, he could be deeply superstitious.

"Something wrong?" Kallik said.

He shook his head.

"No. Nothing. Just need to get my hood up," he said.

Only ten days.

Sam pulled up his hood, and the two men ran back to the dock.

Ray Hollander was on the deck of the *Skippy Lou,* oblivious of the rain, talking to a man in a gray slicker and baggy pants. When Sam saw their new crew member, his step faltered. The feeling of impending doom had returned with a vengeance.

"Looks like you called it," Kallik said. "Guy looks like a bum."

Hollander motioned for the two of them to join him on deck.

"Come say hello to your new mate."

As they approached the ship, the man turned and peered at Sam through a curtain of rain, his sneer creasing the distinctive birthmark on his cheek.

Sam nodded. "Hello, Logan."

Hollander glanced from one man to the other and smiled.

"You two know each other, huh?"

"Oh-ho, yes." Logan Marsh chuckled. "Captain Reed and I are old friends."

CHAPTER 23

Tim Garrett took Emily to the airport on Friday morning. As the two of them rode the ferry to Gravina Island, she resisted the urge to look back at the lush green hills and towering white mountains of Revillagigedo. Emily had promised herself she'd go hiking in the interior before she left, and it was just one more disappointment she couldn't face. Maybe she and Carter would come up there on vacation someday, she told herself. Perhaps, with time and distance, the memory of all that had happened in Ketchikan would have faded.

At least her early departure wouldn't count against her with the internship program. When she told Tim about the call she'd gotten from her mother, he told her not to worry, that judging from the work she'd done already he would be happy to write her a letter of recommendation. He'd lost a brother to cancer the year before, he told her, and knew how devastating it was when all hope was gone.

Emily clenched her teeth, trying not to cry as she pictured her uncle lying in his hospital bed while the surgeon told him that the cancer they'd hoped was confined to the lung had in-stead spread throughout his body. There'd been no need to excise any tissue, the doctor said. The important thing now was for him to get his affairs in order and prepare for the end.

Heavy chop buffeted the ferry as they reached the halfway point, and a few stray drops of rain spattered the windshield—harbingers of the storm that would arrive in a few hours. With luck, Emily would be in Seattle by then, waiting for her connection to San Diego. She was grateful that her mother had found a nonstop from Sea-Tac to Lindbergh Field—even more so because it would be in first class. Sitting cheek by jowl in an airplane full of happy summer travelers was more than she could bear. At least staring out her window in the first row would give her a chance to be left alone.

"Well, here we are again," Tim said as he started the Jeep's engine. "Seems like only yesterday I was picking you up."

Emily nodded. "I know, and I'm really sorry."

"Don't be. At a time like this, you need to be with your family. Who knows? Maybe you'll come back and visit us one day."

"Maybe so," she said. "I'd like that."

The ramp was lowered and secured, and the cars began to inch forward. As Emily glanced across the tarmac at the plane that would soon be spiriting her away, she suddenly felt an overwhelming desire to know the answer to the mystery that she and the other interns had been speculating about for weeks. Was someone making problems for Tim at the cannery? And if so, why? He might laugh and tell her it was nothing, he might even think it was rude of her to pry, but somehow, Emily couldn't leave without knowing.

"Can I ask you something?"

He glanced at her and smiled.

"Sure. What is it?"

"It seems like there have been a lot of . . . issues at the cannery."

Tim wrinkled his brow. "What do you mean by 'issues?'"

She swallowed. Was he going to stonewall? If Tim was the cause of the problems, he'd certainly have reason to.

"Some of us have noticed that you were called away a lot, and it seemed as if you were pretty upset afterward. We wondered . . . I mean, is that normal?"

Tim gripped the wheel in silence as the Jeep shimmied off the ramp and started toward the parking lot. He pulled into a space by the terminal and shut off the engine. Then he turned and looked at her.

"No," he said. "It's not normal. It's been going on for over a year now, and I have no idea who's behind it."

"What is?" Emily said. "I mean, if you don't mind my asking."

"Drugs are being smuggled through the cannery. They come in from offshore and get into our plant and somehow make it through the process without being detected."

He held up a hand.

"I take that back. We *have* detected some of it, but we know there's more that's getting through, and we have no idea who's doing it or how. Just last week, a package of look-alike pain pills found its way into one of our shipments and broke open before it reached its destination. A dozen people ended up in the hospital with Fentanyl overdoses."

Emily's heart was beating wildly. They'd all been thinking this had to do with the interns. It never occurred to anyone that drugs might be involved.

"But surely, no one blames you."

"Not yet, but I wouldn't be surprised if they did. I'm supposed to be the government's eyes and ears inside the cannery, and so far I haven't got a clue how it's happening."

She shook her head.

"I'm sorry. I hope you catch whoever's doing it."

"Well, thanks," he said. "Let's hope we do before anyone else gets hurt."

He put his hand on the door.

"Come on," he said. "Let's get you inside before it starts to rain."

Emily had brought a book along, hoping to discourage conversation while she waited for her plane to board, but no matter how hard she tried, she couldn't concentrate enough to read. Tim's revelation about drugs being smuggled through the cannery had put the problems there in a completely different light. She kept going over her conversation with the woman in the freezer, how she'd told Emily that "he" was the source of the problem, and wishing she'd been able to get a name or even just a description of the man. Was it the guy who'd been working in there with them, or maybe someone else nearby? Whoever it was, she thought, if drugs were involved, the woman might well have been too fearful to say anything more.

Unless, she thought, the woman herself was in on it. In which case, her "information" might just have been an attempt to throw Emily off the scent.

She felt her phone buzz and found a text from her mother: Uncle Danny was sitting up and looking forward to her visit. If her plane got in on time, it said, the two of them would go and see him that evening. If not, they'd have to wait until visiting hours started the next day.

There was a text from Sam, too, wishing her good luck and a safe flight. As she deleted it, Emily grudgingly admitted that he'd been pretty decent about the whole thing. When the shock of learning she was engaged had passed, he told her he'd always suspected there was someone waiting for her back home, as she was "too amazing" to be unattached. The compliment, nice as it was, had left her curiously unaffected. From the second he'd told her he was sailing on the *Skippy Lou,* nothing Sam could say or do made any difference to the way she felt. As far as she was concerned, things between the two of them were over.

She was disappointed that there was nothing from Carter—not that she'd been expecting anything. In the weeks since she'd been away, he'd only called her once, and that was the night he'd asked her to marry him. After she heard about Uncle Danny's prognosis, she'd tried calling him a couple of times but hadn't left a message, knowing how upset he'd be if he heard her crying on the phone. Once she got home, there'd be plenty of time for the two of them to touch base.

The terminal was busy that day with people in vacation mode: expectant faces in the departure areas and happy, sunburned grins on the arriving flights. Emily wondered if she'd ever be that excited to be traveling again. When a blind man with his guide dog walked up and sat down across from her, tears sprang to her eyes. The Labrador retriever looked small compared to Bear, but its protective stance and tender patience were a mirror of the Newfoundland she'd come to know and love. Even if Sam had betrayed her, his dog never had, and the thought that she'd never see him again made her heartsore. The thing she regretted most about leaving so suddenly was having to tell Sam she could no longer watch Bear for him. Emily hoped Tiffany would be good to him while Sam was on the *Skippy Lou.*

The desk attendant announced her flight, and Emily got in line to board. As she handed the gate agent her ticket, she felt drained, so physically and emotionally battered she thought she might never recover. All she wanted to do was go home.

★   ★   ★

"Over here, darling!"

Emily's eyes filled with tears as she rushed into her mother's arms. The two of them embraced, crying as the river of arriving passengers parted and flowed on around them.

"How was the flight?"

"Fine," she said, wiping her eyes. "Thanks for the tickets."

"It's no problem." Her mother took her arm and looped her own through it. "Nothing but the best for my little girl."

They grabbed her bags at the carousel and walked out to the taxi stand. As the two of them slid into the back seat, the driver put Emily's things in the trunk.

"We're going home," her mother said, giving the cabbie the address.

As the taxi pulled out into traffic, Emily stared out the window. The city, she thought, had changed since she left; the hills were browner than she remembered, and the sky didn't seem so blue. And where had all the traffic come from? Even on the surface streets, drivers zipped by them at breakneck speed, weaving through the lanes like fugitives on the lam. The place felt hostile and unwelcoming.

"You haven't had dinner yet, have you?"

She shook her head.

"Good. Maria's making your favorite tamales. Once we've eaten, we can head over to see Uncle Danny."

"How's he feeling?"

Her mother shrugged.

"Who knows? The man always acts as if everything's fine. For now, at least, he says he's comfortable."

Emily sighed. It was hard not to feel sorry for Uncle Danny. When her father was alive, Danny was the kid brother, a nice guy whose star was never quite as bright as his adored older sibling. Nevertheless, when her father died, everyone assumed that his friendly, outgoing brother would take over the helm of the company they'd started together. Instead, Uncle Danny withdrew, selling his interest in the company rather than assuming the CEO's position. There'd been times when she wondered if, had her mother not accused him of causing his brother's death, her uncle might have stepped into his brother's shoes and made them his own, but now, of course, that speculation was moot. Her uncle's time had run out. Whatever he might have been, he would never be more than he was right then. She just wished her mother would be more sympathetic.

"Did you tell Carter I was coming home?"

"No, dear. I thought I'd let you do that."

"I tried calling him last night, but he didn't answer."

"I'm not surprised. Sheila says he practically lives at the hospital these days. Still," she said, patting Emily's leg. "I know he'll be thrilled to see you just as soon as he can find the time."

The taxi pulled into their driveway and the two of them got out. Ever mindful of her mother's bad back, Emily lugged the bags inside and took them up to the guest room. The aroma of Maria's homemade tamales perfumed the air, making her mouth water. As she headed into the kitchen, she realized she'd eaten nothing since the night before.

Her mother was sitting at the table, a G&T in one hand and a single tamale on her plate.

"There you are. I turned around and you'd disappeared."

Emily smiled at Maria and took her seat.

"Those look wonderful, thank you," she said as the older woman placed two plump tamales on her plate.

Maria always said that a full stomach made life's burdens easier to bear.

"Sorry," Emily said as she shook out her napkin. "I was putting my luggage in the guest room."

"You should have left it in the foyer. Maria would have taken it up for you."

Emily took a bite of tamale and almost purred in contentment. She'd promised herself she would not argue with her mother when she got home. Therefore, she would not point out that not only was she less than half Maria's age, she was also fully capable of taking her own things upstairs.

"I see you've started redecorating my room already."

"Do you like it? It's still in the early stages, of course, but Ava has a truly artistic eye. I've been thinking we should hire her to help with the decorations at your wedding."

Emily swallowed. The subject of her marriage was still a sore point. Given the choice, she'd have preferred not to discuss it at all, but it seemed her mother would not be put off.

"That's fine," she said. "But I'm not interested in anything that's too over-the-top."

"Who's talking about over-the-top? All Sheila and I want is for you kids to have something nice. There will be a lot of important people coming to see you and Carter on your special day. You don't want to disappoint them."

"Mom, please don't go crazy with this, okay? Just the thought of a big society wedding makes me cringe. All that fuss—and the money! I'd rather elope."

Her mother's lips thinned.

"Prentices do not *elope,* dear. What would people think?"

"Um, that you didn't want to spend a fortune just so they could eat hors d'oeuvres and watch some guy slip a ring on my finger?"

Her mother gave a pained sigh.

"First of all, money is not a problem, so don't worry about the cost. Second, your father was a very important man in this town. If you don't have the sort of wedding that other people in our social circle are giving their daughters, they'll think he didn't care enough to provide for us. Is that what you want, to make your father look feckless and uncaring?"

Emily stabbed at her tamale.

"No, of course not. It's just that I'm not sure that's the kind of ceremony I want. And frankly, when the time comes, I think Carter should be consulted, too."

"Oh, please," her mother laughed. "Everyone knows that weddings are for brides. Believe me, when the time comes, Carter will do what his mother wants."

Of course he will, Emily thought sourly. Wasn't that what Carter always did?

CHAPTER 24

Tiffany lay in bed, waiting for Seth to fall asleep. The digital clock on his side of the bed cast a greenish light on his face, making him look like some kind of alien, but at least she could see him clearly. As his breathing deepened, she saw beads of sweat break out on his upper lip. It wouldn't be long now. Once Seth dropped off, it took a lot to wake him up. When she was sure he wouldn't hear her, she'd sneak out and check on Bear.

She hated keeping Sam's dog cooped up in the garage. It was only made for one car, and with all the stuff Seth and his brother stored inside, they couldn't even get that in there. Tiffany had dragged out an old bedspread for Bear to sleep on, and whenever they were alone, she let him in the house, but no matter how many times she reminded Seth, he couldn't seem to remember to get dog food at the store.

Bear had been okay the first couple of days. He would eat pretty much anything, and there'd been plenty of leftovers in the fridge, but those were all gone now, and Seth still wouldn't go to the store. Tiffany wished they had a car she could drive. Even with her license suspended, it would be worth taking a chance to get something for Bear to eat. He'd whimpered so much while they were eating dinner that night that Seth had gone out and yelled at him, telling him to shut up or he'd be sorry. Tiffany tried to tell Seth that the dog was just lonely and hungry, but he said she'd be sorry, too, if she didn't stop nagging him.

That's when she decided to wait until Seth was asleep to give Bear some food and water. She'd given him one of her big mixing bowls full of water the first night, but the last time she'd checked, it was empty. They'd had pizza again that night, and she'd made sure to ask Seth to get a large so there'd be plenty left over. He'd probably be mad when he saw that the rest was gone, but she'd just tell him it fell on the floor. Even Seth wouldn't want it after that.

Seth's breathing was slow and even, and every few times he inhaled, he'd snore a little, too. Tiffany slowly pulled back the covers and sat up, resting her bare feet on the floor while she waited to see if he'd wake. If he did, she'd just tell him she had to pee and try again later, but he never did. She stood quietly and tiptoed out of the room.

The light in the refrigerator was so bright it hurt her eyes. Tiffany grabbed the pizza box and set it on the counter, waiting for her eyes to adjust. She wasn't used to being in such a dark house this time of year. Even at midnight, it wasn't pitch black outside, but Seth had insisted they buy blackout curtains for every window in the house, and he checked them every night before going to bed. She took out the three leftover slices of pepperoni and tore them into pieces, using the faint glow of the microwave to see what she was doing, then set them on a paper plate and took them out to Bear.

He was lying on the bedspread in the far corner but got up when he saw it was her. For a big dog, Bear could be pretty shy, and his feelings must have been hurt when Seth yelled at him. When she set the food down, he hurried over.

Tiffany wrinkled her nose.

"*Pee-yew,*" she whispered. "What's that smell?"

Then she remembered: Bear hadn't been outside since he'd gotten there. She felt a pang of guilt, realizing the dog had had nowhere to do his business but in the garage.

"I'm sorry, boy," she whispered. "I guess I forgot. Maybe I can get Seth to buy a paper for you to go on in here."

She'd take him outside in the morning, she told herself. Give him a chance to stretch his legs, too. Sam hadn't left the dog's leash, but Seth must have some rope around there somewhere that she could use.

Bear finished the pizza and started licking the paper plate. Then he held it down with his paw, tore a piece off, and started eating it. Tiffany snatched the rest away.

"No, no," she said. "Paper's not good for you. Seth'll get your dog food soon, don't worry."

She glanced at the empty bowl on the floor.

"Hold on. I'll get you some water."

Tiffany took the bowl and stepped back inside, flinching as the water hissed out of the tap. She turned it off, listening for Seth, but heard nothing. She stared at the bowl. It was only half full, but she didn't want to risk turning the tap on again.

Oh, well. Half full is better than nothing.

Tiffany opened the garage door and took the bowl back out to Bear.

"You be quiet now, okay? I'll see you in the morning."

She tiptoed down the hallway and back into the bedroom. As she sat on the bed, though, the mattress squeaked. Tiffany's heart was in her throat.

Seth snuffled, half-awake.

"Somethin' wrong?"

"Just had to pee," she said, sliding in beside him. "Go back to sleep."

CHAPTER 25

The next morning after breakfast, Emily went into her unfinished bedroom closet and took out her *gi* and *hakama*. It had been almost two months since she'd practiced her aikido forms—she felt rusty and out of shape—and she was hoping to have a word with Sensei Doug. After the visit with her uncle Danny the night before, she craved both the physical exertion and the mindfulness that a session at the dojo required.

Things at the hospital had started out well enough, and Uncle Danny seemed to be in good spirits. Even in the short time she'd been away, though, Emily could see that he'd lost weight, and she wondered if it signaled something more than just an aversion to hospital fare. Since learning that his condition was grave, Emily had been thinking of all the things she wanted to tell him before the end, but once they arrived, she'd hardly been able to say a word. Instead, her mother had hovered nearby, interrupting their conversation and making critical comments about her brother-in-law's historically poor health habits. Whether or not her intention had been to blame him for his own ill fortune, the result was predictable. He grew quieter and slowly withdrew from the conversation, leaving whatever the two of them might have said to each other unexpressed.

Which was why she'd decided to return to the hospital that day and see him on her own. Without her mother's interference, Emily hoped the two of them could finally have the heart-to-heart that was long overdue. With so little time left, she was determined to say her piece.

She put on the *gi*'s white pants and jacket, then tied the black *obi* around her waist and slipped into her *zori* sandals, saving the black *hakama* for the dojo. The loose, pleated pants were fine in the context of her martial arts practice but tended to draw unwelcome attention out in the real world. She set them carefully in her gym bag and headed downstairs.

Veronica Prentice was in the foyer, resplendent in one of her "going to the club" outfits: tailored linen capris, a flowery silk blouse, Chanel espadrilles, and a summer-weight cardigan in case the air con had been turned up too high. As her daughter descended the staircase, she gaped.

"What on earth are you doing in that?"

"Going to the dojo, of course." Emily opened the credenza and took out the keys to her car. "Then I thought I'd head over to see how Uncle Danny's doing."

"No, don't do that," her mother said. "I have a meeting with the gala volunteers at ten and lunch at the club afterward."

"You don't have to come with me. I'm a big girl, remember?"

"Tell you what," her mother said, checking her watch. "We'll go tonight."

"I have plans tonight," Emily lied.

"What plans? You didn't tell me anything about plans."

"Just plans, okay?"

Emily smiled sweetly. She didn't need to have her schedule micromanaged.

"Fine. But don't tire him out."

Her mother opened her purse and took out her car keys.

"By the way, I've taken your phone."

"What?"

"Don't argue; you said yourself the battery's worn-out. I'm going to stop on the way home and trade it in on a new one."

Emily rolled her eyes, but did not object.

"Oh, and don't forget your birthday dinner," her mother added. "We've got reservations at the Marine Room at seven."

The front door opened and Maria came in with that day's mail.

"Ooh, anything for me?" Emily said.

Her mother snatched the entire lot out of the house-keeper's hand and stuffed it into her purse.

"It's probably nothing but bills," she said, snapping her handbag shut. "Now, listen: I really have to go. I'll see you for dinner."

As she swept out the front door, Emily and Maria stood by in helpless bewilderment.

"Well," Emily said. "I hope she's right. I'd hate to think there's an overdue notice in there for me."

Maria nodded, then slipped a hand into the pocket of her apron and drew out another piece of mail.

"Oops," she said, giving Emily a sly smile. "I must have missed one."

As she handed it over, Emily saw that the envelope was addressed to her.

"Why, Maria, you naughty girl. Thank you."

As the housekeeper walked back to the kitchen, Emily tore the envelope open. It was a letter from the family's lawyer asking her to make an appointment at her earliest convenience to discuss the conveyance of her trust fund, something that was scheduled to take place on Tuesday, her twenty-fourth birthday. As she read the letter, Emily's hands shook. She'd heard various estimates of the amount her father had left her in trust. Depending upon the performance of the market and the investments therein, she guessed it must be close to a million dollars.

It seemed impossible that a person her age could suddenly be in charge of such a large amount, and it made the loss of her uncle that much more painful, knowing she wouldn't have his wise counsel to guide her investment decisions. Nevertheless, she knew he'd arrange for someone to take over for him; she'd be in good hands. She called the lawyer's office and arranged to meet him at his office on Monday, then grabbed her gym bag and headed out the door.

Sensei Doug was instructing a class when Emily walked into the dojo. She turned toward the far end of the room where a portrait of aikido's founder, Morihei Ueshiba, hung, and bowed respectfully before making her way quietly to the warm-up area. Careful preparation of the body was an important part of the discipline involved in any martial art, and Emily quickly found herself immersed in the gentle, rhythmic motions. Head and neck, then shoulders, trunk, and last, the legs were stretched, releasing any tightness in her body before she stepped into her *hakama* and joined the others at the mats.

This morning's class consisted mostly of middle-aged women, most of whom were probably new to aikido, and there were none who wore the flowing black *hakama* over their *gis*. Emily kept her attention on their instructor, but it was impossible not to notice the looks of anticipation on the others' faces. Perhaps they wondered why a black belt had chosen to join them that day.

Her sensei, too, must have noticed Emily's arrival, but

nothing in his speech or mannerisms gave away any awareness on his part that his audience had increased by one. It wasn't until the session was almost over that he turned toward her and nodded.

"I see we've been joined by one of my former students," he said softly. "Perhaps she'd like to join me in a demonstration of some of aikido's more advanced techniques."

Emily nodded her acknowledgement, then stood and performed the ritual bows—first to Sensei Ueshiba's portrait, then to Sensei Doug, and finally to her fellow students—before stepping onto the mats. As she approached her teacher, Emily's heart was racing. Other than her brief encounter with Bear, it had been months since she'd practiced any advanced throws. She hoped the master would go easy on her.

He did not.

Ten minutes later, Emily had been thrown dozens of times and was sweating profusely. Her shoulders and back were smarting from contact with the mat, and her wrists and elbows ached from being held to the point of discomfort. The object of aikido might not be to injure one's opponent, but that didn't mean it didn't hurt. When it was over, Emily and Sensei Doug bowed to each other, and she resumed her place on the edge of the mat until the class was dismissed.

"I was surprised to see you walk in today," he said as the last student filed out. "I hadn't expected you to be back from Alaska so soon."

"Neither did I," Emily said. "But some things came up and I had to leave."

His look was searching.

"You seem troubled."

"My uncle's in the hospital with stage four lung cancer. He hasn't got much longer."

"I'm sorry to hear that. Of course you'd want to be with him."

"Also . . . Carter asked me to marry him, so I guess I'm engaged now."

He frowned slightly. "You guess."

"Yeah."

"Most people are happy to be engaged. You don't look happy."

She sighed. "I know."

The truth was, she wasn't happy about the engagement. The way Carter had asked her over the phone while their friends and family listened in was disappointing, and taking it for granted that she'd accept his proposal felt like a slight. Plus, the way he always deferred to his mother's wishes instead of asking Emily what she wanted worried her.

Her sensei folded his arms and gave her a stern look.

"If you're not happy with your engagement, then you need to decide: either fight for what you want or end it."

He was right, she thought. If she and Carter were going to be a team in their married life, there was no time like the present to get started. Maybe after she went to see Uncle Danny, she'd give him a call.

Emily bowed, acknowledging his wise words.

"Thank you," she said. "I will."

"And there's one more thing," he said. "I noticed that your movements were a bit stiff today. You haven't been practicing your forms."

She gave him a sheepish smile.

"I haven't had much of a chance," she said. "The only opponent I've sparred with lately was a dog."

His eyes widened.

"You were attacked by a *dog?*"

Emily laughed. "No, not really attacked. It was running toward me out of control. I remembered our rolling escapes and moved toward him to execute the roll."

"Very good."

"If I hadn't lost my balance and ended up on my face, it would have been picture perfect."

"Considering who your opponent was, perhaps you can be forgiven." The sensei smiled. "I would love for you to stay and tell my students that story. The little ones, especially, would enjoy it."

"No, I really have to go," she said. "Besides, I'm not good at speaking in front of groups."

"Now you're selling yourself short. You're a natural teacher, Emily."

"Ha! More like a perpetual student."

He shook a finger at her.

"It has always bothered me the way you put yourself down," he said. "You're one of the best students I've ever had, and the reason for that is because you were always helping others. Teaching helps you internalize what you know."

She blushed. Sensei Doug didn't hand out compliments lightly.

"You've always been tough in here." He indicated the dojo. "Now, you must learn to be tough in the rest of the world."

"I'll try," she said.

"Do that." He smiled. "It was good to see you again. I enjoyed our demonstration."

Uncle Danny was dozing when Emily returned to the hospital. She stood in the open doorway of his room watching the slow rise and fall of his chest, feeling her own chest constrict. He'd always been there for her. Even when her father was alive, her uncle had been the one she counted on, the one she told her secrets to, who knew the names of all her favorite Kpop singers, the one with whom she celebrated childhood's fleeting victories and mourned its crushing defeats. Emily's father was like a god—all-powerful and remote—but Uncle Danny was her friend.

And now she was losing him.

She rapped on the wall with a knuckle, and he opened his eyes.

"Hey, punkin'," he said hoarsely.

Emily stepped over and gave him a kiss.

He glanced at the door. "Where's your shadow today?"

"I ditched her. She had a meeting at the club." Emily rolled her eyes. "She's running the gala again this year."

"Oh, well. Can't miss those meetings at the club," he said solemnly. "Lots of important decisions to make."

"I know," she said. "Let's see, should we have red streamers this year or crimson? Is platinum in now, or should we go with the traditional gold?" Emily laughed. "Remember the year they used Greenery instead of Arcadia? My God, I'm surprised they weren't arrested by the Pantone police."

He put his hand on hers and did a perfect imitation of her mother.

"This is not funny, dear. These are matters of life and death."

It was done in good humor and Emily appreciated his attempt to join in, but try as she might, she couldn't laugh once the word *death* was out in the open. As tears filled her eyes, Emily placed her free hand on his.

"I don't want you to die," she whispered.

"I know. I know."

He lay back against the pillows and sighed, his energy spent. Slowly withdrawing her hand, Emily pulled the visitor's chair closer and sat down. There was a steady rattling in her uncle's chest that she hadn't heard the day before. How, she wondered, could he be failing so fast?

"I wanted to tell you," she said. "How much I love you."

Uncle Danny smiled. "I know that."

"I'm glad. But I still needed to say it, okay?"

He nodded weakly and closed his eyes. It was like watching an hourglass as its last sands ran out.

"I got a letter today, from Frank Alfano. I'm going to meet with him Monday morning to talk about the trust."

Emily stared at her hands, feeling her lips tremble.

"Thank you for taking care of it all these years. It means a lot that you were always keeping an eye out for me."

She looked up and saw a tear run down his nose.

"Also," Emily said, "I want you to know that the things Mom said, you know, after Dad died—"

"I'm sorry."

"Don't be," she told him. "I never believed any of it."

He took a shuddering breath.

"Forgive me. Please."

"There's nothing to forgive."

Emily waited, but he didn't respond, and after a few seconds she realized he was asleep. She'd said what she came there to say; it was time to go. She stood up and kissed him on the forehead.

"Goodbye, Uncle Danny. I love you."

Emily went back to her car and sobbed, both in sadness and relief. Thank God she hadn't let her mother talk her out of coming when she did. As fast as her uncle was fading, he might not even be alive by that evening. It had been hard seeing him like that, but it felt good to be able to tell him what was on her mind. If she never saw him again, she thought, at least there was nothing between them left unsaid.

She only hoped she'd have as much luck talking to Carter.

CHAPTER 26

Emily drove out to University Hospital and left her car with the valet. She'd been hoping to call ahead and let Carter know she was coming but remembered as she was leaving Uncle Danny's room that her mother had her phone. For a moment, she'd almost changed her mind—failing to warn him seemed like a violation of some fundamental rule of conduct—but decided it was better just to take her chances. Talking with Sensei Doug had made her see how passive she'd been about their engagement, and seeing her uncle had reminded Emily how important it was not to pass up life's opportunities. There were things she needed to get off her chest, and if she didn't do it now, she might never have the guts to do it at all.

At least she knew Carter would be at work that day. On the way to the hospital the night before, her mother had filled her in on the impossible hours he was keeping and made a point of mentioning that he was doing a rotation in orthopedics. As Emily headed into the eleven-story hospital tower and stepped into the elevator, her heart was racing.

She wondered what Carter would do when he saw her; after all, they were engaged now. She wished that he'd abandon his natural reticence for once and sweep her into his arms, but a smile and a chaste kiss would do, too, as long as it was sincere. Her attraction to Sam and the fondness she still felt for him had undermined her faith in the decision to marry Carter; she hoped that seeing him again would dispel any lingering doubts. It wasn't some wild, romantic gesture she was seeking, just confirmation that she'd made the right choice.

Emily headed for the nurse's station and checked in, explaining who she was and asking if Dr. Trescott was available. After a brief consultation with the other people on duty, the woman confirmed that he was not currently with a patient.

"He's probably in the doctors' lounge," she said. "Do you want me to page him?"

"Would you mind if I just head down there? I know the way."

"Fine with me. Just make sure you don't wake anybody up. It was a long night."

"Thanks," Emily said, donning her ID badge. "I'll bring this back when I leave."

She pushed through the double doors and walked down the hall, trying not to glance into the patients' rooms as she passed. Having just been at her uncle's bedside trying to avoid the stares of curious strangers, she had no wish to intrude on anyone else's privacy.

At the end of the hall, she turned left and stopped at the door marked PERSONNEL ONLY.

Here goes nothing.

There were two doctors inside—one sitting at a table playing solitaire, the other stretched out on a couch. On the left was a sleeping area, its privacy curtain drawn. Emily closed the door carefully and approached the man on the couch, an intern she recognized as a friend of Carter's. It took her a second to remember his name.

"Hi . . . Tran," she said quietly. "Is Carter around?"

He and the other doctor exchanged glances.

"What are you doing here? I thought you were in Alaska."

"I was," she said. "But I got back yesterday. My uncle's in the hospital—stage four lung cancer."

"Oh, man. That's awful. I'm sorry."

"Thank you." Emily glanced at the privacy curtain. "Is he taking a nap?"

Tran laughed uneasily. "Nah. Nobody's in there."

As if on cue, the sound of laughter came tumbling out from behind the curtain. High and sweet, it was definitely female. Emily frowned.

"If nobody's in there, who's laughing?"

The doctor at the table flipped over another card. "Maybe you should check."

Emily pursed her lips. "Maybe I will."

As she walked over and reached for the curtain, though, a combination of uncertainty and fear stayed her hand. She could walk away, Emily told herself, turn around, go home, and forget she'd ever come. If she didn't go in there, she thought, she'd never know for certain who was inside. Then she heard another voice, this one deeper, seductive.

Carter?

Emily yanked the curtain aside.

"Hey! What the hell? I told you guys—"

"I'm not one of the *guys,*" she said. "I'm your fiancée."

In the dim light, all she could see was the outline of a pair of bunk beds on either side of the room. As she searched the wall for a light switch, she heard urgent whispered voices.

"Emily?"

"Who else?" she said, switching on the lights.

Carter was standing next to the right-hand bunk in his socks and boxer shorts. Sitting in the bed behind him was a young blond woman, sheets clutched against her bare chest. Emily had been expecting embarrassment and remorse. Instead, he went on the offensive.

"What are you doing here?"

"I came back to see my dying uncle," she said. "What are *you* doing?"

"You can't just barge in here," he snapped. "This is the doctors' lounge. Why didn't you tell me you were coming?"

In the face of her fiancé's outrage, Emily hesitated. For a moment, she even felt as if she were the one at fault. Then something caught her eye: a flash of green coming from the bed. As she narrowed her eyes, the girl slid her hand under the sheets, but it was too late. Emily glared at Carter.

"You gave her my *ring?*"

"I didn't *give* it to her. It's still yours."

The blonde in the bed nodded.

"It's so beautiful, I just had to try it on," she chirped. "I didn't think you'd mind."

In the face of such bizarre logic, Emily could only laugh. She felt giddy and reckless.

"Of course I don't mind," she said. "Keep it, it's yours."

The girl's eyes widened. "Really?"

Carter scowled. "Shut up. She doesn't mean it."

"Sure I do," Emily said.

He took a step toward her and held out his hand.

"Come on, Em, don't be silly. Why don't you go home and I'll call you later? We'll get this all straightened out."

Emily looked at her fiancé, standing there in his sad little socks and matching boxer shorts, and felt a weight she didn't know she'd been carrying lift from her shoulders. She glanced over at the girl in bed and her smile broadened.

"Come to think of it," she said, pointing at Carter. "Why don't you keep him, too?"

* ★ ★

Her mother was in the living room when Emily got home. Sitting stiffly in a wingback chair, her ashen face a stark contrast to the bright coral chinoiserie fabric, she'd obviously been waiting for her daughter to arrive.

"We need to talk."

Emily gave a quick glance upstairs; she'd been hoping to have a few minutes to compose herself before giving her mother the bad news, but judging from the look on her face, she'd already heard. Emily took a deep breath and walked into the room, putting on a brave smile as she took a seat on the couch. She was sorry the grapevine had broken the news before she had and hoped it hadn't been too public or too humiliating.

"So," she said. "I guess you heard."

Her mother nodded. "He called Sheila at the club. When I found out, I rushed right home."

"What did she say?"

"Well, she's very disappointed, obviously. Carter acted like a cad; there's no excuse for what he did."

Emily felt tears sting her eyes. At least her mother understood—and it couldn't be easy for her, either. The perfect wedding she'd envisioned had been ruined, snatched away by the feckless bridegroom in a way both noteworthy and frustratingly banal. The two of them might have disagreed about the size and expense of the ceremony, but Emily had genuinely been looking forward to their planning the day together.

Nevertheless, she thought, a wedding was not a marriage, and even before Carter's betrayal, she'd had real doubts about marrying him. His attitude toward her had always seemed magnanimous rather than affectionate, as if Emily were some sort of charity case; at times, even his family had acted as if she were there on sufferance. No wonder he'd treated her so shabbily, she thought. As far as Carter was concerned, Emily was lucky to have him. It made his betrayal the one silver lining in this whole sorry episode: no one could blame her for breaking off the engagement.

"Thank you for understanding."

"Of course I understand," her mother said. "Believe me, I made it very clear that we expect an apology the minute he gets here on Tuesday."

Emily blinked. "What?"

"Your birthday dinner, remember?"

"Wait a minute. You don't expect me to still have dinner with him, do you?"

"Not now, of course not. On Tuesday. *After* he apologizes."

"I don't care if he apologizes. Mother, I just caught him in bed with another woman."

Her mother's lips thinned.

"Well, now you're just being vindictive."

"I am *not* being vindictive. I'm being realistic. If he'd cheat on me now, he'll cheat on me later."

"Not necessarily."

"Maybe not, but that's the way I feel, and I'm not going to change my mind."

Emily winced. Remembering the scene in the doctors' lounge brought on a wave of pain and humiliation. In spite of her bravado, she really had cared for Carter. Why couldn't her mother understand how hard this was for her?

"Oh, my poor baby." Emily's mother held out her arms. "Come here."

As Emily felt her mother's arms enfold her, the tears she'd been holding back came flooding out. It seemed as if she was losing everything she cared for: Carter, Uncle Danny, Sam, even Bear. She hoped that Sensei Doug was right and that she was stronger than she knew, because at the moment it felt as if she'd been broken into a million pieces.

Her mother patted her back.

"I know it's hard," she said. "What happened to you was terrible, but in fairness, I don't think it was entirely Carter's fault."

Emily pulled back and stared at her mother. She felt breathless, as if someone had punched her in the stomach.

"Are you saying this is *my* fault?"

"In a way, yes. It was you who left him, after all, remember?"

"I didn't leave him. I had a temporary job, which I took, by the way, hoping it would help me get a job in San Diego so that Carter wouldn't have to relocate."

"Yes, but you were gone. Don't you see?"

"No. No, I don't see, Mom. What's your point? That my being gone gave him license to screw someone else?"

Her mother frowned. "Don't be vulgar, dear."

"Oh, *I'm* vulgar? What about Carter? Don't you think sleeping with a student nurse is a bit *outré?*"

"All I'm saying is, don't make up your mind too quickly. Once Carter gets a chance to explain himself and you get the apology you deserve, I'm sure the two of you will be able to straighten everything out."

Emily was aghast. She knew the Trescotts were old friends, knew that her mother genuinely liked Carter, too, but how could she side with them at a time like this?

"Where's your purse?"

Her mother pulled back, flustered by the sudden change of subject.

"In the hall closet, why?"

"I need my phone."

Emily yanked open the closet door and grabbed her mother's purse; her phone was still inside. She checked the remaining battery life—twenty percent—and huffed in frustration. Where had she left the charger? Then she remembered she could charge it wirelessly in her mother's car. She dug out the keys to the Lexus and dropped the purse on the floor.

"I'm going for a drive."

Emily sat on the cliffs overlooking La Jolla Cove, watching the waves tumble in and crash against the rocks below. She'd been sitting there a long time, so long that she saw lights coming on in the houses along the shore and smelled dinners being prepared, so long that people walking by had stopped giving her anxious looks, satisfied at last that she wasn't going to jump. As the sun approached the horizon, she'd watched the sky turn from pale blue to pink and coral. Now, there was only a lilac glow to mark the spot where it had disappeared.

In Ketchikan, it would still be full daylight.

With the sun gone, the temperature plummeted and Emily began to shiver. She looked back along the trail and wondered what to do. She couldn't stay where she was, but she couldn't bear to go back to the house—not while her mother expected her to put a smile on her face and act as if nothing had happened. Maybe some women could do that, Emily thought, but not her.

She swallowed, feeling her lips tremble. Had her mother been one of those women, accepting her husband's infidelity as the price to be paid for a life of comfort and ease? Parents' private lives were a mystery to their children, and rightly so; compared to a child's idealized version, even a good marriage might seem hopelessly flawed. No, Emily thought, whatever accommodation her mother might have made was no business of hers, but neither was it her mother's place to expect the same from her. If things had been different, maybe Emily could have forgiven Carter for what he'd done, but the truth was, she simply didn't love him enough.

At least Sam had been honest with her, she thought, even if he'd told her what she didn't want to hear.

Emily took out her phone and dialed his number. She had no idea where Sam was or even whether she could reach him. All she knew was that she wanted to hear his voice more than anything else in the world. She'd done what Sensei Doug had advised: ended the engagement she hadn't been willing to fight for. Now, she thought, it was time to go after what she did want.

"Hi, you've reached Sam's phone. I'm not here, but if you leave a message I'll call you back when I can."

As Emily opened her mouth, emotion overwhelmed her. It took her a second to get the words out.

"Hey, Sam, it's Emily. Call me when you get a chance, okay? I miss you."

CHAPTER 27

Emily took out her navy blue suit and brushed the dust off its shoulders. The last time she'd worn it was the day she'd graduated from college, and she hoped it still fit. She shuffled through her blouses and took out the cream silk with the shawl collar. As impossible as it seemed, she'd be a wealthy woman soon. She figured she might as well look the part.

Her mother was at the funeral home, making arrangements for Uncle Danny's cremation. Emily hadn't come home until after midnight on Saturday, and she had only a vague recollection of her mother waking her up Sunday morning to tell her he'd passed. She'd accepted the news with a calm that would have surprised her a week ago, but which felt right given their last visit. She felt at peace with his departure, just as she finally felt at peace with the rest of her life.

Marilyn had called after breakfast to tell her that Sam was at sea, but that she was monitoring his voice mail and had heard Emily's message. She was in contact with the *Skippy Lou* via VHF radio, she said, and wanted to know what was going on. Knowing how protective Marilyn was of "Sandy Sam," Emily told her everything that had happened since she'd gotten home, including the scene in the doctors' lounge and the cancellation of her engagement.

"Do you think he'll want me back?" she asked.

Marilyn hadn't hesitated.

"Yeah, I think he will."

"Then can you give him another message for me?" Emily said. "If he hasn't bought that tender yet, tell him not to worry about the money, just buy the ship he wants."

"Why? What's going on?"

"Just tell him," Emily said. "I'll explain when I get back."

She slipped on her stockings and buttoned the blouse, grinning. Emily had come up with her plan the night before. Thinking about the money in her trust fund had put her in a serious frame of mind. It wasn't just a windfall, it was the only material thing she had left of her father: his love and support in the form of cold, hard cash. She'd heard of other people—rock stars, athletes, lottery winners—who'd come into large sums of money and blown it all in a shockingly brief period of time, and Emily had no intention of doing the same. After thinking about it, she'd decided to take some of her inheritance and invest it in a business venture—Sam's, if he'd let her. He had experience and connections in Ketchikan, and she knew what a hard worker he was; as long as he didn't mind having her as a partner, she thought it could work out well for both of them.

The suit still fit. Emily brushed off a few stray hairs and slipped her feet into a pair of shoes, then finished the outfit with the string of Mikimoto pearls her mother had given her for her eighteenth birthday. As she glanced at herself in the mirror, she felt terribly grown up.

The front door slammed as Emily was coming down the stairs. She heard her mother yelling at Maria for some unspecified shortcoming—a tirade that ceased abruptly when Emily came into view.

"Hi, Mom. How did it go?"

She smiled at Maria, who took the opportunity to disappear into the kitchen.

Her mother pursed her lips.

"Well, it's never pleasant having to do something like that, but it's all taken care of. I gave them your uncle's information, and they'll make arrangements with the hospital to retrieve the body. The actual cremation will be sometime in the next few days."

Emily nodded. She'd been trying not to think too hard about the details concerning how, exactly, her uncle would be transformed into a pile of ash.

"Are there any plans for a funeral?"

"No, no," her mother said, removing her jacket. "Why bother? He said he didn't want a big fuss."

Emily felt a pang. It felt wrong not to have at least some sort of memorial, but she had no say-so in the matter. Besides, her mother was right. For all his bonhomie, her uncle had been an intensely private man with no other family but the two of them. She just wished her mother would at least show a bit more distress over his loss. The man had taken good care of them for many years. Surely, he deserved some sort of send-off.

"What about his ashes?"

Her mother sighed helplessly.

"I don't know. I suppose they'll do . . . whatever they do with them."

"May I have them?"

"*What?* Why?" She shook her head. "No, no, no. You don't want them. I'll have them scattered someplace. It'll be fine."

"I can do that," Emily said. "Really, I'd like to."

"I'll think about it."

She paused and gave her daughter the once-over. Evidently, she'd only just noticed the outfit.

"You're all dressed up this morning. Are you going somewhere?"

Emily grabbed her purse.

"I have an appointment."

"Where?"

"Does it matter? It's just an appointment, Mom."

Her mother stared, open-mouthed, clearly unnerved by this change in attitude.

"Don't worry," Emily said as she opened the door. "We can talk about it when I get back."

Emily sat in Frank Alfano's waiting room, flipping idly through a magazine. The last time she'd been there, she was twelve years old, sitting in numbed disbelief as she learned for the first time about the trust her father had set up for her in his will. At the time, the money had meant nothing to her, an abstract assurance of security that paled next to the tangible loss of her big, strong protector. Now, though, she could appreciate the gift she'd been given. The money would never replace her father's love and advice, nor the time together they'd been robbed of, but invested well, it might at least give her a few of the luxuries that marrying Carter would have provided.

The door to his private office swung open, and Frank Alfano stepped out.

"Emily, come in, come in."

She walked over and the two of them exchanged a brief hug. Frank had grown portly over the years and much of his hair was gone, but he was still surprisingly spry.

"I heard about your uncle," he said, closing the door. "I'm very sorry. He was a good man."

"Thank you," she said, taking a seat.

"I was shocked to hear he was gone already. It seemed as if we'd only just heard he was ill."

"I know. I was lucky to get here when I did. We had a nice conversation the night before he passed, though. It seemed that he was at peace."

He sat down behind his desk.

"Can I get you something? Coffee? Tea?"

"No, thanks. Darlene already offered."

"So," the lawyer said. "You've got an important birthday coming up."

"Tomorrow, yes."

"And I hear you're getting married, too. Your mother was in here just last week, talking to me about paying for the wedding."

Emily swallowed hard.

"There isn't going to be a wedding, Mr. Alfano. I've called it off."

"Oh, dear," he said. "I'm sorry to hear that."

"Please don't be. To tell you the truth, I'm relieved."

She gave him a confident smile, hoping to make it clear to him that she had no regrets. Ending the engagement had been the right thing to do; she didn't want anyone's pity.

"Well, good," he said. "To tell you the truth, I'm relieved myself. I think a woman needs to have a bit of money of her own when she marries."

Emily chuckled.

"Well, yes, but I'd say a million dollars is somewhat more than 'a bit.'"

The smile on her lawyer's face stiffened. He frowned uncertainly.

"I'm not sure where you got that figure, but your trust fund isn't worth a million dollars."

She nodded, embarrassed.

"Of course, you're right. I'm sure it's been reduced some-what: college tuition, books, lab fees. It all adds up."

Alfano's look had changed from surprise to wariness. He glanced at the papers in front of him and cleared his throat.

"I'm sorry to tell you this, Miss Prentice, but there's been a lot more than that taken out over the years."

Miss Prentice?

"How much more?" Emily said. "I mean, it couldn't have been a lot, and my uncle was in charge of the investments. The market's up quite a bit over the last twelve years, too. That has to have made up for some of the loss."

"Of course. Yes. But—"

"Well, how much is left?"

He ran his index finger down the page in front of him and tapped the figure at the end.

"Just over seventy thousand."

Emily gripped the arms of her chair, struggling for breath. She felt dizzy and light-headed. What had happened to the money? With a sick feeling of horror, she remembered the scene at her uncle's bedside as he told her he was sorry. Was it embezzlement, not the death of her father, that he'd been apologizing for? First Carter had betrayed her and now her uncle. It felt as if she'd been standing on a trapdoor that had suddenly dropped out from under her.

"I can't believe it," she said. "Why would Uncle Danny do that to me?"

Alfano shook his head.

"No, no. No one's cheated you. Every withdrawal is listed here," he said, patting an accordion file folder next to him. "It was all perfectly legal."

He took another sheet of paper out of the file and handed it to her.

"See for yourself."

Emily's hands shook as she skimmed the list of withdrawals from her trust account: her private school tuition, school uniforms, the never-ending lessons she'd endured. She looked up, her heart pounding.

"Our *swimming pool?*"

"Apparently, it was to help you with your swimming lessons."

She felt her anger build as she continued down the list.

"The trip we took to Europe? That was supposed to be a graduation gift." Emily gasped. "Oh, my God. The *house remodel?*"

He nodded, shrugging helplessly.

"Your mother requested every one of them in writing."

"My *mother?* But . . . but she has her own money. It was stipulated in my father's will. He knew what a spendthrift she is. She wasn't supposed to be able to touch any of mine."

"I understand, but the fact is, your mother was your legal guardian. As such, she had the right to use whatever money was needed for your benefit and well-being. Lessons, schooling, clothing all fall under that heading."

"Sure, I get that," Emily said. "But remodeling the house? A trip to Europe?"

He took a deep breath and gave her a pained look.

"It could be argued that those things were necessary in order to give you a good life, to maintain you in a style that your father would have wanted had he still been alive."

"But—"

He held up his hands as if warding off a blow.

"I'm not saying that I agree, you understand, only that I doubt you'd have a case against either your mother or your uncle's estate if you were to try to recover the money."

The list slipped from Emily's hand and drifted to the floor. She wasn't sure whether to laugh or cry. She'd thought she was rich—she'd spent the entire morning imagining how she would spend her sudden wealth. Instead, she'd be getting less than a tenth of what she expected. Yes, it was a nice nest egg, and far more than most people her age had, but the shock of seeing how much of her money had been frittered away—and why—left her stunned.

"So, when will I be able to take control of what's left?" she said.

Alfano seemed relieved. Perhaps he'd been expecting her to cry or yell. God knows, Emily thought, this couldn't have been the first time he'd dealt with an unhappy client.

"Provided there are no more requests," he told her, "it'll be yours tomorrow morning."

"Don't worry," Emily said grimly. "There won't be."

She stood on shaking legs and snatched the list of expenditures off the floor.

"May I have a copy of this before I go?"

"Of course."

Emily grabbed her purse. Her throat was tight and her eyes stung with unshed tears. How could they have done this to her? Uncle Danny and her mother in cahoots, stealing her inheritance bit by bit while she went blithely along, never suspecting a thing.

"Can I just say something before you go?" Alfano said.

She nodded, too upset to speak.

"I don't want to cause a problem between you and your mother," he said, "but there's nothing in these records that indicates your uncle encouraged her to raid your trust fund. If anything, it appears that he frequently disallowed the requests your mother made. From what I can tell, if he hadn't been such a wise investor, you'd have run out of money a long time ago."

Emily nodded. She wanted more than anything to let her uncle off the hook, but how could she after seeing that list?

Uncle Danny knew what her mother was doing and had let her get away with it.

"So, why did he?" she said. "Why did he let her do it?"

Alfano's look was almost tender.

"If I may hazard a guess, I'd say it was guilt."

"Guilt?"

"Over your father's death."

She shook her head.

"But he didn't have anything to do with my father's death. The investigation proved that."

"I know it did, but I'm not sure either he or your mother ever forgave him."

Emily bit her lip, feeling the weight of her uncle's guilt land squarely on her own chest. No wonder her mother had been so cold to him all these years. With a guilt-ridden brother-in-law holding the key to Emily's trust fund, she could make him give her whatever she wanted. After all, he owed it to her.

How convenient.

"Anyway, that's my guess, for what it's worth." He opened the door for her and handed the list to his assistant. "If you'd just have a seat, Darlene will make that copy for you."

Emily took the list Darlene had handed her and walked out to her car in a daze. She should look on the bright side, she told herself. She'd had her college degree fully paid for, been given advantages and enjoyed experiences most people could only dream of, and she still had some money to start over with. But it wasn't just the money, she thought, it was the betrayal that was devastating, knowing that her mother had been living like a queen all these years while stealing from her in secret. The utter selfishness and disregard for her feelings made Emily sick to her stomach.

How could she do that to me?

No wonder her mother had wanted her to marry Carter. She probably thought the trust fund wouldn't matter to Emily once she had access to the Trescotts' wealth. Who knows? She might even have thought of it as a way to get her own hands on their money. If so, then they should be grateful to Emily for calling off the engagement.

Then she thought of something else, and her heart sank.

She'd told Sam to buy the ship he wanted, that she'd cover the cost. Now she realized there was no way for her to do that. Her mother's treachery hadn't just upended Emily's life, it might have upended Sam's, as well.

CHAPTER 28

Sam stumbled from the deck into the galley and collapsed on a bench. He couldn't remember when he'd been so tired. At twenty-seven, he figured he was at the peak of his physical abilities, but seven days of backbreaking work with little food and less sleep was catching up with him. It wasn't hard to see why Hollander's safety record was so bad. Life aboard a seiner was hard and injuries were not uncommon, but working conditions onboard the *Skippy Lou* made them all but inevitable.

Poor working conditions and lack of sleep weren't the only problems, either. Hollander's short temper and aggressive attitude made him a danger to himself and others. More than once, they'd risked a collision while racing another ship to a prime fishing spot. They'd been lucky so far, Sam thought, but it was only a matter of time. When this job was over, he was going to have a nice, long talk with the Coast Guard. There had to be some way to get the guy out of the water before someone else got killed.

At least Logan Marsh hadn't been a problem. Like every other man onboard, he'd been too busy trying to stay alive to go after Sam. The worst he'd done was to strew the lines in an ankle-grabbing tangle, but that stopped after Ray Hollander took a tumble. Still, Sam remembered the look on Logan's face that day in town, and it was hard to sleep at night knowing the man was only an arm's length away. Thank God he and Kallik would be out of there soon.

Buying a ship while he was at sea was inconvenient, but once he and the seller had agreed on the price, things had begun moving forward apace. The tender had already been inspected when he made his offer and the title was clear; once the Coast Guard registered the bill of sale, the funds would transfer and the ship would be his. He could hardly wait to get back. If there was anything the last two years had taught him, it was that he needed to be working for himself.

But securing his own ship wasn't the only good news. Marilyn had called the day before with a message from Emily: the marriage was off, she was coming home. She was excited about the ship, too, encouraging him to pay whatever it took to secure the one he wanted. With the weather worsening, their radio connection had been weak, and there hadn't been much time for him to reply. He'd had just enough time to ask for a favor.

"See if she can get Bear for me; he's out at Tiffany's new place. The key to the Jeep is in my dresser drawer."

"Anything else?" Marilyn said.

"Yeah. Tell her I love her and I'll see her tomorrow."

Tiffany paced the living room floor as she waited for Seth to return. Her skin crawled and her heart pounded. It felt as if her hair were on fire. If Bear didn't stop whining and barking, she told herself, she'd go mad.

She stormed into the kitchen and pounded on the garage door.

"Stop it, Bear! I mean it, just shut up!"

She went to the bedroom, where it was quieter, and sat

down, hugging herself. She felt cold and hot at the same time. She shouldn't have yelled at the dog, she thought. It wasn't his fault he was driving her crazy. If Seth had just gone to the store and bought the dog food like he promised, Bear would be fine. Instead, he'd been running around with his stupid brother.

Tiffany looked at the time and ran a hand through her hair. He should have been back with the stuff by now. She wrapped her arms around her waist as her teeth began to chatter. Where was he, anyway? He'd promised to get it an hour ago.

A bolt of fear shot through her. What if he'd been arrested? Seth always told her he was too smart to get caught, but that was a lie. Anybody could get caught if they were in the business long enough. He said that keeping it in the family made him bulletproof, but anybody could get turned for the right price. She heard Bear scratching at the kitchen door again and clapped her hands over her ears, crying in frustration. Why wouldn't he shut up? What was she supposed to do?

She felt the room shake as the front door slammed. Tiffany got up and hurried out to the living room. Seth was standing there, breathing hard.

"Can't you shut that damned dog up? I could hear him from down the road."

Tiffany swallowed. She knew how violent Seth could get when he was angry, and Sam would be furious if anything happened to his dog.

"I didn't hear anything," she said. "It must have just been the once."

"Well, once is one time too many. You shut him up or I will."

She nodded, staring at the bulge in his jacket.

"Did you get the stuff?"

He drew the baggie slowly out of his pocket, smirking.

"You mean this?"

Tiffany's eyes widened. Her fingers itched to grab it out of his hand and shove him aside, but she didn't dare. Instead, she feigned indifference.

"Yeah, I guess."

Seth laughed. "Give me a kiss first."

She did, wincing as he grabbed her, hoping it wouldn't go any further. When he was finished, he pushed her away and reached into the bag.

"What are you doing?"

"This one's for the dog," he said.

He raised an eyebrow, daring her to try to stop him. Tiffany was torn. She didn't know what it would do to Sam's dog, but she was hurting real bad, and if she argued, Seth might not give her the rest. She closed her eyes, wishing she weren't so weak.

"Sure," she said. "Good idea."

Seth smiled triumphantly.

"Here you go," he said, tossing the bag to her. "It's good stuff. Don't be greedy."

CHAPTER 29

Emily pressed her nose against the window as the plane neared Ketchikan, trying to peer through the heavy cloud cover to the water below. The first time she'd flown there, she'd hardly given a thought to the men and ships who fished off the Alaskan coast. Now, her entire perspective had changed. She smiled and bit her lip.

Somewhere down there is the man I love.

A voice boomed over the cabin's speakers, reminding the passengers to remain seated with their seat belts fastened as the plane began its descent. Successive storms coming out of the west had made for a bumpy flight all the way up the West Coast and would no doubt make for a tricky landing, as well. Emily put her book away and made sure her seat was upright. Compared to what Sam must be going through, she thought, a little turbulence was nothing.

Rain was pelting down by the time they landed. Once again, Tim Garrett would be picking her up. Emily had hesitated to ask him for a ride so soon after her departure, but with Sam gone and Marilyn on bed rest, there hadn't been a whole lot of options. Luckily, Tim had agreed immediately, telling her it was no problem and dismissing her offer of payment.

Emily hadn't given him an explanation for her sudden change of plans, and he didn't ask for one. Maybe when she felt stronger she'd fill him in on the details, but first she'd have to make sense of them herself.

Things hadn't gone quite the way Emily had expected when she got home from Frank Alfano's office. Not only did Prentices not elope, she was told, they also didn't scream at each other like banshees. Instead, she and her mother had had a tight-lipped exchange of accusations and counterclaims so bloodless that Emily had quickly lost heart—which, on reflection, had probably been the point. Her mother's refusal to admit she'd done anything wrong had effectively robbed Emily of an argument, and without an apology or even an explanation from her mother, Emily found she couldn't forgive her for what she'd done. Things were said that she was sure they both regretted, but nothing was taken back. Instead, Emily had packed her things, arranged to have her car shipped to Sam's address, and taken off. Perhaps time and distance would give them both a different perspective, but at the moment, it seemed unlikely.

She only hoped that Sam wouldn't be hurt by the trust fund debacle. Before leaving, Emily had called Marilyn and asked her to tell Sam she'd changed her mind about buying the tender, but she had no idea if the message had gotten back to him. It had been a foolishly extravagant offer—she realized that now. Unless she wanted to blow through the rest of her trust fund as thoughtlessly as her mother had, Emily would have to learn some hard lessons about spending her money wisely.

And that wasn't the only lesson it had taught her. Looking back at her own feeble attempts at independence, Emily realized that it wasn't just Uncle Danny who'd given in to her mother's demands rather than standing firm. Had she not been so complaisant, in fact, Emily doubted her mother would ever have been able to raid the trust fund as long as she had. Embarrassing as it was, she'd had to admit that Richard Feynman was right: Emily herself had been the easiest person to fool.

Tim waved as she hurried toward the security gate and gave her a tentative hug. They headed down to baggage claim to retrieve her luggage—"Just one this time!"—then tried not to get soaked as they ran to his Jeep.

"Where to?" he asked as they got in line for the ferry.

She gave him Marilyn's address.

"After that," Emily said, "if you could just drop me off at Sam's, that'd be great."

"Sure thing."

As the ferry set out across the water, Emily was filled with conflicting emotions. Coming back to Ketchikan felt deeply satisfying. It had been her choice alone—one that had nothing to do with polishing her resume or improving her chances of getting a job, or anything else other than doing what she pleased. At the same time, though, she was almost sick with fear. What if this was a mistake? She'd spent so much of her life trying to please other people that she'd almost forgotten how to ask herself what it was she wanted. Like a fledgling teetering on the edge of its nest, she wanted to try her wings but couldn't forget that it was a long way down.

"You okay?"

Emily looked over at Tim and nodded.

"Sorry," she said. "Just lost in my own thoughts."

"Oh, hey. Don't let me interrupt you, then."

"No. No, it's fine; I could use the distraction. What's up?"

He grinned.

"I think we're getting closer to finding out who our drug smuggler is."

"Really! That's great. Who's your suspect?"

"Not sure *who* yet, but we've figured out how and when."
He sobered. "We know it's someone inside the cannery, and
we know it started about a year ago last May."

"So, not quite as long ago as you thought."

"That's the way it looks."

"I hope you find them soon. I'm sure the other interns will
be happy to hear it. We were all pretty concerned."

When they pulled up at Marilyn's, Emily hopped out and
ran for the door. Jane was waiting for her with the keys.

"How's she doing?" Emily asked.

"Better," she said. "Tired. Baby's getting big."

"Will she be at the dock tomorrow when the ship gets in?"

"I know she wants to. We'll have to see."

"All right. Tell her to call me if she needs anything."

At Sam's, Tim got Emily's bag out of the Jeep as she ran to
open the front door. He set it inside and gave her a look that
was full of concern.

"You sure you don't want me to go with you to get the
dog? It's no problem."

"No, I'll be okay," she said. "But thanks."

Emily gave him a brief hug, then stood at the door and
waved while he drove off. She hesitated at the threshold, taking
in the unremarkable furnishings. What a difference this place
was from her mother's home: no interior designer had coordi-
nated the color scheme; no feng shui practitioner had decided
where the furniture should be placed; the curtains that hung
from simple brass rods bore no fashionable labels. After the life
she'd had up until then, could she really be happy living like
that for the rest of it? Then she took a deep breath and realized
that there were two things it had that no other place in the
world did: Sam and Bear.

Emily hurried into the bedroom and started rooting through
Sam's dresser, looking for the key to the Jeep. Digging through

his socks and underwear felt strangely intimate, and she felt her face warm. What would happen when he got home? Was this a relationship that would last forever, or just a stepping-stone on the way to another life entirely?

One thing at a time. Get Bear first, then you can think about the future.

The road out to Tiffany's was so rutted and ruined that Emily almost turned around before she reached the house, sure that Jane must have given her the wrong address. When she finally found the place, she rolled to a stop and stared out the window, feeling real sympathy for Tiffany's situation. The place was a wreck, the perfect illustration of just how low addiction had laid her. What a depressing place to live.

She got out of the Jeep and ran to the door, carefully picking her way around the trash and cast-off merchandise strewn around the yard. How must Tiffany feel when she compared this place to Sam's tidy home? Or did none of it matter as long as she stayed high?

Emily rang the bell but got no answer, then rang it again and rapped sharply on the door. She heard whimpering coming from the garage and realized that it must be Bear. When there was still no answer to another series of knocks, she went over to the garage to see if it would open. Grabbing the handle, she yanked and felt the door start to rise.

The first thing Emily noticed was the smell. She held her breath, trying not to gag—urine and feces were everywhere. Emily felt her temper rise as she looked around. The floor was littered with empty pizza boxes and fast food containers, but there was neither water nor dog food—not even an empty bowl—in sight. Had Bear been trapped in there this whole time?

"Bear?" she said, searching the dark room. "Where are you?"

She saw a dark shape cowering in the far corner.

"Oh, Bear," she said, hurrying toward him. "You poor thing."

At the sound of Emily's voice, the dog stood unsteadily. His coat was dusty and his eyes dull. How long had it been, Emily wondered, since he'd been given anything to eat or drink?

"Hold on," she said. "I'll be right back."

The door to the house was unlocked. Emily found a mixing bowl in the sink. She filled it with water and took it back to the garage.

"There you go."

Angry tears filled her eyes as she watched Bear lap up the water. What must the last few days have been like for him, without food, without water, forced to relieve himself on the concrete floor? As the stench increased and his hunger and thirst intensified, had he wondered where Sam was and why his cries were unanswered? A hot tear ran down her cheek. How could anyone have left her sweet boy out there like that?

When Bear had finished the first bowlful, Emily went back inside and got another for him.

"Here you go," she said as she set it down. "Take it easy, though. Don't make yourself sick."

Emily went back into the house to look for something to write on. She couldn't just take Sam's dog without letting Tiffany know where he was. As bad as this situation was, she was sure there had to be an explanation. Sam wouldn't have trusted his ex to watch Bear if he didn't think she'd take care of him. Maybe Tiffany had gotten sick or been injured. It must have been something serious for her to have left the dog in this state.

She searched the kitchen drawers, finding precious little in the way of cooking utensils or even food, much less a pencil and paper. The depressed feeling Emily had when she drove up intensified. It was as if the house had been abandoned and no one really lived there—at least not in a way that seemed normal and rational to her. She walked into the living room and gasped.

Tiffany was lying on the couch, skeletal and pale. Her arms lay at odd angles; a bony leg hung off the edge. She looked like a marionette someone had flung aside. Emily froze in terror, convinced she was dead. Then Tiffany softly snored, and she sighed in relief.

"Tiffany, wake up. I came to get Sam's dog."

There was no response.

"Hey, are you okay?"

She put a hand on Tiffany's shoulder and shook her. The woman's head lolled, but she didn't wake.

Emily recoiled, her heart pounding. Tiffany wasn't sleeping, she was unconscious. She took out her phone and dialed 911.

"I need an ambulance." She gave the operator the address. "Please hurry. I think it may be an overdose."

The operator asked if she could stay there until they arrived, and Emily said she would. She double-checked that Tiffany was still breathing, then went into the bedroom for a blanket to cover her. Once that was done, though, Emily was at a loss. What else could she do? Nothing in her life had prepared her for a situation like that. All she could do was pray that the EMTs would hurry.

She heard the click of claws on linoleum as Bear came into the house. Two bowls of water and a chance to escape his hellish prison seemed to have restored his spirits. When he saw Tiffany, he walked over and nosed her arm, whining, then gently laid his head in her lap. It confirmed Emily's suspicion that Bear's condition had not been Tiffany's fault.

"It's okay. She's going to be all right," she said, hoping it was true.

The sound of an engine approaching sent Emily running for the door, but instead of an ambulance charging up the driveway, she saw a black Toyota Land Cruiser skid to a stop. As the driver got out and slammed his door, Emily gasped.

Noah.

"Tiffany!" he yelled. "Why's the garage door open?"

Danger signs were flashing in Emily's head as she watched him lower the tailgate and start offloading boxes. What had Tim told her about the drug smuggling? It had started a year ago in May—Noah's brother had been an intern then. It was an inside job—the interns had access to everything in the cannery. She remembered, too, how Noah had first pooh-poohed the problems at the cannery, then tried to cast suspicion on Tim when Emily refused to ignore them.

Noah hadn't seen her yet, too busy moving boxes from the truck bed into the garage, but any minute now, he'd see her standing there. Emily glanced back at the couch. Tiffany was still unconscious, Bear at her side, neither one in a position to defend themselves.

It's up to me.

She stepped outside and closed the door behind her. Noah caught sight of her and scowled.

"What are you doing here?"

"I came to get Sam's dog."

He closed the garage and took a step toward her.

"That all?"

Emily shook her head. There was no way Noah was going to let her walk out of there now that she knew his secret. The second she let her guard down, he'd be on top of her.

"Tiffany's passed out on the couch. I'm waiting for an ambulance."

He took another step.

"Maybe you should wait in the truck," she said.

Noah smirked.

"Are you kidding? I live here."

"I don't care. Just stay out there."

Noah laughed and took another step.

"What if I don't?"

Emily nodded. If he wouldn't back down, she'd need to be ready to defend herself. The ambulance would be there soon. All she had to do was keep him distracted until it arrived. She adjusted her stance, willing herself to relax.

"You think you're going to scare me with that aikido stuff?" he said. "Logan Marsh is a wasted old man and he almost took your arm off."

He lunged, and Emily lifted her arm as if to ward him off. When Noah seized it, she drew the arm sharply back, throwing him off balance. As he stumbled forward, she placed her free hand on his shoulder, spun him under her lifted arm, and pulled him over onto his back. Noah made a satisfying grunt as he landed.

"I don't want to hurt you," she said.

Emily had thought he'd back off once he got the wind knocked out of him. Instead, Noah scrambled to his feet and came at her again.

This time, Emily lifted both of her arms in a defensive posture. Noah grabbed one in each hand. She pulled her right arm down hard, raised her left as he fell forward, and pulled Noah's right arm over his shoulder, putting him on the ground a second time.

"Please don't do this," she said as he lay there panting. "As soon as the ambulance gets here—"

He rolled over, glaring at her.

"You think I'm going to let you just drive off after you've seen me here?"

As Noah rose up a second time, Emily took a step back.

After two hard throws, he should have been on the ground, gasping like a fish out of water. Instead, he was preparing to attack again. What was going on?

She noted the pulse throbbing in his neck, the dilated pupils that made his eyes glitter, and realized with dismay that whatever drug he was on had given him more strength and willingness to use it than she'd bargained for. Even as she heard a siren wailing faintly in the distance, Emily realized that stalling for time was no longer an option. Noah was prepared to do anything to keep his secret—even kill her, if necessary. She had to end this now.

He lunged—a feint—looking for an opening. Emily stepped aside.

"You won't hurt me," he taunted. "Isn't that what you said? Hurting your opponent isn't the point of aikido."

He lunged again, this time in earnest, and grabbed her shirt with both hands. Emily jerked in one direction, then the other, but his grip was firm. Unable to break free, she twisted in his grasp and bent forward.

Noah's arms were on either side of her neck now, but she could tell she'd thrown him off balance. Emily reached down, wrapped her arms around his legs, and lifted him off his feet. This time, the air exploded from his lungs as Noah hit the ground. As he rolled over, gasping for air, she placed one foot on his back and twisted his right arm up and around, taking his shoulder just to the edge of dislocation.

"You're right," Emily said as the ambulance came into view. "I don't want to hurt you." She smiled. "But that doesn't mean I can't."

CHAPTER 30

It was the morning of the last day on the *Skippy Lou,* and Sam couldn't wait for it to end. Nine days of backbreaking work had yielded fewer than half the fish they'd anticipated on this run, and morale onboard was low. Everyone was irritable, everyone was tired or injured, and everyone was making mistakes. Adding to their misery, a squall had come up overnight, bringing with it sheets of rain as dense as fog. Most of the fleet had turned for home to wait out the storm, but Hollander had only dug in his heels. Their sonar had found a school of fish half a mile out, and he was determined to take as much of it as he could. Like a gambler on a losing streak, he was betting on one big strike to wipe out his losses.

And then the engine died.

They'd been out only a few days when the problems started, but Hollander had refused to consider putting in for repairs. Since then, their engineer had worked day and night to keep it running, but the man was new, and as the situation deteriorated, it became clear that he was in over his head. It was lucky they had Kallik aboard, Sam thought. No one could coax a diesel engine back to life like he could. When the engine had faltered again that morning, his offer of help had been grate-fully accepted.

While the engineers struggled to get the seiner moving again, Hollander paced the deck, cursing and fuming, oblivious to the downpour. Sam lay on his bunk, listening to the urgent voices coming from the engine room, and willed the ship's en-gine to turn over. It sputtered, almost catching, then died as more curses emanated from above. He held his breath as they cranked it again.

"Come on, come on . . ." Sam muttered.

The engine started—falteringly at first, then steadily, em-phatically. As it roared to life, the men onboard cheered and Sam let out the breath he'd been holding. Once again, the *Skippy Lou* was underway.

Kallik came down the ladder and collapsed on the bottom step just as Sam slipped out of his bunk.

"Way to build the suspense there, pal. You almost had me worried."

The engineer lifted his hand and made a rude gesture.

Sam pulled on a sweater and grabbed his knit cap.

"How far do you think we've drifted?"

"No idea. Why?"

"Just wondering how close we are to the shipping lanes."

Kallik shrugged. "PACTRACS would have warned us if we were too close."

"Right," Sam said. "*If* we've got it."

The Marine Exchange vessel tracking system was the only sure way to know if they were headed into the path of ship-ping traffic, but it required enrollment and a monthly fee.

Sam started up the ladder. "I'll see you topside."

He steadied himself against the main winch, squinting up through the rain to check the power block. He'd been keeping an eye on it with every haul, but so far there'd been no indication that it was unequal to the task at hand. Nevertheless, if the area up ahead was as rich as Hollander said it was, they'd be putting the entire winch under enormous strain. If any part of it was going to fail, that would be the time. Sam wondered if he should mention his concerns to Hollander, but to do that, he'd have to reveal the source of his information, and questioning a captain's authority onboard was always risky.

Hollander was anxiously checking the sonar screen while the others drank coffee in the galley. Even if Sam succeeded in getting the man to reconsider, the rest of the crew might not back him up. More fish meant more money in their pockets, and if the captain was right about the bounty ahead, they'd be as anxious to start hauling as he was. In spite of his record, Hollander had a lot of influence on shore, too, and word of Sam's insubordination would spread like wildfire. With a new ship to man and operate, he couldn't afford to be making enemies.

The engine slowed as they reached their destination. As the wind had died so had the rain, replaced by fog so thick it made Sam feel claustrophobic. The crew scrambled out on deck and made ready to set the seine.

Sam would be driving the skiff this time, pulling the weighted net, or seine, in a wide arc to encircle the fish and form a purse in which to lift them from the water. While the weighted edge of the seine was being secured with metal rings, Kallik and Logan Marsh would plunge poles into the water to keep the fish from slipping away under the keel. Plunging the water was mindless, tiresome work, but it was essential to a good haul and safer than bringing in the net. Once the skiff returned and the purse was closed, Sam could get back on deck to give Kallik a hand when the winch started its first pull.

The skiff was lowered into the water. Sam stood at the rail, watching the rise and fall of the two boats, waiting for the point at which the distance between the decks was shortest before going over the side. Kallik stood behind him, checking to see that the seine unspooled smoothly, its corks staying afloat as they paid out; Hollander was at the winch, ready to set the rings and start raising the purse; and Logan Marsh was braced, pole in hand, ready to beat the water once the skiff was away. Every man knew his job; every man was ready.

The seiner settled and the skiff began to rise. As the decks grew closer, Sam swung his leg over the rail, ready to jump. Then a moderate swell pitched the boat astern, its dark surface white with froth, and a ripple of terror passed through him. The *Skippy Lou* was idling; the wind had died. Where was the white water coming from?

Sam yelled a warning, but it was too late. A wall of churning froth rose up and the seiner listed hard to port, pushed aside by some unseen force. Water poured over the gunwales, and the net began to unspool while Sam clung desperately to the railing. The deck was in chaos. Hollander ran for the bridge as Logan Marsh dropped his pole and dove for the lifeboat. Kallik stumbled toward Sam, lost his footing, and careened across the deck. Then a dark hull loomed out of the fog, struck the *Skippy Lou* amidships, and Sam tumbled over the side.

CHAPTER 31

Bear was glad to be home.

Emily sat at Sam's kitchen table, sipping coffee and watching the big Newfoundland snooze on his dog bed. After leaving Tiffany's, she'd taken him to the veterinarian, where he'd gotten fluids and something to calm his stomach, and she'd gotten reassurance that the dog had suffered no serious aftereffects. For the next week, Bear was to have plenty of water and nothing but bland food, the vet told her; the two of them had left his office with a list of instructions and a bag full of expensive prescription dog food. Emily glanced at the stack of cans on the counter and smiled. After gratefully wolfing down the first two, Bear had turned his nose up at the third—a sure sign, she thought, that he was feeling like his old self.

Unfortunately, Tiffany had not been so lucky. Whatever drug she'd taken had been far more potent than what she'd used in the past, and in spite of their best efforts, the doctors had been unable to revive her. She remained on life support while her parents waited for the rest of the family to come and say goodbye. In the meantime, both Seth and Noah had been taken into custody, each one blaming the other for her condition, and Tim Garrett had spoken to the police about the drugs being smuggled through the cannery. After fourteen frustrating months, it looked as if the mystery had finally been solved.

She looked at the clock, wondering where Sam was at that moment. Between rescuing Bear, taking him to the vet, and giving a statement to the police, she'd been on the go pretty much nonstop since returning to Ketchikan. Now, with nothing much to do, it felt as if time were standing still.

Emily had heard nothing from her mother, nor from Carter or any of their friends back home. The consensus of opinion seemed to be that Emily was in the wrong—a verdict that upset, but did not surprise, her. The Trescotts were rich, important people and their son was a great catch; no doubt they thought she should be grateful he'd chosen her from among dozens of more worthy candidates. Never mind that he'd denigrated her achievements, embarrassed her in front of their friends, and slept with another woman. If Emily had just kept her mouth shut, everything would have been fine.

But it wouldn't have been fine, she thought. Emily wasn't the same person she'd been when she first left for Ketchikan. As horrible as this experience had been, Uncle Danny's death, Carter's infidelity, and her mother's betrayal had done what the previous twenty-four years had not: it had forced her to grow up. The girl who'd foolishly believed that someone would always take care of her was gone. It was time to make her own way in the world, and the first thing she'd decided was that she no longer wanted to be a marine biologist.

Looking back on it now, her choice of major had been unrealistic from the start. The ocean would always fascinate her, of course, but she wasn't the sort of person who could happily spend weeks and months at sea, and the fact that she'd never even considered what the work entailed seemed hopelessly naïve. Perhaps, in the back of her mind, she'd never really believed she would need a job after college. Tim Garrett had offered to help her find something at the cannery, but she'd politely declined. She'd come up with an idea that was far more intriguing.

Sensei Doug had seen something in Emily that, on reflection, felt true: she wasn't just a good student, she had the makings of a good teacher—a sensei—too. It would take time and a lot of hard work, but the last few days had taught her something important. The greatest gift her father had given her wasn't his money, it was his strength and determination to do whatever it took to succeed. The only question now was whether to set up her own dojo or join someone else's, and she wouldn't know the answer to that until she talked to Sam.

According to Marilyn, Sam's tender was in escrow, but Emily had no idea when his offer had been finalized and the thought that her encouragement might have prompted him to pay too dearly for it sat like a weight on her chest. If he had, she'd decided to make up as much of the difference as she could, even if it meant spending the rest of her trust fund. Emily simply couldn't allow him to pay for her own foolish mistake.

She got up to pour herself another cup of coffee. Outside, a ray of sunshine had broken through the clouds, painting a rainbow over the harbor. Emily took a deep breath and sighed. At least she knew now that Sam loved her. After the way they'd parted, she wouldn't have blamed him for being angry. Instead, there'd been no words of recrimination in his last message, only the offer of an open heart. It felt like confirmation that the path she'd chosen was the right one. What better foundation was there on which to build a future?

As she walked back to the table, Bear lifted his head, and Emily stroked it reassuringly. The two of them were right where they belonged, she thought. Now all they needed was for Sam to come home.

The phone rang, and Emily smiled when she saw Marilyn's number on the caller ID. How many other people in the world would understand the mix of eagerness and fear she was feeling?

"Hey, Mar. What's up?"

But it wasn't Marilyn; it was Jane, calling from the hospital. The *Skippy Lou,* she said, had sunk.

Emily pulled out a chair and sat down, stunned.

"What happened?"

"Coast Guard's still trying to find out. I would've called sooner, but I thought you knew."

"Did anyone . . ." She swallowed. "Is everyone okay?"

"Sam's all right, but he's pretty beat up—three cracked ribs and a black eye."

Emily put a hand to her mouth as tears of relief welled.

"And Kallik?"

Jane sighed. "His back is broken—won't know how bad it is until they do the MRI. We got here just before they took him in."

"How's Marilyn?"

"She's strong," Jane said. "Whatever happens, she'll survive."

"And the baby?"

"No problems so far. They put a cot in Kallik's room so she can lie down while she's waiting."

"So, everybody made it?"

"Everybody but the new guy, Logan."

Emily felt a shiver of dread pass through her.

"Logan Marsh?"

"Yeah. You know him?"

"No," she said. "Not really."

"I gotta get back inside. Just came out to give you a heads-up."

"Thanks. I'll be there as soon as I can."

"I'll keep an eye out for you."

Emily grabbed her wallet and the keys to Sam's Jeep. As she snuck out the garage door, Bear was still passed out on his bed.

Jane was waiting outside the emergency entrance, smoking a cigarette, when she arrived. Emily jumped out of the Jeep and hurried over.

"What's the latest?"

"Kallik's back in his room. The other three are waiting to be discharged."

"Any results yet from the MRI?"

Jane took another puff and shook her head.

"He can wiggle his toes, so maybe it won't be too bad."

Emily glanced toward the entrance.

"How's Sam?"

"Driving everybody crazy, asking if you're here yet." She took one last puff and dropped the cigarette, grinding it out with her toe. "Let's get you in there so those people can have some peace."

Emily checked in at the front desk and was buzzed through the double doors. A row of curtained rooms lined the hallway. Sam's was the last one on the left. He was sitting up, his body swathed in warm blankets, when she pulled the curtain aside. The left side of his face was bruised, and she could see the beginnings of a shiner. As she stepped inside, he gave her a lopsided smile.

"Hey, gorgeous."

"Hey, yourself," she said.

Emily stood awkwardly at the threshold. What would he do when she told him about the money? Every instinct was telling her to rush over, hug him, smother him in kisses. Instead, she found she couldn't move. All she could think about was the foolish offer she'd made to help him buy his new tender. How would he react when she told him the money was gone? She knew how betrayed and disappointed she'd felt when she found out that her trust fund had been drained. She couldn't bear the thought that Sam would feel the same way about her.

He held out his hand.

"You can come in, you know. I have it on good authority that broken ribs aren't contagious."

She hesitated a second longer, then pulled up a chair and sat down, trying not to think about the last time she'd visited someone in the hospital.

"What happened?"

"Wandered into the shipping lane and got swatted by a tanker. We were lucky. If the Coast Guard hadn't been doing maneuvers in the area, none of us would have made it."

"I heard about Logan Marsh. Did you know he was going to be onboard?"

"Not until the last minute. Why? You think I should have backed out?"

"No." Emily shook her head. "I was wrong to blame you for trying to help Kallik. I'm sorry."

"Don't be," he said. "I should have tried harder to stop him."

She swallowed hard, tried to keep the tremor from her voice.

"Marilyn says you bought that tender."

"I did," he said. "Thanks for the encouragement."

"I'm so sorry. I never should have told you to buy it."

"Why? I thought you'd be pleased."

There was a box of tissues next to the bed. Emily reached for one and dried her eyes.

"There's something I have to tell you, but please don't be

mad." She blew her nose. "When I left that message, I thought my trust fund had a million dollars in it. I thought I'd be able to help you buy your tender, but it turned out that my mother had spent almost the whole thing and now I can't give you as much as I thought."

Sam struggled to sit up straighter.

"I never asked you for any money."

"I know," she said. "But I wanted to help, and you said you needed the seller to lower his price. If I hadn't told you to spend whatever it took—"

"Whoa, whoa, wait. Can you calm down a second?"

She took a deep breath, nodded.

"The reason I was waiting for him to lower his price was because I didn't want to overpay, not because I didn't have the money."

"Really?"

"Yes. And, no offense, but if I *had* needed money, I wouldn't have borrowed it from you."

Emily frowned. "Why not?"

"Well, considering the situation we're in, I'd say the answer is obvious."

"Yeah, I guess you're right." She paused. "So, you're not broke?"

"Did you think I was?"

"Well . . . sort of."

Sam pursed his lips.

"Why? Because I don't throw money around like your family does?"

Emily drew back. "My family doesn't throw money around."

"Okay, maybe that's a little harsh, but from what you've told me, your mother spends a lot of money trying to impress other people."

She blinked, thought about that for a moment.

"Yeah. I guess that's true."

"Look," he said. "I'm not trying to pick on anybody, but just because I don't live in a big, expensive house or drive a flashy car, that doesn't mean I'm poor. I bought my first duplex when I was eighteen, and I've got three more now. Believe me, I'm doing fine."

"Then why do you work on a tender?"

"Because I love it—and it's good money, too. Buying this ship just means I can work on my own terms with my own crew, Em, it doesn't mean I'm ready to come ashore."

She thought about that for a moment. Could she learn to live with the uncertainty? She'd always promised herself she wouldn't put herself in her mother's position. What if something happened to him and she was left, as her mother had been, alone and brokenhearted?

Emily nodded. "If that's what you want to do, I think it's great."

"What about you?" he said. "Now that you're back, are you gonna stick around?"

"I think so," she said. "See, I met this great guy when I was here before. He's big and strong—a great kisser—and he loves being out on the water. He's also really hairy and he slobbers a lot."

"Should I be jealous?"

She leaned forward and kissed him.

"What do you think?"

EPILOGUE

Bear jumped out of the Jeep and ran ahead, drawn by the faint wail of a baby's cries as Sam and Emily followed him up to the house. When the front door opened, he pushed his way inside, nearly knocking Kallik off his feet on his way to the back bedroom. Sam lunged for him and missed.

"Bear," he said. "Get back here."

Kallik shook his head.

"Let him go, man. She's been fussing all day with those new teeth; we could use some peace and quiet around here."

Sure enough, as the front door closed they heard squeals of delight coming from the nursery. Marilyn trudged out, a diaper slung over one shoulder, and clasped her hands together in thanksgiving.

"The cavalry has arrived. Bless you both."

As she gave Emily a hug, Sam nodded toward the bedroom.

"Kallik says it's been a tough day."

"It *was*," she said, "until Bear showed up. Now, she's all giggles and grins."

"Can I take a peek?" Emily said.

"Sure. Come on back."

They tiptoed down the hall and peered into the nursery. Bear was up on his hind legs, his front paws between the crib slats, staring down at his namesake. Mary Little Bear, now six months old, was lying on her back, holding a chubby foot in both hands and smiling up at him.

"God, she's so cute," Emily whispered, trying not to break the spell.

Marilyn nodded. "That she is."

"And she sure gets a kick out of Bear."

"I think the feeling's mutual."

They stood there watching a while, then Emily glanced back toward the living room.

"How's he doing?"

"Better. Still uses the cane some, but I think it's mostly for reassurance. The PT says he'll be ready to go come salmon season."

"Well, don't let him rush for Sam's sake."

Marilyn rolled her eyes.

"Believe me, it's not for Sam's sake. The man's driving me crazy."

Emily smiled gently. Marilyn might be talking big now, but none of them had forgotten those first days in the hospital. Not that she was going to bring it up; some things were best left unsaid.

They backed away from the door.

"How're things at the studio?"

"Pretty good," Emily said.

She'd found a yoga instructor looking to split the rent on studio space, and the two of them were using it on alternate days.

"I've got a dozen kids signed up for lessons and maybe twice that many adults. Turns out, a lot of people who do yoga are interested in aikido, too."

"Heard anything from your mom?"

Emily felt a tightness in her throat, shook her head.

"Apparently, she's lost interest in wedding plans."

Marilyn shrugged.

"She'll change her mind. You'll see."

A throaty giggle caught their attention. Mary had inched her way closer to the slats, and Bear was licking her fingers. Marilyn laughed as she walked over to the crib.

"Careful, Big Bear. You don't know where those little hands have been."

She scooped the baby out of the crib and turned.

"You want some of this?"

Emily reached out. "Yes, please."

"So," Marilyn said as she handed the baby over. "A fisher's wife. You gonna be okay with that?"

Emily made funny faces for Mary Little Bear while she considered her answer.

"You know, I swore I'd never fall for a risk-taker like my father. I kept thinking: What if I lost him? What would I do? And then I realized how selfish that was. My father could have done something else, but it would have killed him, because he loved his job—and Sam loves his. So, am I scared? Yeah, I am. I'm just not going to let that stop me from loving him as long as I can."

She felt a nudge at her elbow and saw two big brown eyes looking up at her.

"That goes for you, too, Bear."

Turn the page for a delightful excerpt!

When the lumber mill closes, laying off most everyone in Fossett, Oregon, Melanie MacDonald plans to revitalize her beloved but beleaguered homestead by running her border collie, Shep, in Fossett's mayoral race. . . .

Shep wins by a landslide.

A lover of democracy and dog treats, Shep is rapidly earning the goodwill of Fossett's citizens. Tourists are streaming in and everyone wants to glad-paw the new mayor. Suddenly Melanie and Shep are media darlings, with requests for interviews, game shows, and personal appearances through the roof. But there's trouble in paradise. Determined to win back his former wife, Bryce MacDonald discovers a rival in tabloid reporter Chad Cameron, who's in Fossett to dig up dirt on Melanie and Shep. He finds a willing co-conspirator in the malcontent who lost the election. Hounded by the press and desperate to head off a potential dognapping, Melanie unwittingly puts herself in danger. Shep comes to the rescue, proving his mettle to save his faithful human at the risk of his own life . . . and new political career.

PLEASE DON'T FEED THE MAYOR
by Sue Pethick
Author of *Boomer's Bucket List*

Based on a true story. Sort of.

On sale now, wherever books are sold.

CHAPTER 1

Melanie MacDonald woke that morning with a start. Maybe it was a bad dream that had caused it or just the mysterious workings of her subconscious, but the second she opened her eyes a terrible certainty clutched at her heart: Fossett—the town she loved best in all the world—was dying. Blinking back tears, her heart pounding, she groped toward the foot of the bed where her border collie, Shep, was sleeping. As he lifted his head and nuzzled her hand, Melanie took a deep breath and felt the constriction in her chest begin to ease.

"We can't let it happen, boy," she whispered. "We've got to find a way to save this place."

A glance at the clock told her she'd beaten the alarm by twenty minutes—something Melanie would ordinarily have spent on some extra shut-eye—but sleep would be impossible now. Better to get up than to lie there in the darkness and fret, she thought. Plus, it would give her time to think before she headed in to work. There was still time to save her little town, she told herself. The only question was: How?

The brisk October air made her face tingle as she opened the back door for Shep. It was her favorite time of year, a period of growing anticipation between the enervating heat of summer and the first snowfall. Songbirds were emptying her feeders as fast as she could fill them, and in spite of Shep's best efforts the squirrels had already buried an orchard's worth of nuts in her backyard. Down in the river, the last of the late-season Chinook were racing upstream, and the pumpkins she'd planted in July would be jack-o'-lanterns before long. If only other people could see the town the way she did, Melanie thought as she headed back inside, Fossett's problems would be over.

Shep continued to romp in the backyard while Melanie made breakfast. She stood at the kitchen window, watching him zigzag across the lawn, guiding his soccer ball around a stile and into an upturned orange crate. The border collie's previous owners had given him away when he refused to stop herding their small children around like sheep, and she'd made it a priority to channel those instincts toward something less objectionable. Much as she enjoyed having him with her at work, Melanie knew that being inside all day was hard on a working dog and letting him tire himself out a bit first made life at the coffee shop easier for everyone.

When her toast came up, Melanie sat down at the table and began racking her brain once again for ways to save Fossett from extinction. The town's troubles weren't news to anyone; its residents had already spent time and money trying to improve its fading prospects. The old Fossett House, a Victorian mansion built for a railroad baron's mistress, had been remodeled into a bed-and-breakfast, money had been raised to modernize the school, and Main Street had undergone a complete overhaul with fountains, bubblers, and wrought iron benches for people to enjoy during their shopping trips. But in spite of those improvements, folks were still moving away and the future seemed bleaker than ever. If something drastic wasn't done, Fossett would soon be nothing but a historical footnote.

She hung her head and fought the urge to cry. Had moving back there been a mistake? It was so easy at times like that to start second-guessing herself. It wasn't just that she'd sunk her life savings into the coffee shop; she'd given up everything else, too: friends, a good job, even her marriage had fallen to the wayside. Melanie had bet her entire future on making things work in her hometown. If they didn't, it wouldn't just mean that her business had failed; it would also mean she'd sacrificed everything for a foolish dream. She didn't think she could face that.

Melanie looked up and frowned; Shep was pawing anxiously at the front door. He must have let himself in while she was brooding, she thought, but what on earth was he so worked up about? Then she glanced at her watch.

"Oh, my gosh, look at the time!"

She grabbed her coat and the two of them ran out the door.

Ground Central was in the heart of Fossett's downtown, one of a dwindling number of shops still thriving on Main Street. Even as other businesses closed, Melanie had managed to hang on, a fact she attributed to Shep. As the shop's official greeter, he made everyone who walked through the door feel welcome.

Melanie turned on the television and started filling the two large coffee urns while Shep walked through the dining area, nudging chairs into place around the tables. The constant drone of entertainment news hadn't been part of her original plan when she opened Ground Central—she'd been picturing more of a quiet coffee bar like the ones they had in Portland

and Seattle—but resistance on the part of Fossett's populace and the need to meet her financial obligations had convinced her that compromise was necessary to her survival. As frustrating as it felt sometimes, she could at least console herself that Ground Central had achieved its main purpose: to become an informal neighborhood gathering place.

The smell of coffee brewing filled the air as Melanie made a last pass through the shop, refilling stir sticks and sweetener packets while Shep waited patiently for Walt Gunderson to arrive. Walt was the owner of Gunderson's, the grocery/hardware/feed store that had been the heart and soul of Fossett for five generations, and his wife, Mae, made the baked goods that Melanie sold in her shop. Walt had been both mentor and father figure to her the last four years, and as owner of one of the few thriving businesses in town, he was as keen to find a way of improving Fossett's prospects as she was. He was also, as Shep knew, a soft touch when it came to giving out his wife's homemade dog treats.

When Walt's truck arrived, Shep's ears pricked up. Licking his chops in anticipation, he trotted toward the front door to greet his benefactor and, with his head lowered obligingly and his bottom wiggling, Shep stretched his upper lip into an unmistakable doggie grin. Melanie scolded him as she hurried over to unlock the door.

"Shep," she said. "Don't be a beggar."

"It's fine," Walt said, holding the box aloft. "Hold on, boy. Let me put these down and we'll see what Mae's sent for you today."

He set the box on the counter and reached into his pocket as Shep swallowed dramatically.

"Well, well. What's this?" Walt said, holding the bone-shaped biscuit to his nose. "Smells like peanut butter."

Shep whimpered and squirmed impatiently.

"Oh, all right. Here you go."

He tossed the treat into the air.

Shep leaped, grabbed the proffered treat in his mouth, and hurried over to his bed in the corner to enjoy it in peace.

Walt laughed. "I think that's the highest I've ever seen him jump. Mae will be pleased."

Melanie poured Walt the cup of coffee he took in exchange for a discount on the baked goods and pushed it across the counter.

"So," she said, indicating the box on the counter, "what have you brought *me* today?"

"Blueberry muffins and oatmeal scones."

She lifted the lid and felt her mouth form an o in surprise. "What are those?"

"Selma's latest creation. She asked me to include them in this week's deliveries."

Selma Haas was the manager of the newly renovated Fossett House B and B. With business slower than expected, she spent her time thinking up ways to enhance the enjoyment of her imaginary guests.

"She calls 'em Beavertails."

Melanie poked one with her finger. "But what *are* they?"

"Brownies. She told Mae she cooks 'em in a muffin pan and then flattens 'em with a spatula while they're still warm." Walt pointed. "That's what gives them their crisscross pattern."

"And . . . they're supposed to look like a beaver's tail?"

"Something like. She thinks they'll give the tourists 'an authentic Northwest experience.'"

"Assuming we ever *get* any tourists around here."

Walt nodded. "The woman's got an imagination; I'll give her that."

A slow smile spread across Melanie's face.

"Maybe we should call them Eaverbay Ailtays."

The two of them shared a guilty chuckle. Selma had been hired as manager of the B and B on the strength of her claim that she was bilingual. It was only later that anyone discovered the "foreign language" she spoke was pig Latin.

The moment of levity passed, leaving Melanie as dispirited as she'd been when she woke up that morning. She sighed and slumped against the counter.

"Oh, Walt, what are we going to do? I've been cogitating till my brains are scrambled, trying to figure out how to save this place."

He shook his head. "I'm not sure there's anything we can do. At the moment, my plan is to wait till Social Security kicks in, then close up shop and move to someplace warmer."

"You can't mean that."

"Why not? This place has broken my heart too many times, Mel. There comes a time when a man has to admit defeat."

She shook her head, unwilling to adopt his pessimistic attitude. There had to be a way, Melanie thought. She just hadn't found it yet.

Walt reached across the counter and patted her arm.

"I know how you feel, but at this point, I'm not really sure this place is salvageable. Look at the folks we've lost: professionals, small-business owners, families with children—the people a town needs to build a foundation on." He looked askance at the Beavertails. "Aside from the two of us and the guy who owns the bar, the most successful people in town are a pet psychic and the gals with the pot farm."

Melanie held up a hand in protest.

"Okay, first of all, it's not a pot farm; they grow *medicinal* marijuana."

Walt rolled his eyes as she continued.

"And sure, Fossett's got its fair share of oddballs—maybe

even more than its fair share—but that's just local color. People like Jewell Divine add a dash of whimsy that's charming," she said. "We just need to find a way to attract some normal people to Fossett, to sort of . . . dilute the ones that are already here."

Walt wasn't buying it.

"People don't want to live around a bunch of weirdos," he said. "I'm sorry, but short of a miracle, I don't think Fossett's got a chance in hell."

The morning breakfast crowd started arriving as soon as Walt drove away, and it was almost ten o'clock before the place emptied out again. Someone had cranked up the volume on the TV set and with no human voices to cover the sound, the reporter's voice was giving her a headache. She grabbed the remote and was about to turn it down when she saw the headline at the bottom of the screen:

English Town Elects Cat to Local Council

"This is Chad Chapman, reporting to you from the tiny English village of Croton-by-the-Sea, where its single seat on the county council has been given to Reginald, a ten-year-old tabby cat belonging to Miss Pansy Suggitt."

The camera angle widened to show an orange-and-white tabby, lying on a pillow in what appeared to be a tobacconist's shop. A man with a microphone stood next to him, facing the camera.

"Since his election, 'Reggie' has become something of a celebrity in his little town. Dozens of tourists arrive by bus each day, hoping to meet the new 'councilfeline.'"

Dozens every day? Melanie thought. A shiver of excitement passed through her.

"Cards and letters addressed to 'Councilman Reggie' quickly overwhelmed the local postal authorities, who have had to bring in extra help

to handle the overload, but few people are complaining, as sales of merchandise with the tabby's likeness have boosted the local economy and put this sleepy little hamlet on the map."

Melanie's heart was racing. This was exactly the sort of thing that Fossett needed: a bold move that would get people excited again. They might not have a town council, but they could figure something out. All they really needed was the right animal to fill the position. And that, she thought, glancing over at Shep, would be easy.

CHAPTER 2

Melanie's hands shook as she set out the last of the folding chairs. In the three days since she'd come up with her plan, she'd lost two pounds and chewed off all but one of her fingernails. If this town hall meeting didn't go well, she feared she'd never come up with another idea as promising. There'd be no other option then but to watch Fossett continue its downhill slide.

A bead of sweat snaked its way down her temple. Melanie wiped it away as she counted the number of seats crowding the floor of her coffee shop. How many people would show up? she wondered. Folks in Fossett weren't particularly "churchy," but most still thought of Sundays as sacred, even if all it meant was getting an extra hour or two of sleep. She'd posted flyers on every street corner and several people had told her they'd be there, but saying and doing were two very different things. What she needed was a representative sample of residents to test her idea on, but with five minutes to go and no one in sight, she feared even that modest goal had been too ambitious.

If only she'd been able to convince Walt.

In spite of his admission that her plan had merit, Walt

Gunderson remained stubbornly convinced that any idea—even one as unconventional as making Shep the mayor—was doomed to failure. The last time they'd spoken, he advised her not to look for him at the meeting. As Melanie grabbed another chair and set it in place, she tried to ignore the knot in her stomach.

"Where do you want these cookies?" Kayla said.

Melanie looked up at the girl in the heavy metal T-shirt. For the first few years after opening Ground Central, Melanie had labored alone, unable to afford even part-time help. Then five months ago, she'd finally hired her first permanent employee. Kayla Maas might be only eighteen and her fashion choices somewhat questionable, but she showed up on time, didn't cop an attitude with the customers, and adored Shep, for whom the feeling was mutual.

"The front counter is fine," Melanie said. "Are the coffee urns ready?"

"Yep. Regular on the right, Unleaded on the left." Kayla set the tray down and covered it with plastic wrap. "How many people will come, you think?"

"Who knows? Twenty? Thirty? None?"

There was a handprint on the front door. Melanie walked into the back room to get some vinegar water and a rag.

"You think Mr. Gunderson will change his mind?" Kayla said.

She shook her head.

"I doubt it."

"I don't get it," the girl said, dusting crumbs off the counter. "That story about the cat said it brought a lot of people into the town. If it worked there, why not here?"

"It's not that he thinks having Shep as the mayor won't work," Melanie said. "It's just that, well, he's not sure that anything will help save Fossett at this point."

"Why not?"

She bit her lip, wondering how to paraphrase Walt's position without giving offense. After all, it wasn't as if his objections were unfounded.

"Because we don't just need people to come and visit; we need for them to move here permanently. I think he's afraid that most folks won't find Fossett all that appealing."

Kayla scrunched up her nose.

"What's wrong with it?"

"Oh, you know. It's a small town. People in small towns can be a bit . . . different." She chuckled. "I mean, it's not every place that has a pet psychic."

"But people love Jewell!" Kayla said. "And she's really good, too. When our cockatiel, Stevie, stopped eating, Mom asked Jewell to come over and take a look at him. Right away, she knew what was wrong."

Melanie nodded feebly. She could just picture Jewell Divine, showing up on Kayla's doorstep in one of her tie-dyed caftans, ready to reveal the thoughts and feelings of the anorexic bird.

"Jewell told us that Stevie had been smuggled in from South America in some guy's smelly coat and then sold to a pet store where the other birds were mean to him. It was real sad."

"And did he start eating again?"

"Oh no, he died," Kayla said. "But at least we understood him better, and Jewell said sometimes that's all an animal really wants. Plus, after all he'd been through, we could sort of understand why he'd want to end it all."

"So . . . it was suicide?"

"Yeah, I guess so."

Melanie was about to say something about the chances that a bird would willfully self-destruct when the girl's phone rang. As Kayla went off to answer it, Melanie started cleaning the window, going over what she planned to say at the meeting as she wiped away the handprints. Now wasn't the time to worry about whether or not Walt was right, she told herself. Making Shep the mayor was going to be enough of a stretch without complicating matters, and it was important that the idea get more than a grudging endorsement. For her plan to work, Fossett's residents would need to know they had a stake in the outcome. The last thing she wanted was for anyone to feel they'd been buffaloed.

Kayla returned and glanced at the door.

"I'm surprised there's nobody here yet."

Melanie felt the knot in her stomach tighten.

"Yeah. I guess free coffee and cookies weren't as enticing as I thought."

"Mind if I take off, then? I told Cal I'd go kayaking with him today."

"No, you go on," Melanie said. "I appreciate your helping out. See you tomorrow."

As Kayla disappeared around the corner, Melanie sauntered up to the front counter, lifted the plastic wrap from the cookies, and slid one off the tray. To help keep her strength up when everyone arrived, she told herself, taking a bite. Or as consolation, if no one did.

Then, like the first drops of rain after a long drought, people began to arrive. A trickle at first, then groups of two and three came in, chatting amiably as they surveyed the cookies, poured themselves some coffee, and found a seat. Selma from the B and B came, taking an extra cookie for the boy who was watching the front desk, along with her twin sister, Helena, and Jewell Divine, in a pair of harem pants and a tie-dyed vest. Rod Blakely arrived in his usual attire—jungle fatigues, combat boots, and a flak jacket—and Francine and Everett Stubbs had left their herd of goats to take their places in the front row.

When the flow of friends and neighbors finally abated, fifty-one people—more than twice as many as expected—had shown up. Melanie searched the faces carefully, but Walt's was not among them. She told herself it shouldn't have been a surprise. Nevertheless, his lack of confidence felt like a blow.

She stepped up in front of the counter and cleared her throat.

"Thanks for coming, everyone," she said, loud enough to be heard over the din.

As the room quieted, all eyes turned toward her. Seeing so many hopeful faces made Melanie feel weak at the knees. These were her friends and neighbors, people hoping for a way out of a desperate situation, and what did she have to offer them? An absurd idea based on something that had happened half a world away. What if Walt was right and Fossett was already beyond salvation? All she'd be giving them was another dose of false hope. Melanie looked down at her ragged fingernails and felt the weight of their expectations pressing down on her. Perhaps, she thought, it would be better just to admit defeat and go home.

A whoosh of air and the sound of chairs being shuffled caught her attention. She looked up and saw the door close as Walt Gunderson slipped inside. He leaned against the back wall, arms folded, and gave her an encouraging nod. Melanie felt tears of relief and gratitude well up. Maybe this wasn't a lost cause after all.

"We all know that things around here have been going downhill since the mill closed. Shops are closing, people are moving away, and the changes we thought would bring more people into town haven't worked out the way we hoped."

Heads nodded. There were murmurs of assent.

"I have an idea that I think might help, something that would get us some attention and bring tourists into town."

"We don't need tourists," Rod Blakely grumbled. "We need jobs."

"You're right," Melanie said. "We do need jobs, but we need people, too. Folks who have jobs in Corvallis or Albany—even Salem—might just be looking for a small town where they can raise their kids. If we can get the word out about what a great place Fossett is, I think folks like that will want to come here and buy houses, settle down, and fill our school with their kids so we can reverse the downward spiral we've been in."

"The mill's closed," someone said. "Those jobs aren't coming back."

"No," she said. "But if we can increase our numbers, Fossett will be a more attractive place for companies to come to. We've got a lot of empty storefronts to fill."

"Retail jobs don't pay enough to live on," said another.

"Yeah," Rod Blakely added. "Minimum wage won't help anyone."

Melanie was tempted to point out that rents were dirt cheap in Fossett and having any job was better than being unemployed, but she didn't want to get pulled into an argument before she'd had a chance to share her idea. Making Shep the mayor was never going be the entire solution to Fossett's problems, but it could be a step toward helping the town rehabilitate itself. If they got bogged down in the details now, people might give up before they'd even given it a chance.

"So," came a voice from the back. "What's your idea?"

Melanie gave Walt a grateful smile. He might be a skeptic, but he'd come and shown his support. Whether or not he'd ever change his mind, it seemed he at least wanted people to hear what she had to say.

"I think we need a gimmick," she said.

At once, the air of excited anticipation died. Heads shook and eyes began to roll. Melanie felt panic rise up in her chest.

How could they dismiss her so quickly? They hadn't even heard what she had to say. She gave Walt a pleading look, hoping for some backup.

"Quiet down!" he said. "You all sound like a bunch of geese. Let the lady finish."

The effect was immediate. Against the moral weight of their most prominent citizen no one was willing to argue.

"So, what's the gimmick?" Selma said.

Melanie paused. Thinking about making her dog the mayor was one thing, but saying it out loud almost made it seem like a joke. She didn't want people to think she was making fun of their plight or minimizing the amount of effort it would take to drag them back from the brink of disaster. What made her think that her plan would work when so many others had failed?

Then Melanie glanced at Shep, sitting beside her, alert but unruffled by a crowd whose emotions were wavering between hope and despair, and it occurred to her that he was exactly the sort of leader they needed. Maybe having Shep as Fossett's mayor wasn't so crazy after all, she told herself. Maybe, under the circumstances, it was the sanest thing they could do. She just had to hope that the people who saw him sitting there would realize it, too.

"I think we need a mayor."

"A *mayor?!*"

"Oh, come on."

"What the hell kind of gimmick is that?"

"Hold on!" Walt said. "Let her finish."

"*And,*" Melanie added, "I think it should be my dog, Shep."

For the first few seconds, no one moved. The coffee shop was so quiet she could hear the clock ticking on the wall behind her. Melanie swallowed, and the sound seemed to fill the room as she waited for a response.

I am never going to live this down.

Then everyone began to talk at once.

"That's a great idea!"

"A dog mayor! We'll be famous!"

"It's perfect!"

"Three cheers for Mayor Shep!"

As the crowd continued to smile and voice their approval, Melanie glanced at Walt, who shook his head in wonder. The folks there had not only taken her seriously; they also seemed to think her plan could work. It wasn't the end of Fossett's problems by a long shot, but it was a start.

And it was already catching fire.

"He should wear a badge that says: 'Mayor Shep.'"

"And carry a briefcase!"

"Why don't we give him an office in the old City Hall building?"

"Yeah, people could come and see him passing laws."

"Mayors don't pass laws; they enforce them."

"No, the police do that!"

"Well, Fossett doesn't *have* a police force, does it?"

"Good thing, too, or you'd be in jail!"

"Wait!" Melanie shouted, waving her arms. "Hold on! Shep wouldn't be doing things that a real mayor would do. He'd just be the *honorary* mayor."

Disappointed looks were exchanged among the audience members.

"What's the point of that?"

"The point is, he'd be *called* the mayor and people would come and see him."

"But if he's not a real mayor—"

"He would be a real mayor," Melanie said. "A real, *honorary* mayor. Cities do it all the time."

Nevertheless, the air of skepticism remained.

"But what would he *do?*"

"The same thing he does now: greet people at the coffee shop and nap on his dog bed."

"Who'd want to come all the way out here just to see that?"

"Lots of people," Melanie said, her confidence waning. "He's a dog. People love dogs."

Now that they were talking about the actual details of her plan, she had to admit that the idea sounded awfully flimsy. The story on the television hadn't said anything about Reginald the cat doing anything special, but that was in England. Maybe Americans needed something more exciting to get them to come to a place like Fossett.

"I don't know," Selma said. "I still think he needs to do some mayor stuff."

"Well . . . maybe he could be a real mayor," Melanie conceded. "But before we decide about that, we need to agree that this is something we all want to do. If people here in town don't take this seriously, no one else will believe it and the whole thing will fall apart. What we have to decide today is, should we do it or not?"

"You can't decide something like that on the say-so of a couple dozen people," Rod Blakely said. "That ain't fair."

Melanie ground her teeth. Leave it to Rod, she thought, to stop her momentum in its tracks.

"All right," she said. "What would you suggest?"

"We should put it to a vote."

"Right now?" She looked around.

"No. On Election Day."

"But that's silly. He'd be the only candidate."

"Not necessarily." Rod gave her a mutinous look. "There might be others who'd like to be the mayor."

She should have seen this coming, Melanie thought. Rod

Blakely was not only the most disagreeable person in Fossett; he was also under the impression that he was the smartest, most competent, and best-loved guy in town. The man was delusional.

"Look, I really don't see why we should hold an election. After all, the point is to have a *dog* as our mayor."

Rod crossed his arms. "No, the point is to make the process *fair.*"

Melanie was dismayed to find several people nodding in agreement. Folks in Fossett might not be terribly sophisticated, but they had a keen sense of right and wrong; fairness and playing by the rules meant more to them than reason and logic. She glanced at Walt, hoping for some sort of intervention, but he simply shrugged as if to say, *You got yourself into this mess. Better figure your way out.*

"All right," she said. "We'll hold an election."

"On Election Day?" Selma said.

"Uh, sure, I guess. If we can manage it."

"But we don't have a mayor *now.* How do we elect one?"

Melanie shook her head, feeling the optimism that had carried her thus far begin to falter under the weight of reality.

"I–I suppose the first thing we'll have to do is talk to an attorney and find out what the legal requirements are."

Francine Stubbs scowled.

"And how much will *that* cost?"

"Yeah," her husband said. "I thought this was supposed to *make* us money, not *cost* us anything."

As the rumbles of dissent grew, Melanie knew she'd have to act fast.

"It's all right," she said. "I know a lawyer who'll do it for *free.*"

And just like that, the tide turned back in her favor. Hopeful smiles broke out all over the room and people came forward to shake Shep's paw, promising him their votes. Walt Gunderson gave her a thumbs-up and she nodded her thanks. She'd done it! And once the people there went back to their homes and families, the idea would percolate and grow until everyone in Fossett would be eager to have Shep as their mayor.

Sure, they'd have to hold an election and Rod Blakely might insist that his name be on the ballot, but no one in their right mind would vote for him, so why worry? All she needed to do was figure out how to hold an election that was legally enforceable in the next two weeks. Never mind that the only lawyer Melanie knew was her ex-husband, or that she hadn't spoken to him in years, or even that they'd broken up over his refusal to move to Fossett. That was history, over and done with. The two of them had moved on ages ago. He'd be happy to help her out, right?

Connect with U s

Visit us online at
KensingtonBooks.com
to read more from your favorite authors, see books
by series, view reading group guides, and more.

Join us on social media
for sneak peeks, chances to win books and prize packs,
and to share your thoughts with other readers.

facebook.com/kensingtonpublishing
twitter.com/kensingtonbooks

Tell us what you think!

To share your thoughts, submit a review,
or sign up for our eNewsletters, please visit:
KensingtonBooks.com/TellUs.